BLOOD BONDS

STRIKE FORCE ZULU

Book 2

Laura Acton

ISBN: 978-1-951713-06-5 (paperback)
ISBN: 978-1-951713-07-2 (ebook)

BLOOD BONDS is a work of fiction. Names, characters, places, and events are products of the author's imagination or are used fictitiously. Any resemblance to actual persons, living or dead, events, locales, or organizations is entirely coincidental.

Three Fates Publishing

By Laura Acton

Strike Force Zulu series

ZULU SIX
BLOOD BONDS

Beauty of Life series

FORSAKEN: On the Edge of Oblivion
SOLACE: Behind the Shield
BELONGING: Hope, Truth, and Malice
OUTLIER: Blood, Brotherhood, and Beauty
PURGATORY: Bonds Forged in Hellfire
SERENITY: A Path Home
GUARDIANS: Mission to Rescue Innocence
SECRETS: Passion, Deceit, and Revenge
OUTCAST: Trust, Friendship, and Injustice
WHITEOUT: Above and Beyond
BREAKPOINTS: Slow Spiral Down

Acknowledgments

Where would I be without Kate?
Still stuck on chapter one, I suspect.
Thanks for your daily inspiration and friendship.

Kate, Martha, Lisa, Valarie, and Angel
you ladies are all awesome. I sincerely appreciate
your continued support and keen eyes.

THANK YOU!

Contents

BLOOD BONDS

Chapter One

FURY and frustration built as Master Chief Jake Marshall glared beyond his second-in-command at the blond, curly mop of his rookie, who now swung in a hammock. "What the hell am I gonna do with him? Did I not clearly outline my expectations and rule four?"

"You did." Senior Chief David Katz agreed, disappointed their new teammate ignored rules set forth less than ten hours ago.

"Yes, I did. He blatantly ignored me, and that shit doesn't fly on my team." Jake's gut twisted as he wondered yet again if he erred by selecting Stirling for his team.

Attempting to defuse his best friend and team leader before he did something he might regret, Dave said, "To be fair, he was celebrating, and we didn't expect to be spun-up so soon. Let him sleep it off. He'll be sober enough by the time we land."

Jake turned steel-blue eyes on his friend. "Not good enough! If he doesn't possess the maturity level to cut himself off and abide by my rules, he doesn't deserve to be on our team. Not only did Stirling break rule number four, he deliberately tried to hide the fact he arrived stinking drunk from us. That is breaking rule one too—don't lie to me."

Returning his gaze to Stirling, Jake declared, "He's a liability in his current state."

"Perhaps we can leave him on base," Dave suggested.

Desire to teach the impudent kid a life-lesson grew as Jake bit out, "No. I got a much better idea." He rose and sought out the source of his anger. Crossing the distance in long strides, Jake flipped the hammock, dumping Stirling to the aircraft's floor. "Rise and shine, cupcake. Time to sweat out the alcohol. You do NOT show up drunk off your ass."

Max blinked after smacking the ground. His headache from before increased after he whacked the metal grating. His stomach rolled, and he fought the need to hurl as saliva filled his mouth. The world around him swam as Marshall yanked him to his feet. Max barely managed to focus on the face of his pissed-off boss before he lost the battle.

The gagging gave Jake only a brief second to react. He spun Stirling around and shoved the kid's head towards a box of something—he didn't care what, only that it would catch whatever Maxwell spewed.

Roused by the commotion, Finn eyed Jake as he manhandled Stirling. "Glad I'm not him right about now."

"Who? Boss or Stirling?" Zach asked as he petted Rocketeer, who hopped up in his hammock.

"Both." Finn yawned and closed his eyes. None of them expected to be called for this mission, and wouldn't have been if Charlie Team had not ended up with some version of the flu. That would be the only defense their rookie would be able to offer for reporting while three sheets to the wind.

Grant shook his head. "Appears the kid can't hold his liquor."

On his knees, Max upchucked his stomach's contents, the excellent dinner he enjoyed with Cali making an unappetizing return. The abdominal cramping and hurling intensified his headache, which began on the drive to base.

If Max could've formed words, he would've told Marshall he was not drunk. He didn't consume alcohol at dinner. Plus, he only drank only half a beer with his Sierra buddies before Babcox tripped while carrying the tray of drinks to their table and bathed him in rum and beer.

Max didn't have time to go home to shower and change since the text told him to report directly to the airfield, and Draper packed his gear for him. Upon reaching the tarmac and overhearing Lockwood inform Marshall the team would be briefed after they arrived in Afghanistan, Max hurried to the head to take an urgent leak.

By the time he finished peeing, the pilots were ready to take off, and he sat in the first available seat, far from the rest of the team. When airborne, Max hung his hammock and crawled in, hoping sleep would rid him of his pounding headache.

Not wanting to let Marshall down, Max managed to rise after regurgitating his last meal. He swayed and opened his mouth to explain, but Marshall cut him off with a tirade. Every time he attempted to speak, his team leader became louder and more irate. Reasoning with the man at this point seemed to be futile.

So, Max sucked up his pain, dropped to the ground, and began doing pushups per Marshall's orders. When he reached one hundred, Max flipped over and did an equal number of crunches before being instructed to run laps around the plane. Disappointed and disgusted eyes tracked him on his journey. Lockwood, Farris, Draper, Dave, Finn, Grant, Zach, and even Rocketeer, the team dog, scowled at him.

After an hour of back and forth, soaked in sweat, smelling like a distillery from the spilled alcohol, Marshall finally allowed him to stop running. The master chief shoved a bottle of water into his hands and told to drink it all. Max downed the entire contents in several gulps … wrong thing to do. He pivoted and bent over the same revolting box as his body rejected the liquid.

"Get in your hammock and sleep," Jake directed after the kid finished puking again. He strode to the rear, as far from Stirling as possible so he wouldn't wring his neck.

Plopping down in a seat, Jake blew out a breath as he eyed his rookie crawling back into the swinging bed. He had done all he could for now. Keeping his men safe was hard enough with them sober. He didn't need the added weight of dealing with a hungover newbie.

Lieutenant Nicole Farris, Zulu's primary intelligence officer, shifted her position to face Jake. "You think he'll be up for the op when we arrive?"

"He better be. Why the hell were we tagged for this mission? Alpha or Bravo could've covered for Charlie."

Nicole sighed. "They don't have anyone who speaks Nazeri's dialect. Stirling does, so his language skills are necessary."

"Could've sent a terp with them," Jake challenged, ticked off they were throwing the kid right into the fire without the two weeks of integration training Kendrick allotted them.

"Not enough time to locate one. As it is, you'll scarcely arrive in time to execute the mission as Carlson planned."

Jake eyed Nicole. She tended to keep her distance from them, but he developed a working rapport with her in the two years she'd been assigned to Zulu. "How well do you know the spook?"

Nicole exhaled heavily. "Carlson's brought actionable intel to my office one or two times. Other than that, I haven't had any interactions with the CIA agent. But we've been after Sina Nazeri for years, and missing this opportunity isn't an option. You should grab some shuteye, Jake."

Crossing his arms and slumping in the seat, still not confident he wouldn't wring Stirling's neck for disobeying the rules, Jake settled back, trying hard to sleep. However, his mind wouldn't shut off as thoughts of Stirling mixed with his son.

His new teammate was only six years older than his son Jamie, and Jake realized he was old enough to be Stirling's father. That notion kicked up a strange feeling.

Jake stared at Stirling as the rookie made a trip to the head. *Perhaps I should've given more weight to Finn's point about Stirling being too green. Ignoring rules and arriving drunk is an indicator he needs to mature. Did I make a mistake selecting him as Zulu Six?*

At the front of the aircraft, Max returned to his hammock after peeing. As he lay back, he clamped his eyes shut, swiped sweat from his forehead, and fought the renewed nausea as his head throbbed. *I'm not drunk, but what the hell is wrong with me?*

Chapter Two

Forward Operating Base (FOB) – Tarmac

MAX woke as the C-17's wheels touched down, his hammock swinging crazily. *No one woke me for landing. Guess they don't give a damn about my safety. Nothing new.* The movement caused his unsettled stomach to roll, but he managed not to ralph again. When the aircraft came to a halt, he climbed out and held the fabric for stabilization as a sharp pain stabbed his lower back.

Hammocks are not the most comfortable, but they never left me sore before. Probably a kink from all the running and crunches Marshall made me do. Max stretched to relieve the ache, glad the hammering in his skull subsided to a dull banging.

As the rear of the plane lowered, a blast of heat rolled in along with bright sunlight, which caused him to squint. He squared his shoulders as Marshall approached, now dressed in his uniform instead of the civvies they all arrived wearing. "Boss, I wasn't—"

"I don't want excuses. You got five minutes to change and grab your gear before the bus leaves. If you miss it, you'll be running to the briefing." Jake picked up his bags, pivoted and strode out the back with the other four members of Zulu and Rocketeer.

Yanking the desert uniform from his ruck, Max changed swiftly. He fought the headache and backache, wishing to ask for a couple of pills, but Draper scowled at him, and he reasoned no one would believe him if he told him he had not been drunk.

They all made assumptions, and Marshall confirmed them by reaming him and letting him sleep the remainder of the flight. Max understood team dynamics well enough to comprehend that with this being his first official mission as a member of the elite team run by Jake Marshall, he was low man on the totem pole. As such, he must do what was expected, when expected, as expected with no questions or complaints.

Max wanted to earn the respect of his new teammates, so again, he sucked it up, grabbed his pack, and barely made it to the white bus within the time limit. He found an open seat in front of Grant Beckett, the team's medic, and across from Finn McBride, their breacher and heavy weapons specialist.

Grant tapped Max on the shoulder. "So how much you drink last night?"

Without thinking, Max answered, "Only part of a beer."

Finn smirked. "Lightweight."

"Told you, the kid can't hold his alcohol." Grant chuckled.

"Sure the hell reeked and acted like more than one beer," Zach muttered from behind Grant.

Deciding to keep his mouth shut since it would likely only increase their razzing, Max clenched his jaw. He shifted to relieve his back pain, swiped at the sweat beading on his brow, and braced himself for all the shit that came with being the team newbie once again.

FOB – Tactical Operations Center (TOC)

As he continued the briefing, laying out his plan, Percival Carlson scanned the unit Nicole claimed to be the best. By the looks of them, he possessed other opinions. His eyes landed on Jake Marshall, who, with his chair tipped back on the rear feet only, appeared bored and not paying any attention to the details.

The man came with a reputation for being a royal pain-in-the-ass and demanding to the point of insubordination, that is if Lieutenant Commander Lockwood didn't fully support him, which Lockwood always did according to Carlson's sources.

Marshall was one reason Carlson had expressly requested and worked with by-the-book Master Chief Hanson for this operation. He didn't want the headache of dealing with Marshall. But when three members of Hanson's team became ill, including the soldier with knowledge of the local language, he was forced to go with Zulu Team because Farris indicated they possessed a multi-lingual shooter fluent in the dialect.

Sneezing several times, Carlson eyed the dog. "Get that mangy mutt out of TOC. I'm allergic to dogs."

Zach smirked as Jake responded.

"Deal with it, Carlson. Rocketeer is a member of my team and stays with his handler." Jake dropped his chair on all four and reached for the bottled water Draper placed on the table for him. As he twisted off the lid, he noted Draper produced tissues from somewhere. Their logistics specialist always had whatever they required, and in this case, what an annoying CIA agent needed.

After giving Carlson the packet of tissues, Kira continued passing out water to the guys. Today was scorching and humid, causing her uniform to cling to her in all the wrong places. The room had become stifling with so many bodies crowded in the small space, and everyone appeared uncomfortable and overheated.

She stopped next to Stirling to hand him one and reconsidered her thoughts. Stirling looked absolutely miserable with the way his eyes squinted as he focused on the presentation. *Serves him right for coming onboard drunk. Must have one helluva hangover.*

"Water?" Kira said to garner his attention when he didn't notice her holding out a bottle.

Concentrating on the agent, Max glanced to the left, surprised Draper offered him one after her scowls on the plane. "Thanks." He shifted in his seat, trying to alleviate his still aching back as he wiped the sweat from his forehead again. "Can I have two?"

"Sure." Draper shoved another one at the rookie. *Yeah, he needs to rehydrate before going on a mission. If he keels over, Jake will eat him alive for putting them all at risk.*

Shooting a glance at their rookie, Grant noted Stirling appeared to be flushing his system of alcohol by consuming extra water. The sweating would assist in that process. *So he's not a complete idiot. At least Stirling is taking the right steps to prepare for the mission.* Grant returned his focus to the front as Lieutenant Farris took over from Agent Carlson.

Max guzzled one bottle but slowed his consumption when his stomach rolled. Hot, achy, sweaty, and all-around miserable, he attempted to concentrate on the briefing. The last thing Max needed to do was hurl in here and garner more unwanted attention. Making a spectacle of himself is not how he wanted his first mission with Zulu to go down.

Nicole said, "We must take Sina Nazeri alive. This is the first chance we've had in two years. The intel we can glean from him will help us take down the Hamood Network."

"Explain again why this requires a daylight raid, and my rookie specifically?" Jake challenged, not liking what he heard so far. "We don't need to talk to snatch Nazeri under cover of darkness."

"Or to wipe out all his lackeys in the process," Finn added with a grin as he rolled his lucky coin between his fingers.

Carlson scowled at the red-headed heathen. "My plan doesn't include creating an international incident."

"The world will be thankful if we schwack the scum who sell explosives to terrorists who blow up elementary schools and hospitals," Finn retorted.

"Nazeri is a middleman who can provide the names of those in charge. However, I don't expect a knuckle-dragger like you to understand such a complex situation," Carlson haughtily replied.

Finn laughed. He dealt with too many pencil-pushing cake-eaters in his years to allow the pompous remark to bother him.

"I'm waiting. Why daytime and why Stirling?" Marshall crossed his arms as he leaned back again.

"This is the plan I approved. Nazeri visits his father once each month, and we need to take him as he arrives. He will be without his main compliment of protection," Carlson reiterated.

"Still doesn't answer my questions." Jake stood, not liking this squirrely agent. In general, he didn't trust CIA agents, as many had their own agendas.

Carlson's strategy to grab Nazeri made no sense. A daylight mission was suicide. *Does the moron expect us to waltz into a village deep in a Taliban controlled area and stroll out with Nazeri? How in the hell did this shitty plan get approved? Hell, Hanson might not be the brightest team leader, but he's not stupid enough to agree to something like this.*

Dave recognized Jake's tension, and the fact Carlson was no tactician. He reviewed the aerial photos of the rugged landscape surrounding the village nestled in a valley. "I don't like the terrain. We are too exposed for a day op. We should—"

Frustrated, Carlson cut him off. "You are soldiers. You do as commanded. This plan's been in the works for months. This is our only opportunity."

"Sailors," Finn corrected.

Bryan Lockwood eyed Carlson, before gazing at Farris, trying to glean her take on this agent. *Who does this guy think he is?*

Ignoring both Carlson and Finn, Dave continued, "Jake, if we went in tonight and situated ourselves here." He pointed to a building. "We would be in a position to snatch Nazeri as he arrives and avoid issues with a daytime infil. We only need to work out a fast exfil after we nab him."

Jake moved forward and scratched at his beard. "Might work. Clear a home close by and wait." His eyes shifted to Lockwood. "HALO infil and helo exfil?"

"That can be arranged," Bryan said, hearing the first decent suggestion for getting his men in and out in a reasonably safe manner with a higher probability of keeping their target alive.

Carlson argued, "Hanson and I worked out all the plans for this operation."

"Hanson isn't in command of Zulu. My men, my op, my decision," Jake stated in a no-nonsense manner which appeared to rile the sweating man in front of him.

Carlson fumed as everyone completely ignored him, and Lockwood and some woman made arrangements for the HALO.

Jake relaxed somewhat as Draper arranged for a flight. The team determined the best infil drop zone, and a landing zone for the helo exfil. Both would require his team to trudge up and down ravines and hike several clicks.

Once satisfied with their planning, Jake stood to address his teammates. "It will be a long night. Rack out for a few hours and grab something to eat."

As his men rose to comply, he observed the rookie's slow motions and chalked it up to the aftereffects of too much alcohol. He noted Stirling's wet shirt but discounted it as they were all sweaty today. However, a gut reaction brought on by his memory of his son Jamie passing out in their backyard after he came home drunk, caused Jake to call his name. "Stirling."

Max halted, pivoted to face Marshall, and waited.

"Make sure you hydrate properly. Don't want you passing out during the op and becoming a weak link because you decided to drink excessively."

Though he should try again to correct Marshall's assumption, Max didn't want to risk being sent for another run or doing calisthenics, so he only said, "Copy." He waited a moment longer, and when his team leader turned to speak with the lieutenant commander, Max shuffled out with the others to find his bunk.

FOB – Zulu Quarters

Following Zach and Grant, the third to enter the rectangular storage container, which would serve as their quarters, Max set his pack on the bottom mattress of one of the two bunk beds. Although he slept almost the entire flight, he was fatigued and ready to rack out instead of going to the mess tent as most of the team planned to do after dropping off their gear.

Glaring at the pack on *his* bed, Finn allowed his sometimes-used Scottish brogue to come out in full force. "Yer aff yer heid if ya think I'm sleeping up top, boy."

Max whirled to face McBride, incensed by the last word, tired of the man's snarky attitude and comments, and sick of being the butt of his jokes. "I'm no one's boy! First come, first choice."

Finn smirked. "Seniority has privileges. I get first dibs." He reached around Stirling, snagged his rucksack, and tossed on the top bunk before dropping his on the lower one.

Taking an exaggerated sniff of Stirling, Finn wrinkled his nose. "You stink like a brewery. Hit the showers before we head out tonight. Otherwise, the Taliban will smell you coming. And I ain't gonna die because some eejit rookie decided to break rule four and go on a bender."

Fed up, Max bit back, "I wasn't drunk."

"Aye, right, and my nana's the Queen of Scotland." Finn turned and strode out.

Max stood and watched as Grant and Zach stowed their bags and exited too. Once alone, his shoulders sagged, and he peered at the short ladder to the upper bed. A rebellious part of him wanted to knock McBride's gear to the floor and lay in the bed he claimed, but the rational piece of his mind curtailed that act.

The nauseous sensation he fought off and on returned and his lower right side throbbed with a renewed vengeance as he climbed up, pushed his pack aside, and plopped his head on the thin pillow. Although the room had no air conditioning, the open door provided a little airflow, so it was not as stifling as the TOC.

Disappointed with the beginning of his first mission as a member of Zulu, Max drifted to sleep, telling himself he would not be the weak link. He would prove to Marshall that he belonged on Zulu, and perhaps find a way to make them all eat crow for believing he would break team rules.

Chapter Three

FOB – Zulu Quarters

JAKE rose from his rack and glanced over at Dave, who still slept in the second bed. As senior team members, they rated a two-person accommodation with a fan, which moved the stifling air around a bit. He stretched and moved to his pack to retrieve and change into his black uniform.

After sending his guys off for a nap, he and Dave poured over the mission details again before grabbing shuteye too. His gut still didn't like the setup, but the strategy they worked out would keep his men as safe as possible and still net the HVT.

Having not eaten earlier, Jake decided to wake Dave so they could head over to the mess for some food. He shook Dave's shoulder, and when his second-in-command cracked open an eye, he said, "Time to eat."

Dave pulled his pillow over his head and groaned. "Not hungry. You go."

After ripping the pillow away, Jake tossed it to his cot. "We've got a hell of a hike ahead of us. You can't go on an empty stomach."

Groaning again, Dave swung his feet to the floor as he sat up. "I'll wake the boys on my way over."

"Think they ate already." Jake tucked in his shirt.

"Well, they'll want coffee and a snack before we HALO."

FOB – Mess

Although the sun set over an hour ago, Max still felt somewhat overheated. And though his afternoon siesta and a quick shower revitalized him, wiping away the residual headache, a sense of nausea made a return appearance as he entered the mess. He didn't feel like eating, but since he had not eaten in over twenty-four hours and his delicious dinner with Cali ended up in a box on the plane, he recognized he must force something down.

The last to arrive, Max filled his tray with bland options and grabbed several packets of crackers, hoping they would calm his unsettled stomach. Taking a seat at the picnic-style table where his teammates congregated, he nibbled on the saltines as he listened to the guys shooting the shit.

Max poked at the unappetizing chicken a la god-knows-what with noodles and opted to take a mouthful of pasty mashed potatoes instead. He eventually managed to swallow several bites of chicken, cushioning each with half slices of bread. When Finn glanced his way, Max moved things around on his plate, giving the impression he consumed more than he had.

He filled the empty crevices in his stomach by drinking a carton of milk, and two bottles of water, telling himself he had power bars and MREs in his pack if he got hungry later. When the others rose, signaling the end of the meal, Max stood with them, and luckily, no one seemed to notice he dumped three-quarters of his dinner in the trash barrel.

As he geared up with his team, Max gave thanks he didn't receive any heated glares from Marshall or more razzing from anyone. When a twinge his right flank flared again, he pressed a hand to his back, wondering if he tweaked a muscle when Marshall flipped him out of the hammock. It was the only change in his routine that would account for the intermittent pains.

Inhaling deeply and exhaling gradually, Max tucked away his discomfort, giving his full focus to the upcoming mission. He needed to prove to Marshall and the rest of Zulu Team they made the right choice. *I will not be the weak link.*

Zulu Aircraft

Taking his role as 'rookie babysitter' grudgingly to heart, Finn jerked on Stirling's chute, ensuring he buckled properly. This was not the colt's first jump with them, but the previous one he'd been a member of Sierra. Though a bit banged up after being knifed in the sewer, Stirling never complained about being thrown into a follow-on mission to blow Massi's weapon stockpile in Algeria.

The kid saved Dave's life that night, which was one of the factors he weighed when voting. But Stirling also pulled a stupid stunt by not listening to Jake and continued after Massi, which is how he ended up in the cesspool in the first place. Though this young stallion, who ran like the wind, shot as well as Dave, and spoke numerous languages, might be green broke, he would require a firm hand to finish his training.

Finn grinned. *Perhaps being Zulu Three isn't so bad. I'm just the person to halter and rein him in, so he doesn't end up dead in the prime of his life.* Assured their rookie had strapped in correctly, Finn asked, "You good?"

Gritting his teeth against the pain the yanking caused in his back, Max only nodded.

"I asked if you're alright. Expect a verbal response." McBride pinned a glare on the rookie.

"Yeah," Max managed. Though his intention to focus solely on his job was admirable, his body decided to rebel and make this mission suck. Since they boarded the plane, he fought constant nausea and hoped he wouldn't puke in his mask as they did a HALO jump.

Jostling into position when the pilot indicated they would be at the jump zone soon, Max received several inadvertent jolts to his back. He suppressed a groan and clenched his jaw. A voice in his mind told him to tell Marshall he was not fit for duty, but a louder one shouted he would be kicked off Zulu if he backed out. Several deep breaths and one mental pep talk later, his pain subsided, as did his stomach's roiling. *This is nothing. I've worked through worse pain. I'm Zulu now. I can do this.*

The flight tech signaled they were approaching the drop zone before opening the rear of the aircraft. Once the green light displayed, Zach, with Rocketeer strapped to him in a taco sling and wearing a specially designed doggie oxygen mask, and doggles was the first out, followed by Grant, Dave, Max, Finn, and lastly Jake. When they reached the right altitude, each man pulled his cord, and six rectangular canopies unfurled.

Familiar tranquility settled in Max as he floated down. He enjoyed night jumps and took a moment to appreciate the beauty of the universe. The stillness before the coming chaos always helped him focus, and this time was no different.

Landing Zone

The jarring touchdown dropped Max to his knees as pain ricocheted across his back from his right flank. He panted several breaths as it ebbed to a manageable level, and thankfully his riotous gut didn't embarrass him in front of the others. Though at present, everyone was busy rolling their chutes and stuffing them in bags to bury the evidence of their presence.

Max rose and swiftly completed his task, sensing the heat of Marshall's eyes on him, even in the dark, as he finished last. So much for redeeming himself … though he was innocent of reporting drunk.

"TOC, Zulu One, passing Sapphire. What does ISR show about our surroundings?"

"Copy. Passing Sapphire. All quiet and clear," Draper said as Lockwood marked off the infil step on their tracking board.

Max lowered his night vision into place, casting his world in green. He moved out with his new team as they began their eight click trek through rough mountain terrain to reach the village. Each man silently maintained their grueling pace after Jake reported into TOC.

Slipping into combat mode and finding refuge in the physical exertion, Max ignored and overrode the lingering ache in his back and slight nausea. *My first mission with Zulu won't be my last.*

Target Village – Building Near Nazeri Residence

Jake used hand signals, and like a well-oiled machine, Zulu prepared to silently breach the doors so as not to alert anyone in this Taliban held village to their presence. Teamed with Finn and Grant at the rear entry, Max drew in a breath, glad his stomach finally settled, and he had not backed out of the op.

His mind in the zone, prepared for action, Max no longer dwelled on useless worries and what-might-have-been if he had notified Jake of his upset stomach during dinner. The possible lecture, glares, or taunts from his teammates he imagined while hiking didn't matter now. The only thing that did was doing his job to the best of his ability.

Executing their entry plan, Max moved stealthily, protecting their rear as Grant and Finn began clearing the rooms at the back of the abode. Not finding anyone thus far, the trio returned to the stairs in the first room.

On point, Finn started up the steps in the darkened room with Grant a few paces behind and Max covering their six. After Grant passed an alcove to the right of the staircase, Max spotted a man with a knife stepping out from the shadowy recess.

In a flash, Max slammed the tango's skull into the wall, needing to take him down without alerting the household. He covered the target's mouth as he utilized a chokehold to silence him before he could warn the others.

Finn turned at the commotion, ready to help, but realized Max didn't need any when the rookie released the unconscious hostile, guiding the body to the floor to prevent unwanted sound. McBride grinned and nodded. *Kid did well.*

Grant knelt to secure the combatant's hands and ankles with zip ties before gagging him. As he rose, Grant patted Max's shoulder in silent thanks. *Guess Stirling can add me to his growing list of Zulu members he's saved. At this rate, we're all gonna make his list in short order.* Grant shelved his thoughts and refocused on their task of securing this two-story building so they would be in a position to snag Sina Nazeri alive.

Finn continued up the stairwell, followed by his teammates. The three worked together clearing the second-floor rooms, securing the four sleeping men they located, as did Jake, Dave, and Zach on the first, trussing up five they found.

Leapfrogging positions, the trio on the upper level made it to the last room just as Jake notified them the first-floor had been cleared. Entering first, Max didn't have time to react when a dark-clad figure lunged out from behind a tall bookcase. The impact sent both men to the dusty wooden floor with Max underneath his attacker. Max's back rammed into something solid and sharp, sending shockwaves of agony coursing through him.

Finn sprang into action, wrapping his arm around the tango's throat and pulling him off the kid. When the assailant fought back, McBride snapped his neck, letting the limp body crash down, without a second thought as his attention turned to Max.

Riding wave after wave of pain, gasping for breath, Max was assaulted by nausea again, and this time he couldn't control it. He rolled to his left side and began puking.

As Grant covered them, Finn took a knee beside his teammate, wondering what caused him to toss his cookies. "Hey, Six, what's wrong?"

Somewhat disgusted by the vomit, but more concerned, Finn reached out to check for wounds, and his glove came in contact with something on Stirling's back just below his vest. His touch knocked it loose, and the thing clunked on the flooring.

Flicking on the light attached to his helmet, Finn searched for the object. He spotted a bloody, pyramid-shaped chunk of glass, reminiscent of prisms used in the decks of tall-masters to bring light below. "Shit!" Tugging Max's shirt up, Finn discovered a fast bleeding puncture wound. Applying pressure with one hand, he keyed his comms with the other. "Zulu One, we got a problem."

"What?" Jake headed for the stairs, leaving Zach and Dave to maintain overwatch on the entry points.

"Six is down. Bleeding from a wound in his back and puking his guts out."

Jake made haste, taking two steps at a time and appeared as Max finished ralphing. "What the hell happened?"

"Kid landed on that when the tango took him down." Finn pointed to the pyramid. "Punctured his back."

Pain radiating around his wound, Max stifled a moan when Finn pressed harder. His eyes locked with Jake's as his leader peered down at him. "Give me a sec … I'll be good."

Jake's concern notched up as he snorted and shook his head as he assessed the situation. "Yeah, right."

Taking the words not as intended, believing Marshall was displeased, or worse, thought him a liability and incapable of pulling his weight, Max began to rise to prove himself.

"Lay still," Jake barked.

Finn held him down, and Max couldn't stop the moan as McBride pushed on his flank.

"Grant, take a look," Jake ordered, and when their medic swapped with Finn, his glare landed on McBride. "I told you to take the kid under your wing. I realize you don't like your role as number Three, but shirking duty and letting him get hurt on the first damned mission isn't what I expected from you."

"Not his fault. I didn't react in time." Max refused to allow McBride to take the blame for his screw up.

Finn and Jake both stared at Max, and a moment later, Finn pointed to the shelving unit as he said, "The tali-monster popped out from behind that! And if that fucking thing hadn't been lying on the damned floor, nothing would've happened."

"Guys, not the time," Grant growled.

Jake blew out a breath. "What do you need?"

"More light and to move him away from the stench."

"The previous room had a mat on the floor. We can move all the detainees to the first room," Finn suggested.

"Do it," Jake said to Finn as he knelt to help Grant with Stirling. "How do you want to handle this?"

"I can stand." Max tried to rise again, but Jake placed a hand on his shoulder. "We do this how Grant decides."

Holding a pad to the still oozing wound, Grant said, "You help him up while I maintain pressure."

Max shifted to a seated position first, then allowed Marshall and Beckett to assist him to his feet. He sharply exhaled as pain lanced his back, and he seized Jake's forearm when he swayed.

"Got you. Whenever you're ready." Jake slung Max's arm over his shoulders and slipped a steadying arm across his upper back.

Shuffling forward, breathing through the pain, Max made his way to the other room with Marshall's and Beckett's assistance. Used to fending for himself, Max hated relying on others and putting this operation in jeopardy. He needed to dig deep and pull himself together.

Thoroughly ticked off at himself as they settled him on the futon type mattress on the ground, Max gruffly said, "Tape it up, and I'll be fine after a few minutes."

"Quiet. Lie down and let me take a better look." Grant dropped his medkit beside the mat and took a knee as Stirling complied, and Jake shut the window's shutters so he could turn on a brighter light to examine the wound.

Fifteen minutes later, Max lay on the pad, his wound now packed with quickclot gauze. Marshall insisted he stay put for the remainder of the night. Max didn't argue with the order because he was too busy fighting the desire to paint the dusty floor with watery bile and gain control over his pain.

Out of earshot of Max, Jake pulled Grant aside. "How is he doing? Can he make the assault and exfil?"

"Not sure. The puncture is near the kidney and might've nicked it. I slowed the bleeding by packing the wound, but Max seems warm to me, and I don't have a thermometer in my kit to verify. As for the puking, intense pain can cause that, but …" Grant trailed off as his mind sifted through several thoughts.

Noting Grant's contemplative expression, Jake asked, "What are you thinking?"

Grant sighed and shared his concerns. "We've only rolled with him twice."

"Four times if you count Argentina, Libya, and both Algeria missions," Jake corrected.

Grant glanced over at Max. "Yeah, four, but I'm not sure how his body reacts. I rechecked the knife wound he got in the sewer, and it doesn't appear inflamed. Though with the fever and vomiting, both here and on the plane, the kid might be fighting an infection. He could've picked up almost anything wading around in all that waste. We got spun up so fast that I never had a chance to ask Dr. Irving about his blood workup.

"On the bus, I asked him what he drank, and he said only part of a beer. He slept almost the entire flight and all afternoon after we finished the briefing. I also noticed he tossed most of his dinner away, and he didn't eat lunch. I think he's sick in addition to the wound, which might complicate things."

Blowing out a frustrated breath, Jake mentally chastised himself. *Dammit, I missed something. I should've let Stirling explain on the flight. I allowed my issue with Jamie's excessive drinking to cloud my judgment.*

Never one to back down from a problem, Jake strode over to Max, squatted beside him, and demanded, "How much alcohol did you consume before we were upped? I want the truth."

Startled by the harsh tone, Max blinked open and stared at Marshall as he fought renewed nausea. "Only half of one beer."

"Why did you smell like a brewery when you arrived?"

"Was with Sierra Team at the Barnacle. Babcox tripped and spilled a tray of rum and beer on me right before I got the page. Didn't have time to go home to shower." Max's abdomen muscles clenched as he lost the battle for control, and he began to retch, but nothing came up.

Jake braced Max as he dry-heaved, noting the excessive heat radiating from him. *Damn, the kid is sick and injured.* Grant took over when Max began shivering. Worried Zulu Six's condition would deteriorate, and they'd lose him on his first official op, it was not a risk Jake would willingly take. He keyed his comms and said, "TOC, this is Zulu One. We need to abort."

Chapter Four

SHOCKED by Marshall's statement, and uncertain she heard correctly, Petty Officer Draper responded, "Zulu One, say again, your last."

"We must abort. Zulu Six is down, and hot exfil with him is a no go." Jake leaned against the doorjamb as Finn entered the room after securing the detainees.

Ripping the mike from Draper's hand, Carlson barked, "You are ordered to complete your mission. One man is expendable. Leave him and grab Nazeri when he arrives."

Farris and Draper glared at Carlson as Lockwood stepped forward and took the handset from the CIA agent. "TOC to Zulu One. Sitrep."

"Six sustained a puncture wound to his back, and Four believes it might've nicked his kidney. The kid is also feverish and vomited, possibly fighting an infection. Four's done what he can with limited medical supplies. Six's condition is deteriorating. Suggest we move to exfil now for early extraction and go after the HVT next month."

Ticked off, Carlson exclaimed, "You will NOT abort this mission! A single loss for Nazeri is acceptable. Besides, if he is a little sick, he should still be able to run. Don't they train for stuff like this?"

Nicole scowled at the callous spook as words failed her. She spoke with him one or two times before, but never realized him to be this ruthless and uncaring. Draper grabbed her attention in the next instant.

"Zulu One, be advised, incoming. Six figures are approaching the back of the building."

Nicole and Bryan both focused on the monitor showing six heat signatures closing in on their team's position.

Carlson frowned. *Goddammit, they showed up. This isn't going as I planned.*

Inside Building Near Nazeri Residence

"Copy," Jake said. *This op just went from bad to worse.* He turned to the others. "Four, stay here with Six. The rest of us will deal with our unwanted company. Let's move." He hurried out, heading downstairs with McBride following.

Max pushed up, resting against the wall, trying to pull his shit together as he peered at Grant. "Shoot me some morphine and give me my weapon. You go with them. I can take care of myself."

"Not countering Boss's orders." However, Grant did pull out an injector and gave Max a partial dose of morphine to ease his pain. "Only taking the edge off, don't want you out completely. How long have you been feeling like shit?"

Waiting for the drug to take effect, Max answered, "Had a headache when I boarded, the reason I crawled into the hammock after take-off. Got better, then worse. Didn't feel this bad until we began trekking here."

"Should've told us about this on the plane or before we rolled out," Grant admonished.

"Tried to, but Marshall didn't want to listen and made me run." Max's head lolled to the side, hoping Grant didn't question why he didn't try again before the mission. *I screwed up. I should've said something instead of keeping quiet.*

Nodding, Grant refrained from asking more. Stirling spoke the truth. Jake had not let Max get a word in edgewise on the flight.

He stood and moved to the door, ready to cover Max since the rookie was in no condition to be handling a gun. Silently scolding himself for his role in this situation, Grant glanced back at their new guy. *I'm a medic. I shouldn't have assumed the kid was drunk, especially after learning Max consumed only a partial beer. I also should've talked to Jake earlier when I noticed how little Six ate.*

Max shouldn't have been spun up with us until Dr. Irving cleared him. Did the doc clear him? If so, Irving might've missed something because a fever wouldn't come on so fast with a puncture wound. And Max said he had a headache when he arrived.

Grant continued to review the symptoms he observed with the new knowledge and came to one conclusion. More than one person screwed up, and now Max was paying the price, and this mission would turn into a total failure. Neither Lockwood nor Marshall would be pleased.

Downstairs, the five men and Rocketeer prepared for the incoming hostiles as Jake instructed in a quiet voice, "We allow them to enter and take them down inside, quiet-like, so we don't give away our position."

Outside Building Near Nazeri Residence

Approaching the location they planned to conceal themselves in until time to take out their targets, Blaze hoped this wouldn't be another trap. They'd been run ragged lately with a slew of false intel that cost them too many good men.

Though this appeared to be vetted by several sources, including the CIA. In a briefing with General Broderick and Colonel Sutton three weeks ago, they revealed Canadian and American covert operatives shared mutually beneficial information, then devised a combined mission to capture Sina Nazeri.

Blaze agreed to the mission because it would also net him and Winds one of the lowlife bastards on their personal hitlist. Their list had been sanctioned by the general and compiled over the years as they tracked down and killed the animals responsible for torturing Blondie for three excruciating months.

They learned one of the scumbags who almost killed Blondie, Yel Malik, now worked for the Hamood Network as security for Nazeri. They now had two objectives for this mission, a dead Malik and a live Nazeri, who they would turn over to an American counterpart per an agreement Sutton worked out.

And although this should've been a joint op, Agent Carlson became wishy-washy with Sutton at the last minute and informed them the American team would not be ready until next month. Not wanting to allow this opportunity to snag Nazeri or kill Malik pass them by, Sutton sent them as initially planned.

While en route, due to six fewer men without their U.S. contingent, Blaze and his unit devised a new strategy. Instead of landing at Bagram Air Base and linking up with the other team, they did a HALO jump and patrolled to the village.

Blaze didn't like the idea of a daylight mission, but with Sina Nazeri set to arrive mid-morning and leave by early afternoon according to intel, he didn't have much choice. After his men stacked up at the door, ready for a silent breach, he gave the signal to Winds to execute. His best friend opened the door, allowing all six men to slip inside.

Inside Building Near Nazeri Residence

Five SEALs and one dog surrounded six JTF2 soldiers. Had any of them been trigger-happy, a terrible incident would've occurred, but both teams being well-trained, they ended up with guns pointed at each other, astonished as they peered at allies.

Jake exclaimed, "What the fuck?" as Blaze expressed, "What the hell?" when the two leaders faced one another.

"Who are you, and why are you in our AO?" Jake demanded as he began to lower his rifle.

"Could ask you the same questions," Blaze responded as he lowered his weapon. "Didn't think the U.S. was sending a team to deal with Nazeri. Leastwise, that is the intel I had."

"You're here for Nazeri?" Dave asked as he took his cue from Jake, who moved his gun off the other warrior.

Winds noted the arm patch and realized the man speaking was the second-in-command like him. "Yeah, and another bastard, though he won't be leaving here alive like Nazeri." He clenched his left palm, which contained the thin, white scar from his blood oath with Blaze to seek justice for Blondie.

Jake took control of the conversation. At least for his men, as he spoke with the leader of the Canadian JTF2 unit, a Major Blain, who preferred to be called Blaze. The two men shared details, and it became clear something smelled fishy.

Pressing his comms, Jake provided a sitrep. "TOC, Zulu One. Hostiles turned out to be friendlies … Canadians. They're here to snatch the HVT. We may be able to Charlie Mike, but there is some apparent miscommunication we must sort out." He relayed the information gleaned from Blaze.

FOB – TOC

"Copy. Once you work out a plan, I'll make contact with Sutton, and we'll coordinate from here," Lockwood said as he pinned Carlson with a glare.

Draper contacted the Canadian operations center, connected Lockwood to Colonel Sutton, then sat back and watched as the lieutenant commander dealt with the colonel. Her attention shifted when Nicole went after Carlson.

"Why in the world would you tell them we would be waiting until next month?" Nicole demanded as she rounded on Carlson. "Are you that much of a glory hog you would risk the lives of all those men? Had someone opened fire, they might all be dead, and we would miss grabbing Nazeri!"

Carlson found himself backed into a corner as Farris harangued him. He had nothing to counter her accusations with because she nailed his motivations. He wanted to reap the rewards of being the one to bring in Nazeri, and they didn't need the Canadians to do that.

Inside Building Near Nazeri Residence

Blaze sent Russ, his sniper, to the rooftop to maintain overwatch and left Angus and Hal on the first floor as he, Winds, and Duncan went to the second floor once he learned one of the Americans had been wounded and was ill.

Jake led the way into the room and said, "Max is over there."

Shucking his pack, Duncan moved forward to the injured man and took a knee. "My name is Duncan, and I'm gonna take a look at you. Alright?"

Grant moved to Max, not liking someone he didn't know taking care of his teammate. "I'm a medic. What can you do for him that I haven't?"

Duncan stopped his visual assessment, turning to the other man. "No offense meant, but two heads are better than one. Your CO indicated he might be running a fever." He unzipped his medkit and grinned. "Got a bunch of non-standard items in my kit. A holdover from my predecessor. Shea used it all the time until Broderick left the unit."

Producing a tympanic thermometer, Duncan added, "We can find out how high his temp is."

Grant smiled. "Gotta get me one of those."

As Duncan gave the device to Grant, and they discussed what happened to Stirling and his earlier symptoms, Jake laced his hands on top of his head while observing.

Directing his query to Max, Duncan asked, "Besides nausea, headache, and fever, did you experience any other symptoms?"

His eyelids opened a crack, and Max's world appeared hazy and unreal as he tried to focus. Somewhat confused, when something poked in his ear, he attempted to pull away.

"Hold still, kid. Taking your temperature." Grant stuck the probe in Max's ear again, and after reading the digital output when it beeped, he relayed, "Not good. One oh three point five."

Turning his head towards Duncan, Max reached out and touched a solid mass. His face screwed up in confusion. "Dad?"

"Um, no, I'm Duncan."

Jake's gut twisted. Stirling was bad off if he was hallucinating. And damn, the young buck's glassy eyes appeared as vulnerable as one of his kids when they were ill. Moving forward, Jake crouched beside Max and placed a hand on his shoulder as he softly said, "Relax, kid. Close your eyes and rest for now."

Without warning, Max slid to the side, toppling into Jake.

When the master chief ended up on his butt with the injured SEAL's blond head in his lap, Winds snickered, earning glares from Zach and Finn. Winds put up his hands, palms out. "Whoa, I'm not laughing at him. Your kid only reminds me of our younger brother."

"Blondie." Blaze fondly smiled as he peered at Jake and Max, seeing himself and Dan. This team was in for one hell of a ride if Max was anything like Blondie.

Finn arched a brow. "Blondie? What kind of name is that?"

"An uninspired one. We suck at naming. Hence, we gave up the practice. Blondie had terrible reactions to morphine and experienced some weird-assed hallucinations. The kid kept us on our toes for six years."

"Six? Did he …" Finn didn't finish the question. If this Blondie person died, he really didn't want to know.

Blaze supplied an answer anyhow, "Blondie's with the Toronto Tactical Response Team now. Better place for him."

Unconsciously, Max gripped Jake's sleeve and twisted as a sharp pain stabbed his back, overriding the dose of painkillers.

"Easy, kid." Jake gently patted Stirling's shoulder, offering comfort similar to how he used to for his eldest son Jamie. In the past few years, they had butted heads so often that Jake almost forgot the quiet, sensitive side of his son. *Perhaps it's time I re-examine our relationship and make some changes, or I'm going to push Jamie away.*

After completing his exam, Duncan sat back on his heels and rubbed his chin with his index finger and thumb as he considered everything. "I'm not a doctor, but given his symptoms and what you told me about the cesspool, I'm guessing kidney infection."

Grant nodded. "The sudden onset of vomiting, shivering, and fever, coupled with his original back pain leads me to the same conclusion. Though I would like to find out the results of his blood work from the doc."

"So what are we going to do, Jake? Exfil under fire with Max is out of the question given this." Dave waved toward the two, hiding a slight grin at the absurdity of Max lying in Jake's lap. He was certain if Stirling were aware, he would've pulled back. The things he read in Stirling's jacket and his limited interactions with the kid gave him the solid impression he didn't rely on anyone.

Blaze suggested, "How about Duncan and Hal take him to the exfil location under darkness? We can rig explosive on Nazeri's house tonight. My guys will take out Malik while your team snatches Nazeri. We'll provide cover for you as you move Nazeri out, then set off the explosives as a diversion and exfil ourselves."

Finn snorted. "I thought Canadians were all friendly."

Winds eyed the man, liking what he saw, someone not afraid to speak his mind. "Depends. Piss us off and were as bloodthirsty as Americans. And Malik made it to the top of my kill list."

"What did he do, kiss your mother?" Finn joked.

"Tortured Blondie for three months, before we rescued the kid," Blaze said flatly.

Finn drew in a sharp breath. He recalled rumors of a Canadian JTF2 soldier who survived months in the hands of terrorists. Apparently, it was true.

Jake considered the plan but was not comfortable leaving Max in their hands alone. *Stirling is my responsibility.* "I agree, but your medic and Finn will be the ones to take Max."

Blaze nodded, understanding Marshall's decision. He wouldn't hand off one of his men to another unit, either.

Although Finn didn't relish the idea of playing nursemaid, he accepted Jake's decision without complaint. As Jake rose to discuss plans with Blaze, Finn took his place, becoming a cushion for Max. Somehow, their rookie got under Finn's skin and made him act as a protective older brother.

Chapter Five

Inside Building Near Nazeri Residence

CROUCHING in front of Max, Jake studied his rookie. The kid looked wretched with his brows furrowed, and pain lines etched around his eyes. However, given a dose of antipyretic to reduce his fever and a half-hour to rest, Stirling was lucid again, and this might be as good as he got.

So, although Jake had misgivings about sending only two men to help Max traverse almost five miles of rugged terrain to their exfil location, Jake stood and said, "Time to go, Six."

Eschewing offers of help, Max batted away Finn's hand. With effort, he pushed up to his feet. Wobbling a bit but standing, Max leaned his left side against the wall to steady himself.

Finn took no offense. He would want to rise unaided if it were him. He waited close by to catch Max if he started to fall, but would allow him the dignity of doing what he could for himself.

Jake eyed Finn, his message clear. *Keep our boy safe.* Out loud, he said, "Check-in when you arrive at the exfil pos."

"Copy," Finn replied before following Zulu Six out the door.

Reaching the staircase, Max gripped the rail, determined to make it to exfil under his own power. He took a deep breath and started down the steps. Max sensed Zulu Three right behind him and appreciated his teammate didn't treat him like an invalid, though everybody knew he was damned close to one right now.

Four treads down, sharp pain caused him to gasp, lose his grip, and start to lean forward. If not for his burly, red-headed teammate grabbing the loop on the back of his vest, Max would've tumbled the rest of the way to the ground floor.

"Easy." Finn decided to maintain his hold as they made it down the remainder of the stairwell.

Jake observed from the top, his gut twisting as he wished to send more than only Finn with Max, but this operation was too vital, and he already lacked two shooters. His mind caught up, and Jake scowled as he did the math and realized his idiocy. Six plus six minus three meant he was actually up by three men. *I can spare one more man.*

"Zach, go with them," Jake ordered and received a nod in acknowledgment from Zulu Five.

Rocketeer's ears perked up as his handler moved from his position, and he needed no command to fall into step.

Dave turned to Jake. "Why send Zach?"

"Early warning detector. They won't have a drone over them. Rocketeer will alert them of any potential incoming hostiles."

Winds grinned at Blaze. "Sure wish we had all the toys these Americans do."

Blaze chuckled. "What would be the fun in that? Old school tactics serve us well, my friend."

"Just saying, we could've used the eyes in the skies and a canine sniffer many times, especially with all the shit Blondie got into."

"True." Blaze turned thoughtful eyes on the master chief. "You might have the newest version of Blondie. If you do, you've got your work cut out for you, but mark my words, you'll thank the lucky stars you have the privilege to be his brother."

Not quite sure how to take that bit of information or warning, Jake only nodded. He turned and strode over to the window to take up watch. The Canadian team would rack out first.

Peeking out at the sleeping village, his thoughts went to when the kid grabbed his sleeve and hung on as pain engulfed him. Jake mentally kicked himself for jumping to conclusions on the plane.

He behaved no different than those COs who had written unsubstantiated notes in Stirling's jacket because he was Preston Stirling's son. The kid's history demonstrated he had to grow up fast, and never had a family to support him. It also didn't help this situation that they didn't get to do the two weeks of integration training with their newest member.

With that knowledge, coupled with his actions, Jake gave Stirling slack for not being forthcoming about his less than stellar health. Though once they got back to base, he would make it clear to Max the team rules were in place for everyone's protection—his included. The kid also needed to learn that as a member of Zulu's family, they would always have his back.

En Route to Exfil Location

His environment swathed in green again, Max stumbled along at a sorry pace. *If I crawled, I might go faster.* Finn, never more than a grasp away, saved him from face-planting more times than Max wanted to count in what seemed like endless hours.

He lost track of time and distance because their exfil took them on a different route. Though the first part had been flat, most of their path took them up and down multiple ravines as treacherous as their infil. Several times his boot slid on loose pebbles, but he kept going, refusing to be more of a weak link.

Max accepted his tactical error would've aborted the entire mission if the Canadians hadn't shown up. He also understood why Marshall sent him packing before any action started. In his condition, he would be a liability after they snagged Nazeri. If not sick and injured, he would've led everyone up and down the gulches and gullies and not even broken out in a sweat or breathed heavily. But now, he dripped with perspiration, panted, and wondered if he would be able to complete the journey.

At his current speed, they might arrive only moments before the rest. That would be humiliating since the other guys had to wait until Nazeri showed up mid-morning, and it was currently still pitch black with the stars shining in the sky.

With Finn at his side, and safely sandwiched by Zach on point using Rocketeer to secure their path, and Duncan guarding their rear, Max's pride took a huge hit, and he remained worried about repercussions once Marshall laid into him for breaking a rule.

Although Max had not violated number four, no excessive drinking, he broke rule six. He failed to inform Marshall of an injury. Max halted his thoughts and recalled Jake's exact words. *Sixth and equally important as the others, never hide injuries. They can be a liability to the team.*

A glimmer of hope entered his mind. *Technically, I did not hide my injury, and I didn't realize I was so ill.*

Cresting another hill, Max's thoughts flew out the window as he experienced another excruciating stab of pain in his right flank. He couldn't keep the gasp silent this time and found himself halted by Finn's grip.

"Time for a quick rest," McBride ordered as he guided Stirling to a handy cluster of rocks and forced him to sit.

Duncan moved in and took a knee. "Health status?"

Eyeing the medic, Max didn't understand his query but settled on saying, "Same as before."

"Sorry, shorthand for my unit. Something my predecessor started," Duncan explained. He learned Blaze expected a lot from him. He had big shoes to fill after taking over for Patch as the unit's medic. "What is your pain level?"

"Three."

"Liar," Finn scoffed. He held out water to the kid.

Not willing to admit to more, Max took the bottle and sipped, hoping like hell the liquid would stay down.

Duncan grinned at Finn calling out Max, and he believed Blaze to be right. This blond was another Blondie. "Kidney infections are quite painful, so I'll double what you tell me. Six it is. Don't consume much water. Only wet your lips and mouth for now. If your kidney function is compromised, we walk a fine line."

After a five-minute break, Finn reached down and assisted Max to his feet, noting the soft hiss. *Damn, the kid is hurting ... bad.*

At a snail's pace, they made it to the bottom of the gorge and began a steeper trek up the other side. Halfway, Max stumbled on loose shale. Seizing Max's arm to steady him, Finn's boots, unfortunately, slid on the unstable rocks too. With Max's weight off-balance, both pitched to the right.

"Shit!" Try as his might, Finn couldn't change his trajectory mid-fall. Max hit the ground first, on his injured right side, and Finn landed on top of him.

A strangled yelp and short, "Aaaargh," emitted from Max as his back slammed into the hard-packed, rock-strewn earth. He would've released another cry when Finn's full weight crashed down on him, but the air expelled from his lungs, leaving him nothing.

It only took Finn a second to roll off. "Son of a bitch! Stirling?"

Rocketeer reached Max before Zach, but only by a moment. "Breathe, kid. Breathe."

Max sucked in a lungful of air and began panting through waves of agony. Nausea assaulted him, and he gagged. Three sets of hands turned him to his left side, two hands holding his shoulders, and the other four tugging his shirt up as the little water he consumed only minutes ago made a return appearance.

His body began shivering, not a damned thing he could do to stop the vibrations, which spiked his agony and caused more tremors—a vicious cycle Max was powerless to escape. Vaguely aware of a pinprick in his thigh, Max realized Duncan shot him up with more morphine.

When the heaving stopped, spent, Max didn't fight the fact Finn cradled his head in his lap. He concentrated on breathing, attempting to gain the upper hand on his pain. A hard-fought battle only won with the aid of meds. As his gasping evened out, Max managed to mumble, "I'm good."

Zach sat on his heels. "Yep, you're tough as nails, Kid." He rose and gave a soft verbal command to Rocketeer before he said to Finn, "I'm gonna scout the area while Duncan gets the bleeding under control."

Finn nodded, then turned his attention to Duncan. "What damage did I do?"

Putting a fresh gauze pad over the now gushing wound, the old one soaked through, Duncan didn't want to add guilt to the man holding his teammate. "Packing dislodged. Gotta apply pressure to aid in clotting." Duncan swapped out a second pad when the first became saturated.

By the sixth soaked pad, Finn realized he did more harm than the medic indicated. *Aw shit, Jake isn't going to like this one damned bit. Hell, I don't like this. I fucked up.* He caught Duncan's gaze and realized things were going downhill. In his arms, Max stilled, but the heat coming off him could almost fry an egg. *Fever's up again. Can this get any worse?*

Duncan couldn't pretend any longer. "He's losing blood too fast. I can't be certain, but if his kidney got nicked, all this blood makes me suspect a ruptured renal hematoma. I need light to work. He won't make it to exfil if I can't stop this hemorrhaging."

"Light out here will be a beacon to hostiles who patrol the area," Zach said as he returned.

"Did you find any indication of tali-monsters in our vicinity?" Finn asked.

"No, but that doesn't mean they aren't there." Zach took a knee and gazed at Max, noting he didn't move or open his eyes. "I spotted a rock outcropping not too far from here. The opposite direction of exfil and all uphill. We'll need to carry him, but once there, we can create a shield, and Duncan can help Max."

Finn pressed his coms. "TOC, this is Zulu Three."

"Go ahead, Three," Draper answered.

"Deviating from the original course." Finn provided the direction, approximate coordinates, and the reason for the change.

"Good copy. Be advised another drone will have eyes on you in about fifteen minutes."

"Copy." Finn shifted, rocks poking him in the ass, making sitting uncomfortable, but he didn't complain. His discomfort nowhere near Max's. "Wrap him tight, and I'll carry the kid."

Duncan did as required, packing the wound and wrapping gauze snuggly around Max's torso. When he finished, he held Stirling as McBride stood.

"Alright, kid, no complaints. I'm carrying you." Finn adjusted his vest and rifle, then squatted, preparing to hoist Max over his shoulder in a fireman carry. He became worried when Max made no response. "Kid?"

Glazed eyes blinked open and stared only a moment before his lids lowered again.

"I gave him a full dose of morphine. If he was six before the fall …" Duncan trailed off.

"At least I won't be hurting him too much then." Finn lifted Max, noting the kid was heavier than his frame indicated. *The young stallion is all muscle.* Picking his way up the slope, Finn moved with care, so he didn't fall and hurt Max again.

Chapter Six

Rock Outcropping

ZACH assisted Finn in laying an unconscious Stirling on the flat rock, while Duncan knelt and shrugged off his pack. A scan of the area indicated this place provided them with the ability to spot approaching hostiles. The overhang also offered protection from the elements with a location for overwatch on top. Almost as if it were made especially for their purposes.

With three of the four sides solid rock, Finn and Zach set about creating a blind that would allow Duncan to use a light to assess Max's condition. Finn kept taking peeks at the kid as the medic positioned Max on his left side and pulled up his shirt again. Once they finished providing a small but workable cover, he asked, "How's our kid doing?"

Duncan grabbed his penlight and cupped a hand around it to help with concealing the rays.

Finn took a knee and offered, "I'll hold that for you, so you have both hands free."

As much as Zach wanted to stay, he didn't. "I'm going up top to maintain overwatch." A hand signal later, Zach moved out, and Rocketeer lay at Max's feet, resting his head on his newest packmate's boots and released a soft whine. Rocky took a whiff of the odor ... one he didn't like. *If too much red stuff leaks out, we might lose the new golden-haired pup.*

With both his hands freed, Duncan removed the soaked outer dressing. He grumbled, "Not good," before pushing more sterile gauze in Max's wound. Filling the void with material to reduce available space to bleed into, he pressed hard, applying pressure to the damaged vessel or organ to arrest blood loss.

"Anything else I can do to help?" Finn met Duncan's eyes and read something that scared him. *Kid's in serious trouble.*

Not worried about causing pain since Max was out cold, Duncan continued to apply significant pressure because stemming the blood flow was more critical. "Grab an IV kit for me."

Finn did as requested. "Want me to start it?"

"No, you apply compression. I need a set of vitals after I insert the line." Duncan swapped positions with Finn and set the light on a rock to provide illumination. He worked swiftly, and Max didn't flinch as the needle entered, not that an unconscious man would feel the prick. Duncan taped the port in place and hung the saline bag from a short, collapsible pole he extended.

After retrieving the tools of his trade from the medkit, Duncan set about taking Max's vitals. When completed, he withdrew a smaller unit containing a vial and syringe from the pack.

Meeting Finn's gaze, Duncan noted the worried expression was identical to those on Winds, Blaze, and Jim when they pulled Blondie out of a ravine in Toronto after a gang war. "I'm going to insert a volume expander. It will help counter the blood loss."

Still holding the packing firmly, Finn asked, "So, how's the kid doing? He's gonna make it, right?"

Not pulling any punches, Duncan replied, "Fever's up again. One hundred two point eight now. Although the saline drip buys us some time, due to the hemorrhaging, he's showing signs of hypovolemic shock. Fast, shallow breathing, low blood pressure, rapid pulse, and clammy skin. I don't carry blood products, and his volume needs to be replaced now."

Finn swallowed hard as unexpected emotion rolled through him. *Damn! Kid's too young to die.* "When I got the IV out, I saw a field blood transfusion kit. I'm willing to tank him up."

"Are you the same blood type?"

"Aye. This is the kid's first official mission with us, so Grant made sure we knew that info."

Somewhat relieved when he confirmed the ABO and Rh groups on their tags, Duncan said, "I'll hold pressure while you sit down. I need to draw from you first."

"Okay. Give me a sec to update TOC and Bossman." Finn lifted his hand, and Duncan took over as he repositioned. Once Max's head rested in his lap, Finn pressed his comms to check-in. "Zulu Three to Zulu One and TOC."

Duncan checked the flow and determined he could release pressure on Max's wound. He pulled off soiled gloves and reached into his bag for the FBTK. After rolling up Finn's sleeve, he donned clean gloves, opened the donor kit, and grabbed the latex-free tourniquet.

Inside Building Near Nazeri Residence

"Sitrep," Jake demanded, continuing his pacing since learning they needed to deviate when Max started bleeding profusely.

"Six is holding on. Bleeding slowed but not stopped completely. Started an IV, which buys him time, but he's got signs of hypovolemic shock. Duncan is setting up a whole blood transfusion. Damn glad I'm a match, but I can only give him one unit, and if he needs more, we're SOL. Evac needs to come to us, moving him too much might kill him."

From TOC, Bryan responded, "Been working on a solution for an earlier exfil for Six, but getting ahold of General Havershash to authorize another helo is proving difficult. Captain Franckle is working under orders not to send additional flights due to the sizable cache of RPGs the hostiles in the area possess, but—"

Jake's fist clenched as he cut off Lockwood. "So, the cake-eater is willing to let the kid die?"

Though as frustrated as Jake, perhaps more so, Bryan kept his tone neutral. "I'm not giving up. Hold what you got. We'll figure something out."

When the communication ended, Jake itched to punch the wall but stopped himself—breaking his hand would only create more problems in an already shitty situation. As he paced, he muttered, "Options. I need options. Something workable that doesn't end up with Six bleeding out."

Winds peered at Blaze as an old memory surfaced. Something niggled in his brain when they learned the coordinates to where the others deviated. "I think they're at the rock overhang Blondie scouted for us after we crashed."

Blaze nodded. "Sounded familiar to me too." He turned to Marshall and said, "Our kid picked a prime spot and dragged our asses there when an RPG knocked out the engines in our plane." Blaze meant literally in his case. Blondie hauled the travois with his unconscious body on it though the kid suffered a lower back injury from the crash, a down-to-the-bone laceration on his palm, and a knife wound on his shoulder.

"Freshwater stream close by," Winds added, then grinned and quipped, "Nice place except for the horde of one-eyed, purple people eaters."

Blaze chuckled at the memory as the others stared at him and Winds. "Morphine caused Blondie to hallucinate." He put away the thought, and his mind shifted, working the problem.

Coming up with an option, Blaze focused on Marshall. "I'll contact Sutton. He and General Broderick will authorize our exfil to come now if we can hitch a ride back with you later. Sutton is aware of the terrain, the RPG concern, but most importantly, where the helo can set down safely for a faster extract."

Jake smiled. "Sounds like a plan to me."

Both keyed their comms to relay the idea to their respective commanders. They impatiently waited for twenty minutes as Sutton and Lockwood worked out the final details.

Bryan responded, "TOC to Zulu One and Zulu Three. Canadian helo is en route and prepared for the medical situation. ETA one hour."

"Good copy." Jake leaned against the wall, somewhat relieved.

Rock Outcropping

Finn watched his blood drip into Stirling. Extract couldn't come soon enough in his mind, though they still had forty minutes until they would arrive. Heat radiated off the kid, even as Duncan doused a roll of gauze in water and wiped Max's face to cool him. "Here, I'll do that. You take a break."

Handing over the wet gauze, Duncan sat and took a drink as he studied the two men and the dog who stayed close. "He's rather young, isn't he? I mean for a top tier team."

Though he might bitch about the kid's age, Finn was a team guy through-and-through so he would defend his teammate against all detractors. "He's damned good. One of the best shooters I've seen in years. Stirling earned his spot."

"No offense meant. Just thinking out loud. I can understand why Blaze took to Blondie so fast ... he was young too. To hear Winds talk, it's like Blaze became Blondie's dad. Wonder if the same will happen to your CO."

Finn snorted. "Jake? Nah. Don't get me wrong, he's all about getting us home in one piece, but Stirling becoming like a son ... I don't see it happening."

Not willing to push the point, but having a different opinion, Duncan shifted so he could check Max's back. Noting no change, which at this point was good because the treated packing appeared to stop the bleeding, he believed the young SEAL would make it out of this alive. "He's had one helluva first mission."

"Aye. I ken the wee nyaff won't be forgettin' this one soon."

Up top, Zach snickered. "Laying the brogue on a bit thick, aren't ya, Finn?"

"Chan eil mi beagan dragh," Max mumbled as he blinked open his eyes and found his head lying in someone's lap.

Duncan laughed.

Relief surged through Finn when Max's eyes opened. "What did you say?"

"He said he isn't a little nuisance," Duncan translated after he took a quick sip of water.

"How do you know what he said?" Finn asked.

"Mason."

"Who is Mason?"

"He used to be with Blaze's unit but got his own team several years ago. He speaks Gaelic, and I learned a few things from him on a boring recon op last year."

Finn peered down at Max. "You speak the Gaelic?"

"What?" Max tried to focus, but found it too difficult and let his eyelids shut again.

"Hey, Kid. Open them purdy blue eyes," Finn urged.

Struggling to lift his lashes, Max managed to crack them halfway.

"Welcome back. You are a nuisance, almost getting yourself killed. You're gonna make my job difficult, aren't you?"

"Job?" Max didn't follow all the words, too hot, miserable, and fuzzy for them to make sense.

Duncan moved forward, picking up his stethoscope as he addressed Max. "Gonna grab another set of vitals. I need you to stay immobile, finally got the bleeding stopped."

"Bleeding?" Max mumbled.

When Finn eyed him with concern, Duncan said, "Transfusion is working. He's getting an oxygen rush which brought him around, but the fever or morphine, maybe both seem to be causing him confusion." He attached the blood pressure cuff to Max's arm and inflated it.

To cover his emotions, because Finn didn't do touchy-feely crap well, he teased, "You're getting a premium McBride fill-up and a special ride to the hospital, but don't let that go to your head. You'll be running the hills once you're better, 'cause we gotta teach you not to be stupid." Finn left his next thought unsaid. *We'll all be sprinting right along with you because we were stupid too.*

"Uh?" Max blinked again, struggling to understand through the dense fog surrounding him.

Dabbing Max's forehead with the wet gauze, Finn said, "Rest. Just rest, Kid."

FOB – TOC

Used to long nights and monitoring Zulu's positions, Kira reached for her coffee, never taking her eyes off the split-screen of two locations. She loved her job, enjoyed working with the guys, and ensuring they got whatever they required when needed. Often before they even realize they need it, but tonight she was upset with herself and believed she failed the team.

When Stirling asked for two bottles of water during the briefing, she assumed he was trying to rehydrate after drinking too much. Had she used her keen powers of observation, she might've recognized he was ill, not hungover. And if she had, the newest member wouldn't be in a life-threatening situation now.

They all needed to do better for him. Stirling saved five members of Zulu before he even joined them. Levi still lived because Max volunteered to rescue him from the rooftop. Finn and Axel lived 'cause the kid came to their assist in Massi's compound. Max also saved Dave's life, taking out two creepers in Algeria. And although not a Zulu operator, Nicole shared with her that Max protected her at Guantanamo Bay.

Stirling deserved better from them, and Kira vowed to take the time to observe and understand what made Max tick. To find his telltale signs, no matter how obscure, to be prepared for the future. Pulled from her thoughts, she turned to glance at the CIA agent as the man poured another coffee.

She got a bad vibe off the man. He seemed a tad old to be in his position, almost as if his career stalled, and he didn't possess the wherewithal to be promoted. Kira wanted to throttle the spook when he insisted they leave Stirling. He had no concept of how valuable these operators were … both intangibly and monetarily.

Though a bit crass to think about the money aspect, the Navy did expend an enormous amount of money training SEALs. Though the figures weren't exact, it cost between 350,000 and 500,000 dollars to train one SEAL. And to keep him operational and deployable, the cost was around one million dollars per year. So deliberately leaving one behind to die would never happen.

With only forty minutes left until the Canadian helo would arrive to extract Max, Kira dismissed Carlson as a donkey's ass and refocused on the monitor. Her eyes widened as she noted a worrisome change at the very edge of the ISR's perimeter. "Sir, we have a problem. A huge one."

Lockwood turned and peered at the screen as Draper pointed to what concerned her. With years of experience, Bryan kept his voice neutral as he picked up the handset and said, "Zulu One and Three, a force of approximately fifty is moving on foot towards Three's position from the west. Can't tell if they're armed, but I'm guessing so given the territory. If they stay the course, they'll arrive in twenty or thirty minutes."

Carlson stayed back and contemplated if he should speak up now. If Nazeri's men found the four, he might deviate from his normal behavior and leave without visiting the village tomorrow. But then again, fifty against four, Nazeri might eliminate them and keep going. The loss of four soldiers was nothing compared to the value of his career for bringing in Nazeri.

He took a seat and chose to maintain secrecy. He would keep this piece of intel to himself as he had done when he got the operation greenlit. If he had shared with anyone that Nazeri camped outside his father's village with a large portion of his army, but only took a few with him when visiting, then he wouldn't have received approval.

Carlson sipped his coffee, assured his plan would go as he wanted, and the promotion he'd been denied for many years would at long last be his. And, Captain Athole might also thank him for ridding the world of Preston Stirling's son. Though that had not been part of his plan or his intention, it would be a satisfying bonus. If dead, the brat would never be able to make waves about Preston's last mission.

Chapter Seven

Inside Building Near Nazeri Residence

JAKE turned to Dave, who already pulled out the map to determine the distance between them and the outcropping. Their eyes met, and Dave nodded, if they went now, they would arrive before the force. Jake no longer cared about grabbing Nazeri. Well, technically, he did, but three of his men would be outgunned in a matter of minutes, and he needed to do something to ensure their safety.

Blaze understood Marshall's hard glare. He'd been in the same boat too many times himself. "The location is defensible."

"How defensible?" Jake asked.

"Clear line of sight, high ground, multiple egress directions," Blaze shared. "Go. We'll handle Nazeri."

Nodding, Jake noted Dave and Grant were preparing to leave, rightly assuming he would choose to go since the Canadians would complete the Nazeri snatch. "We owe you one, Blain."

"Nothing owed. Keep Duncan safe for me," Blaze shot back as Marshall hurried out.

"Zulu One to TOC, heading to Three's position. Keep me updated." As Jake adjusted his NODs, he recognized one positive in tonight's misadventures. Due to Max's condition, the boys traveled only two miles. So, even with the rough terrain, he would arrive in time to mount a defense if necessary.

FOB – TOC

Kira continued to monitor the horde of heat signatures moving towards her team, ready to convey any changes to Jake. She refrained from mentally asking, what more can go wrong because she didn't want the guys jumping from the pan into the fire.

Carlson seethed. "What the hell? Call him back. Marshall is abandoning the mission. I will lose Nazeri. The high-value target is more important than a few soldiers."

"Sailors," Nicole corrected and noted the use of 'I' in his statement. Her gut roiled, not liking this slimeball with no regard for the lives of honorable men who risked everything to combat terrorism.

"Whatever!" Carlson bit back.

Bryan rounded on the disgusting CIA operative. "I trust the Canadian team to grab the HVT. I will not sacrifice my men when they can be saved. Their lives matter whether you think so or not."

Prioritizing, Lockwood dismissed the agent from his mind and picked up the secured phone. He needed to contact Sutton to convey the change in circumstances and prevent the colonel's QRF team from blindly walking into a sizable enemy force.

Huffing when the lieutenant commander turned his back, Carlson shifted his mind to how to spin this if the Canadians did bring in Nazeri. He could still claim the catch, though he would need to do some covering up since his ploy to keep this a U.S. only op had gone out the window when Sutton's team showed up.

Cover-ups were a specialty of his, so Carlson didn't think he would have any difficulty. His first significant operation eighteen years ago went south, and to this day, nobody ever questioned the story. His solution had been a stroke of genius and flawless, as he helped to successfully place the blame on someone else.

Well, not entirely true, but no one who mattered or who would be believed suspected the responsible party was anyone other than Preston Stirling. He thoroughly destroyed the evidence, so there was no proof except the stuff he and his two buddies concocted to point the finger at Stirling.

Rock Outcropping

After dousing the light and flipping their night vision into place, Finn assisted Duncan in carefully repositioning Max at the back of the alcove, providing him more protection. Unfortunately, Max woke as they were doing so, and emitted a pain-filled hiss.

Kneeling to place a pack under Max's head, Finn let his hand rest a moment on the kid's feverish forehead. "Stay down and quiet. Unwanted company is coming."

Glazed eyes fixated on the shadowy figure in front of him, as Max tried to make sense of Finn's comment. Their fall came back to him, though he appeared to be in a different location now.

"You understand? No movement. Stay quiet as a church mouse," Finn reiterated, hoping Max was a bit more with it now.

"Where are we?" As his vision cleared, Max glanced around without moving, taking in his location and spotting Rocketeer and Duncan beside Finn.

"Partway to exfil, but tali-monsters decided to crash our party, so you need to be quiet."

"Give me my weapon."

Finn snorted. "Not such a bright idea, Princess Peach."

"I'm not going out without a fight." Max attempted to push up, but two sets of hands stopped him.

"If you promise to remain still, okay. Move, and you start leaking. You can't afford to lose too much more. I gave you all I can, and neither Zach or Duncan are a match." Finn put Max's pistol in his hand. "Boss is coming, so you hold tight. This time we got you covered, little buddy. Got it?"

Blinking to keep his heavy lids open, Max said, "Copy."

Finn motioned upward with his chin to Duncan. "Go topside with Zach. I'll cover Max from here."

Duncan nodded and climbed up the rock overhang. He lay flat next to Zach and peered out into the night, searching in the direction of the hostiles. "Think we can hold off fifty?" He wouldn't have asked if his unit were here. Blaze and Winds always ensured they came out on top.

Zach smiled. "Fifty are no match against a pissed off Marshall."

"Is he pissed?"

"Most definitely. The kid is hurt and in danger."

Duncan chuckled. "Just like Blaze when Blondie is in trouble. Blaze still goes all Papa Bear whenever he finds out Blondie gets hurt. But I don't blame him. They developed a bond forged in six years of hell."

Down below, Finn listened as the whispers funneled down to him. He reconsidered Duncan's earlier words and wondered if Jake would ever take to Max as Blaze supposedly did to their Blondie. *Nah, I still don't see Jake in that role with Max. Brother, yes, father, no way ... Jake has his own kids.*

Several minutes later, Finn put aside his thoughts when Rocketeer's ears perked up, alerting him the dog perceived something he had not. He scanned the area but relaxed when Jake's voice came through his headset.

"Zulu Three, have your position in sight. Coming up."

Struggling to keep his eyes open, Max realized the morphine dulled his pain and left him fuzzy, but did nothing to quell his fever. He lifted his empty hand to wipe away beads of sweat from his forehead and saw the IV. *When did that get there?*

When a rustling sounded close by, Max brought his gun up, preparing to fire. No way in hell he wanted any of them to die because he fell on some stupid-assed pyramid thing and poked a hole in his back. He pointed at a figure emerging from the trees, wondering why Finn didn't react.

"Whoa, Kid. Just me," Jake whispered as he approached.

Finn turned back to Max. His gut twisted, viewing the handgun aimed at Jake. "Damn, shouldn't have given it to him."

"Easy." Moving slow, Jake knelt as he reached out to cover the loaded pistol and push the barrel down and away from him.

Blinking, Max registered Marshall. He allowed the gun to be taken from him, realizing he could've shot his team leader. His hand shook a little at the thought and hoped if Jake noticed he would attribute it to his current condition.

Joining the others, Dave took a knee beside their injured rookie and noted the kid's earpiece dangled near his chest. "Max didn't know we were approaching." Dave shifted the earbud back in place. "This should help."

Though he trusted Duncan, Grant moved forward to do a once over on Max as Jake contacted TOC to get the enemy force's latest position and determine his strategy.

FOB – TOC

Draper prayed the huge group would deviate or walk right past her guys. She breathed a tiny sigh of relief when three images converged on Finn's location, Jake, Dave, and Grant had arrived in exceptional time. When Jake asked for an update, she reported, "The group appears to be slowing and adjusting course. They might miss you if we are lucky."

Bryan hung up the phone after communicating with the Canadian force. He put their QRF team in a holding pattern six miles from his team's location so the sounds of the inbound helos wouldn't alert the unknown group to their presence. Mulling over the details, something didn't sit right with his gut. Turning to Farris, Lockwood said, "Something doesn't fit. Nazeri isn't supposed to be with a large contingent, but could this be him?"

Nicole pursed her lips as she assessed Carlson, who continued to sip his coffee as if nothing was amiss. She'd been asking herself the same question for the past few minutes. "Although all intel points to only ten guards traveling with him, it is possible we're missing a piece of the puzzle. It would make more sense if Nazeri traveled with his full force. Perhaps he does, and only a few go into the village while the rest wait nearby."

"If that is the case, our boys could've been slaughtered on exfil because they might've run smack dab into this group," Kira chimed in as she shot a glare at Carlson. She didn't trust the weasel since he remained unnaturally silent and didn't offer any input as Lockwood and Farris discussed the possibilities.

Farris pinned her eyes on Carlson. "What is your take?"

Setting down his mug, Carlson began to lay the groundwork to redirect any blow-back from him. "All accounts I received from my Canadian source is Nazeri only travels with a small number of men when visiting. It appears their lackadaisical recon put this mission in jeopardy."

"*Their* intel? You're the one who got the op greenlit. Didn't you bother to vet the information?" Nicole blurted out. She couldn't believe Carlson was putting this on the Canadians … this was his baby from the get-go.

Lockwood cleared his throat, taking charge. "It is what it is. We need to deal with the situation at hand." With Stirling stable for the moment and help only minutes out once the area was secured, Bryan picked up the handset and communicated with Zulu and both Canadian teams. He informed them Nazeri might be with the approaching group and directed them to develop a coordinated plan to identify if the HVT was among them and to snatch him if at all possible.

Once Bryan finished, Kira communicated, "Zulu One, the group halted about two hundred yards from your pos. They appear to be making camp. Several individuals have moved away from them in four directions, perhaps to act as sentries."

Canadian Helo

Sergeant Murchadh Ailpein Srònaich O'Naoimhín, Mason to everyone because saying his name was impossible for most people, listened on his comms as the American commander explained the issues. With the arrival of an excessive number of Taliban, their approach and landing zone changed. When Lockwood finished, he engaged with Blaze and Zulu One to outline a new strategy.

His unit would now fast-line down about seven clicks away and high-tail it to Zulu's position. Running flat out, they would arrive shortly before dawn and be able to help the Americans. The second helo with medical personnel would maintain in a holding pattern until further notice. Blaze would remain in the village on the off-chance Nazeri was not with the larger group.

Turning to his second-in-command, Mason grinned and spoke loudly over the engines, "Ready, Pirate?"

"Aye. Time to maraud."

The ropes dropped, and Mason's six-man unit rapidly descended. Before taking off at a run towards the familiar outcropping, Mason let Marshall know they were now en route to their position.

Near Rock Outcropping

After making a new plan, Jake left Finn, Zach, Rocketeer, and Blaze's medic at the outcropping to protect Max while he, Grant, and Dave set out to recon the encampment. Draper had been right. There were small fires in the clearing, and the armed men appeared to settle around them.

With Max in a precarious condition, Jake didn't want to engage the enemy combatants unless discovered, or they located Nazeri. The sky would be lightening soon, which would allow them to search for Nazeri, but before losing the cover of darkness, they had a little work to do.

Jake, Dave, and Grant moved, and with Draper's assistance identified the location of the posted sentries. Stealthily, they approached their quarry from the rear and applied chokeholds, rendering the guards unconscious. After lowering them to the ground, the guys shoved leaves in their mouths and used the fabric of their turbans to gag them, dragged them to trees, and zip-tied their hands behind them around the trunks.

Before twilight, they silently incapacitated ten of the fifty, without being discovered. Moving back to their defensive position, Jake squawked his comms twice to alert the others they completed their task and now would wait for Mason's team to join them before taking further action.

As he waited, Jake's mind returned to Max. Stirling had been pretty out of it when he pointed the gun at him, and he wondered if Max would even remember. *I need to talk to Finn about giving the kid a weapon when dosed up on morphine. Not a smart idea.*

Rock Outcropping

When the comms came alive with a deep, yet quiet voice indicating the Canadian QRF team was almost in place to assist if they located Nazeri, Finn glanced at the kid whose eyes had shut again. Though he regretted Max pointing the firearm at Jake and expected a lecture from the boss when this was all over, the thought of leaving the kid unarmed in the face of so many bloodthirsty jihadists seemed the greater of two evils.

Finn pulled the pistol from the back of his pant waist, where he tucked it after Jake handed it over to him. Crouching close, Finn patted Max's shoulder and waited as his lids flickered up. He whispered, "How ya doing?"

Though Max found it exceedingly difficult to keep his eyes open, he gave Finn a thumbs up. As he shifted slightly, hoping for a more comfortable position, the motion caused a sharp pain to slice through his flank. Max's eyes squeezed shut as he gritted his teeth, only partly successful in preventing a moan from escaping.

The expression of agony made Finn's decision. Sadly, the kid was in no condition to be armed. He leaned in close, only a few inches from Stirling's face. "I said not to move," he growled in a hushed but authoritative tone.

Copy. Moving sucks. Responding with only a blink and slight nod, Max held still.

From up top, Zach's quiet command filtered down to Rocketeer. "Protect."

Finn grinned as Rocky took up a position in front of the kid. If he went down and couldn't cover Max, Rocketeer would guard their kid until his last breath. Their badass pup would happily sink his canines into any tali-monster stupid enough to come anywhere near his new packmate.

Chapter Eight

Near Rock Outcropping

LIFTING his night vision as the first rays of a new day illuminated the horizon, Mason halted behind the cover of a tree on the left flank of the Americans. He scanned the area, sighting the hostile's location before keying his comms. "Kilo One to Zulu One. We are in position."

"Copy. Hold," Jake whispered as he breathed easier, knowing the unit led by Mason reached them before the missing sentries had been noticed. If their luck held out, they would be able to determine if Nazeri was present before anyone sounded a warning. Although mission-focused, part of Jake hoped Nazeri wouldn't be here so they could evac the kid undetected.

A bit selfish, Jake didn't want to lose another teammate so soon. Though neither Levi or Axel died, Zulu had been through the wringer, and his team needed stability. Jake acknowledged any blame for this mission snafu, caused by not allowing Stirling to explain on the plane, would fall on him. Jake determined to do his damnedest to fix his screw up if they got Six out of here alive.

Glancing over to Dave, who with his high-powered scope, searched the encamped men for their HVT, Jake closed the lid on all non-essential thoughts, preparing to take action if necessary. "See anything?"

"Possible. Second fire to the south," Dave answered.

Using binoculars, Jake trained his eyes on the location. He spotted five men standing, surrounding one man sitting on a rock near the fire and facing him. Jake had stared at the ugly mug long enough during briefing to recognize and positively identify him as Sina Nazeri. "TOC, Zulu One, HVT confirmed in the group."

Jake's attention shifted from Lockwood's transmission confirmation as a man yelled after finding one of his comrades trussed up to a tree. The quiet morning erupted in noise as the camp surged to life, and Nazeri barked orders to his men.

"Zulu Two, target those around Nazeri as soon as we engage. We want him alive," Jake instructed, no longer bothering to keep his voice to a whisper as the enemy spread out searching for their other sentries.

Talking became non-existent as Zulu and Kilo engaged in a full-on firefight hoping the element of surprise would even the odds of twelve against forty. Having the high ground provided an advantage if only slight in the face of so many. The real advantage was their training and accuracy in firing. One after another of Nazeri's force met their maker after a well-placed bullet.

Jake shifted position, moving up the hill as Nazeri's men rushed him. Making a dent in the numbers still didn't mean they would be victorious. He dove behind a rock right before a shower of shots rained down around him. A burning sensation across his left bicep told Jake he had been hit, but he didn't have the time to check as he began targeting the hostiles moving in on him.

Sniping those surrounding Nazeri, Dave took out all five guards. Though they must apprehend Nazeri alive, Dave figured the best course of action would be to hobble the man with a minor leg wound to prevent him from running. He fired as Grant provided him cover from those approaching his location. Once Nazeri went down, he bugged out, too many advancing on him for Grant to protect him any longer.

Mason and his team tried to draw the force away from the rock outcropping to safeguard Zulu's injured man and managed to lure at least twenty, but half still moved on Zulu's position.

Rock Outcropping

Still vastly outnumbered, Zach, Finn, and Duncan sent out a torrent of bullets providing cover for Jake, Dave, and Grant as they pulled back. After the three attained new positions, they dialed back to directed shots to conserve their dwindling supply of ammo.

Though their barrage safeguarded their teammates, regrettably, the muzzle flashes from their weapons provided the insurgents with their location. More shots zinged in their direction, smashing into and ricocheting off the surrounding rocks.

Rocketeer moved, putting himself in front of Max, sensing one of his humans was in danger and doing as his partner instructed … protect.

A yelp caused Finn to twist his head in time to witness Rocketeer fall back on Max. "Shit, Rocky's hit!"

"How bad?" Zach yelled down, wanting to go to his dog but unable and unwilling to leave his post.

The sustained gunfire brought Max around, and he witnessed the dog jerk and fall. Without regard for his well-being, he reached out to Rocketeer, who now lay next to him, and found the wound. His soft groan mixed with the pup's whine as Max pressed hard to stem the flow.

"In the thigh," Max said as he struggled to stay conscious, striving to ignore the pain in his back. His four-legged teammate needed help, and he would give it for as long as possible.

"Kid's got him for now," Finn called out as he returned his attention to the dozen or so men who dug in, taking cover and still firing at them.

Rocketeer's soulful brown eyes locked with the ocean blue ones of his new packmate. He whimpered but licked his face, thanking him and commiserating in their agony.

After Rocky's tongue ran across his scruffy cheek, the pup settled his head on his paws and stared at him. Max never experienced a connection with an animal before, but he would swear complete trust reflected in Rocketeer's eyes.

When a burst of fire kicked up dust around them, Max shifted, pulling Rocketeer closer. With a grunt, caused by intense pain, Max used the last tendrils of consciousness to lift and drape his body over Rocky to shield him from the bullets.

Near Rock Outcropping

Finally realizing they were outgunned, the remaining eight turned tail and retreated, leaving their wounded and dead on the ground, including Nazeri, who yelled for them to take him with them and when they didn't, cursed them as cowards.

Jake, Grant, and Dave went on the offensive, unwilling to allow the fleeing men to escape to gather reinforcements. They engaged them in the next gorge, and all eight chose death this time instead of giving up when Dave called out one of the few phrases he spoke in their language telling them to surrender.

On their way back, they met up with the Canadians, who killed those they lured away from the outcropping. As Grant halted next to Nazeri to render first aid, applying a compress to the minor wound on the terrorist's leg, Dave's gaze traveled upward at the massive six-foot-seven man who introduced himself as Mason.

"Damn glad you were able to help," Jake said as he shook Mason's hand, noting the scar across his cheek.

Mason's response was drowned out as Finn's voice cut across the comms. "We need evac now! Can't stop the bleeding. We're losing the kid. Rocketeer's down too."

Jake ran like the devil bit at his heels, leaving Dave to handle things with Mason and Nazeri.

Rock Outcropping

Reaching the alcove, Jake boomed, "Son of a bitch," as he witnessed Finn's bloody hands pressing down on Max's right flank while Zach did the same to Rocketeer's thigh as Duncan attached a new bag of saline to Stirling's IV port.

Finn's eyes met Jake's. "He moved. The little shit moved."

Jake didn't need more explanation, and he keyed his comms. "TOC set the helos down as close as you can. I'm not losing Zulu Six. Package also acquired."

He knew Lockwood and Draper would do all in their power, so he knelt next to Max and tapped the kid's cheek, hoping to elicit a response. When fever-glazed eyes opened, Jake admonished, "You weren't supposed to move."

Using the last of his energy, Max mumbled, "Saving a teammate. Would do it again." His eyes rolled back as he gave way to sweet oblivion again.

Zach held pressure on his dog's hindquarter as he stared at Max. "Damned kid risked his life for Rocketeer."

When Duncan took over, pressing more packing on Max's wound, Finn rose and paced as anger and concern warred inside. He snapped, "Rocketeer would be dead. Kid took four rounds in the vest covering the dog."

"Zulu One, evac four minutes out." Draper then rattled off the coordinates, which was a close as they could land, but she wished it could be closer.

Jake peered at Duncan. "Wrap him tight. I'm carrying him." Turning to the others, he said, "Prepare to move."

Finn shook his head. "You're hit, Jake. I've got him."

"It's nothing. He's my responsibility."

Although he didn't argue further, Finn would not be far from either on exfil. "I'll hold pressure as we go, might give him more time."

Jake nodded.

Once Duncan did everything possible to stem the flow, Jake squatted and, with assistance, carefully lifted Stirling to his shoulder. Ensuring his grip was firm Jake stood, and Finn placed a hand over Max's back.

When they reached the clearing, Jake readily agreed with Mason when he offered to stay to secure the area and guard the few living detainees until Blaze arrived, so Zulu Team, along with Nazeri and Duncan, could continue to the evac location.

Landing Zone

Arriving as the helos set down, Jake moved to the larger one as two corpsmen hopped out. With their help, he lowered Max to a waiting stretcher. He stepped back, making room for Grant as his medic began calling out Zulu Six's status over the sound of the rotors.

When Duncan began to assist Nazeri toward the medical helicopter, Jake stopped him and pointed to the smaller one as he yelled, "The asshole goes on that one. Rocky's life is more important to me, so he's on this one." Jake motioned for Zach to join him as he directed Finn, "Go with the HVT."

Though wanting to go with the kid, Finn nodded and didn't argue with Marshall since they would need room in the tight quarters to save the kid's life. He followed Duncan and Dave to the other helo with one of the medics who grabbed a kit.

With assistance, Zach climbed aboard the helo and settled Rocketeer in his lap; grateful Jake prioritized Rocky over Nazeri. The last to board, Jake barely sat on the floor near Stirling before they were in the air. Though he left prayers to Dave, he did peer down at Max's pale, lax features, and hoped like hell the kid survived the hour flight to the hospital.

Helo

Kicking to the surface with all his might, his lungs burning with the need for air, Max fought against the unseen forces trying to pull him down. Breaking through the surf, he gasped, drawing in a life-giving breath. Disoriented by a cacophony of sounds, he fought to open his eyes, and his legs attempted to scissor kick to keep his head above water.

When someone or something grabbed him, fear washed through Max as he struggled not to drown. He twisted one way and another, kicking his feet and flailing his arms even though the action caused him significant pain. Max struck something solid, and a vice seized his hand, preventing him from moving.

Fifteen minutes into the flight, as Max began coming around, he thrashed when Grant and the other medics tried to strip him of his clothing. Jake grabbed Stirling's hand to prevent him from pulling out the IV. Leaning close to Max's ear, he shouted to be heard over the blades, "Stop fighting. You are safe."

A loud, stern voice filtered in, and Max stilled, obeying the command. The water around him evaporated, but his body remained drenched, and his mind discombobulated. Max's lashes fluttered up, and he found a familiar face only inches from his, but the expression didn't match the harsh tone.

"Relax, Kid. We got you. Let Grant do his job." Jake softened his tone as he peered into confused, glassy, pain-filled orbs. His gut did another flipflop witnessing the vulnerability in those young eyes. They reminded him of Jamie's eyes, though they were not the same shade of blue. He reduced the strength of his hold on the kid's hand but gave it a reassuring squeeze. "You're gonna be okay."

Max allowed his eyes to close, unsure why Marshall's presence chased away his demons. He clung to Jake's hand with a crushing grip when pain rippled through his chest as he inhaled a deep breath. Heat consuming him, Max attempted to reopen his eyes but slipped unconscious again.

Jake listened to the medical jargon flung around by the two men in charge of Max's care. Things he didn't understand, but he watched Grant, who continually nodded and often chimed in with other details. He did comprehend when one said, "Temp is too high. One hundred four point six."

Shit! This isn't good. Jake's eyes flickered to Rocketeer as the dog whimpered in Zach's lap. His ordinarily stoic hair missile handler had tears in his eyes as he gently petted Rocky while Grant shifted to examine their canine teammate.

When Max became restless again, he followed Zach's lead, essentially petting Max's blond locks and scratching behind his ears. Amazingly, it calmed their rookie. He caught Grant's amused expression. "I'll deny this if you so much as breathe a word."

"No one would believe me, so I'll save my breath." Grant chuckled, despite the stressful situation. He peered up at Zach. "Rocketeer is gonna be alright. It's in the fleshy part. Don't think the bullet did too much damage."

Grant's short laugh and assessment broke Zach's tension. He smiled and drew in a deep breath; relieved Rocky would be okay. His gaze transferred to Max and hoped the same could be said for their newbie.

The flight seemed to take forever as Jake reassured Max each time the fever's delirium caused him to become restless. By the time they arrived at Bagram Airfield, Max's head lay in Jake's lap, and one hand brushed the kid's fevered brow while Max grasped his other hand. Though semi-conscious, Stirling's grip remained firm and truthfully a little painful as Max squeezed his fingers.

Tarmac

Once they landed, more medical personnel rushed forward with gurneys for the wounded. As they transferred Max, he started to thrash again when Jake let go of his hand.

"Go with him," Bryan ordered after assessing the situation.

Jake didn't object, though he wanted to find Carlson and put his fist into the man's face. There would be time enough for that once Max had been attended to by doctors. He ran alongside the stretcher, as did Grant, not willing to be shoved off.

After climbing in the ambulance, Jake glanced back, and his eyes met Dave's. A silent conversation occurred in the brief moment before the door shut. Jake trusted Dave to keep an eye on Finn. They had enough experience with the hothead to predict he would be seeking blood from Carlson, and if not stopped would cost McBride his career.

Dave turned to Finn. "Grab Stirling's gear."

"Got other plans." Finn's fists clenched, itching to pulverize Carlson. *The CIA asshat sent us on a mission with shit intel, that could've gotten us all killed. And the kid didn't even need to be there ... fucking Nazeri speaks English.*

"No, you don't. Jake will handle Carlson," Dave's tone brooked no defiance.

"I'll take whatever is left then." Finn stormed over to the other helo and grabbed the kid's vest and weapons. The sight of blood covering the floor caused his fury and guilt to rise. "Damned kid!"

Duncan stopped near McBride. "Need a hand?"

Finn peered at the man who kept Max alive. "No, I got it. Thanks."

Shaking his head, Duncan said, "None needed. Catch ya on the flip side." He strode toward Sutton, surprised to find the colonel at Bagram. Coming to a halt, Duncan stood at attention. "Sir, wasn't expecting you to be here."

"At ease, Duncan. I hopped a flight from Kandahar to be on hand for a combined debrief with the Americans." Sutton needed to gather as much detail from his men before attending, so he said, "Give me the status on the injured."

"Nazeri's wound is minor though by his bitching and crying you'd think he was dying. Stirling is in bad shape, but having blood products en route helped. I'm confident he will make it now that he'll receive the right care. Their dog too. Damned if he doesn't remind me of Blondie."

Sutton chuckled. "Which one the canine or the man?"

"Well, both actually. Each one shielded the other. When will Blaze and Mason exfil?"

"The American helos are almost there. A little allied shaming went a long way in getting a certain American general and captain off their asses to authorize the flight. Our units should return in about an hour with the detainees."

Duncan nodded and followed Sutton to a waiting vehicle. He spied McBride lugging the extra gear and smiled. He believed Stirling's unit would protect their kid as fiercely as Blaze, Winds, Patch, Mason, Brody, and Ripsaw had protected Blondie.

Chapter Nine

Hospital – Waiting Room

PACING for the past twenty minutes, Jake took fifteen steps one way and fifteen back. His hands alternated between clenched fists and lacing them behind his neck and squeezing. In the short, swift ride to the hospital, Stirling had gone downhill fast. By the time they arrived, two IVs were going full bore, and his temp had risen more.

The scariest moment, yes, macho SEALs experienced fear, was when Max's heart quit beating. Jake stopped breathing at the same time and only began again when the medic found a pulse after shocking Max with a defibrillator.

Bryan entered, followed by Finn and Dave. He noted Jake's demeanor, which told him things were grave. "How is he?"

Jake halted, and his burning glare landed on Lockwood. "He died ... almost died. I'm gonna plow my fists in that ass, Carlson. Did you know Nazeri speaks English? The kid didn't even need to be on this fucking mission. And, had we grabbed Nazeri in the village, we would've run into his men upon exfil. My men might've been slaughtered because of shitty intel."

Unable to hold back any longer, Jake slammed a fist into the thin wall. His other fist followed. He beat a hole the size of a face, envisioning Carlson, landing one punch after another until Dave and Finn pulled him away and shoved him into a seat.

Nicole Farris watched and wished she could do the same. But unlike Jake, she possessed restraint and a more effective method of dealing with Carlson. The man would be eating dog food as far as assignments went. He would never leave the basement of the most backwater, least influential CIA office once she got done with the bastard. That is after Jake bruised him up because although Nicole would never strike a physical blow, she privately admitted she wanted the idiot bloodied after glimpsing the floor of the helo stained with Max's and Rocky's blood.

"Where is Grant?" Draper asked as she arrived.

All eyes turned to Jake.

Waving his hand toward the door, he answered, "Back there with Zach. Some shit about this not being a veterinary hospital and the doctors not wanting to treat Rocketeer. They are making them see the light … probably at gunpoint … that Rocky is a teammate in need of care, regardless of the fact he has four legs."

Finn growled, "I can go help."

Kira couldn't help herself as she smirked. "Finn's more of an attack dog than Rocketeer."

Arching a brow at Draper, Finn conceded, "Maybe not more, but I agree we're kin. Let me sink my teeth into Carlson."

A door opening caused the group to turn, and they spied Grant exiting as Dave asked, "What's the word on both?"

Grant inhaled and released his breath gradually. "Nothing yet on Stirling, but Rocketeer will be fine after a couple weeks of rest. They removed the bullet after giving him a local anesthetic. Nothing major hit. The doc is scared shitless of Rocky, so Zach's staying with him as they finish bandaging up his leg."

Kira tapped Nicole's arm. "Sounds like it might be a long wait. I'm going to grab coffee and such for the guys, would you help?"

Nicole nodded, and they headed back the way they entered.

Three hours later, the haggard group all stood as a doctor approached them. He launched into gibberish as far as most of them were concerned. When he stopped, they all looked to Grant for translation of the medical speak.

"Dr. Bajwa said Max is suffering from a severe kidney infection, which caused the fever and is most likely the reason for his nausea and headache too. The tip of the pyramid nicked his right kidney. The doctor suspects a hematoma formed and ruptured when Max fell.

"When the kid moved to cover Rocky, he dislodged the packing, disrupting the coagulation process. Fortunately, although his actions reopened the lesion, which led to additional blood loss, he didn't bleed as profusely. They surgically repaired the damage and are transfusing him now."

"Damn, this is my fault," Finn grumbled. "If I hadn't landed on the kid."

Grant shook his head. "Could've ruptured on its own."

Jake asked, "How the hell did his kidney get infected?"

"Based on the onset of his symptoms, my best guess is he picked up the bacteria while in the cesspool. He shouldn't have been on a mission until Dr. Irving reviewed and signed off on his blood work." Grant eyed Lockwood, believing he screwed up by not pushing back when Max's language skills became the deciding factor in choosing Zulu for this operation.

"Duly noted," Bryan said, aware he dropped the ball and put one of his men in harm's way. Something he wouldn't do again. Though, he also acknowledged, as terrible as this turn of events were for Stirling, it likely saved the entire team.

Weary, Jake slumped into a chair. "So, will he be alright?"

"Yes. They are treating the infection, too."

"What about the bullets he took for Rocketeer?" Dave asked.

"Bruised ribs. I'm amazed none are cracked or broken, given the placement. His back will be colorful and sore for a while," Grant explained.

"Thank God, he survived." Dave sighed.

Peering at the doctor who still stood with them, Finn groused, "Why can't you explain things in plain English like Grant?"

Incensed, Dr. Bajwa said, "I speak English quite well. Perhaps you should learn your own language."

"When can we visit him?" Though Jake didn't quite understand his reaction, he didn't want the kid to wake up alone.

"He will be moved to a room within the hour, but you must wait for visiting hours," Bajwa stated.

Bryan captured Jake's gaze and prepared for the challenge. "Go clean up. Sleep. Stirling will be fine in their care."

"Hell no. I'm not letting that kid out of my sight," Jake challenged, again surprised at his gut reaction. One he might've had if it were Jamie, Eve, or Tommy in the hospital.

"Don't make me pull rank." Lockwood straightened up.

"A shower, food, and a bit of rest will do you good, Jake," Dave urged. Finding no softening, he added, "Perhaps a little talk with Carlson, too."

Jake's eyes flared as they landed on his second in command. Annoyingly, Dave knew him all too well. "Fine."

Finn grinned and fell into step with Jake's long stride, eagerly anticipating watching Carlson piss himself when his ticked off boss found the CIA weasel.

FOB – Carlson's Quarters

Cramming his meager belongings into a duffle bag, Carlson desired to make it out on the next transport, hopefully, before a raging Marshall found him. Farris, Lockwood, and Sutton cornered him in TOC and read him the riot act before notifying his boss of the clusterfuck of a mission.

His career now in shambles, none of his plans to shift the blame would work. Those bastards worked too damned fast for him to cover up his missteps. The long-overdue promotion he expected and worked so hard for evaporated and Carlson doubted he would ever be assigned another field position.

Another fucking Stirling cratered my career. Like father, like son. I'll have my vengeance once again. I'll make sure Maxwell dies just like Preston. Athole will help me ... he owes me one ... and he wants to be rid of the whelp too. Carlson grabbed his bag and laptop, opened his door, and stepped out.

Carlson took two strides before being abruptly slammed up against the wooden wall of the temporary housing. The air in his lungs expelled rapidly with the impact, and by the time he inhaled a ragged breath, amber eyes of a lion bore into him, and the man wearing a tan beret unleashed a verbal hurricane.

Sutton strode up to Blaze, observing Winds giving Carlson a piece of his mind. Nonchalantly he said, "Damn glad you accepted the promotion, but also happy you were in the field on this one. Did you get Yel Malik?"

Blaze kept his gaze on Winds, ready to intervene if his best friend moved into territory that would result in a demotion or court-martial. He needed Winds to take over the team, so the days of his unbridled storm of words had to be tempered.

Rubbing the faded, thin line on his left palm, Blaze answered Sutton. "Not us, we have the Americans to thank. The filthy animal was among five taken out by Zulu's sniper. Unfortunately, we still have a couple more bastards to find and put down."

"We will locate them, and as you know, the general and I fully support the vow you and Winds made."

Blaze turned to peer at Sutton, and a grin grew. "A few years ago, I didn't believe Blondie's father gave a rat's ass about him. Now, truth be told, I firmly believe if he could, General Broderick would return to the field to personally take out the bastards who tortured his son."

Sutton nodded. "He keeps his sniper skills sharp. If the opportunity presented itself, you are right, William wouldn't hesitate to pull the trigger."

A commotion caused Blaze to turn back to where Winds harangued the slimy weasel. "Whoa, I do believe Carlson is in for more than Winds's verbal lashing."

Sutton pivoted. "Can't watch, or I'll be forced to intervene. Tell me later what doesn't officially happen." He strode away with a smile. At his rank, he would need to put a stop to this, but he had no desire to do so. He was done putting up with deceitful men who didn't care about soldiers.

He lumped Carlson in with men like Plouffe. If Sutton had his way, Carlson's career would be buried six feet under—along with his decomposing body.

A smug grin formed on Blaze's face as he observed five pissed off SEALs, striding towards one screwed CIA operative.

Approaching the base's temporary quarters, Jake overheard someone yelling at Carlson well before he viewed who was letting loose a torrent of biting words, saying much of what he intended. Jake would've grinned at the cowed figure trapped by Winds, but he was too furious and planned more than words.

Still in stride to his intended target, with anger controlling the timbre of his voice, he brokered no interference. "Thanks, Winds. We'll take it from here."

"The asshat is all yours." Winds acceded, presenting Carlson to his brothers-in-arms with a slight bow before joining Blaze to enjoy the show as the Americans doled out a bit of unit justice.

Jake's fist flew, connecting with Carlson's nose, creating a satisfying crunch of cartilage as he shouted, "You son of a bitch! You nearly killed my men with your shit for brains intel!"

Finn stepped forward next. "You lying motherfucker, I should shoot you here and now, but I'll settle for this." He landed a powerful punch to Carlson's solar plexus, causing him to bend over and gasp for breath.

Furious this asshole's plan got Rocketeer shot, Zach lifted Carlson's head by using an uppercut to his jaw. As the back of the man's head whacked the wood wall, he barked, "My dog is more human than you. If Rocketeer could be here now, I'd let him tear you to pieces."

Grant and Dave stood behind the other three, prepared to step in if their teammates moved beyond a few punches. With Jake and Finn, that was entirely possible.

Reeling, gasping, hurting, Carlson's hand covered his bleeding nose as he whined, "My plan would've worked if you stuck to it, and your worthless rookie didn't screw up. He's as stupid as his father, and he'll be the reason you all end up dead."

Jake's restraint, what little he still held, snapped when Carlson laid the blame on Stirling. He let loose with a barrage of strikes to Carlson's midsection before Dave seized his arm and pulled him back. Jake still saw red as Carlson dropped to the ground holding his stomach and moaning.

Grant grabbed Finn, preventing him from taking Jake's place. When McBride struggled to loosen his grip, he said, "The asshole isn't worth your career."

"FINE!" Finn twisted away, putting space between him and the spook before he lost all control and pummeled him to death.

Picking himself up, Carlson's fear-filled eyes landed on Marshall. *The man is a menace and will pay.* "This is assault. I will ensure you are all arrested and court-martialed."

"Your word against ours. You think anyone will believe you after the lies you told that almost cost the lives of thirteen warriors?" Jake declared.

"Twelve," Carlson dared to correct.

Landing another blow to Carlson's face, Zach snarled, "Rocketeer is a warrior, you asswipe!"

Dazed by the strike, Carlson sank to the dirt, and his head lolled to the side.

Grant squatted and, by the hair, lifted Carlson's head. He checked his pupils and then stood. "He's had enough. Any more, and he'll be concussed."

"I would prefer him to be dead." Finn couldn't resist planting a well-placed kick to the asshole's right flank wanting him to feel pain exactly where Max had been injured.

"We're done here." Jake pivoted and strode away. He agreed with Finn. *Dead would be better.* But he needed to shower, grab some food and head back to the hospital ... he would sleep there. *Anyone tries to kick me out of the kid's room, and they'll find out it isn't happening.*

The rest of the team each kicked Carlson as he sat in the dust, before following Jake. A bit of justice served for Max and Rocketeer.

Tarmac

Lieutenant Farris stood with Draper and Lockwood as their gazes tracked a disheveled Carlson limping towards a plane. Nicole couldn't stop the slight upturn of her lips. "Appears Carlson got his comeuppance."

Kira snickered. "Too bad, he took a tumble out the door of his quarters. He really should be more careful."

Chuckling at Draper's explanation for the man's bloodied and dusty appearance, Bryan shook his head. "Must be a klutz as well as a crappy agent."

Becoming serious, Kira focused on Lockwood. "Not happy Stirling is hurt, but Charlie Team would all be dead now had Carlson's original plan been enacted."

"He won't be planning ops ever again," Nicole stated before turning her eyes on the group of Canadians heading for their helos. "Glad they showed up. Stirling might not be with us anymore if they hadn't."

Bryan nodded. "Colonel Sutton, General Broderick, and their JTF2 units were an immense help."

Kira grinned. "I arranged to send them a thank you gift."

"Do I want to know what?" Bryan eyed the logistics specialist who did more than her occupational specialty. She was as valued an asset as the men of Zulu and made his job easier by taking care of their needs.

"Nothing big. A case of beer and a bottle of the finest Scotch I could find." Kira turned her eyes back to Carlson as the idiot boarded the plane. "If you will excuse me, I need to round up some things for our boys too."

Once Kira left, Nicole said, "She's officer material. Think Draper might be interested in OCS?"

Bryan shrugged. "I agree and perhaps. Though, selfishly, I would hate to lose her as logistics support."

"It would be hard to fill her shoes. I'll be going too. Nazeri should be ready to interrogate now. If lucky, we'll have a few more targets to hit before heading home."

Chapter Ten

Hospital – Max's Room

ORCED to sit in a chair and finally allow Grant to clean the graze on his arm, Jake kept his eyes on Max. The kid lay motionless as sweat beaded, combined into pools, and trailed off his forehead. His fever still in the range of one hundred and two, even with the help of meds, concerned Jake.

Rocketeer occupied the second bed in the room, much to the hospital staff's dismay. The nurses gave the dog a wide berth, approaching Max on the opposite side since Rocky growled at anyone, other than the team, who dared come near Max. It didn't matter to Rocky that they were helping the kid.

Grant finished wrapping gauze around Jake's arm. "Another scar to add to your list. Not too deep, you were right, didn't need stitches."

Nodding, Jake asked, "Shouldn't the fever be down?"

"It is. Antibiotics need time to work." Grant closed his medkit and glanced at one of the chairs Finn stole from other rooms, so they all had somewhere other than the floor to sit. Though, the ground might be more comfortable than the tiny wooden chairs.

Grant chose to continue standing and visually assessed each of his teammates. They all needed sleep, but none of them wanted to leave the new guy. When his perceptive gaze halted on Finn, he noted distress in his countenance. *He's feeling guilty.*

Finn maintained his position between the beds, his green eyes never leaving the young buck. Guilt ate at him. Regardless of Grant's claim that the wound could've ruptured on its own, he knew his weight crushing on top of Max caused the excessive bleeding and nearly cost the rookie his life.

So much for taking him under my wing and protecting him. I'm the reason he is lying here half-dead. A hand landing on his shoulder caused him to turn, drawing him out of his self-flogging.

"Not your fault. I should've taken point into the room. If I had, Max wouldn't have landed on that damned pyramid thing," Grant said.

"We alternated. It was the kid's turn," Finn responded.

Jake rose and pinned a hard gaze on both men. "If anyone is to blame, it is me. I fucked up. I should've let him explain on the plane instead of jumping to conclusions and making assumptions. If I had listened, we would've determined he was sick and not drunk. He wouldn't have gone on the mission."

"Jake, we all thought the same thing. He smelled like a friggin' distillery and the way he climbed into the hammock after take-off, well—"

Cutting off Dave, Jake shouted, "Well, nothing! I would've given each of you the chance to explain. I didn't with him, and I don't know why."

As the truth of his statement rang in their ears, each man turned inward. Jake would've listened to them. A moment later, Max's moan drew their attention as he started to twitch.

Jake was at the kid's side in an instant, gripping his hand. "Be still. You're safe," he intoned close to Max's ear as his rookie's body twisted in the bed. "Stay still, or you might undo all the doctor's work."

Hot, so damned hot, yet freezing. And I fucking hurt. Max grappled and clawed his way up to consciousness. A challenge as his brain wanted two disparate things. One part wanted to stay in blessed oblivion where pain didn't exist. The other needed to wake to defend his team from the onslaught of hostiles.

As he fought to move a body that wouldn't respond appropriately, his first conscious thought came out in a dry, raspy voice, "Rocketeer, gotta protect Rocketeer."

"Rocky is right here. He is safe. You saved his life." Zach glanced at his dog, who whined and endeavored to rise. "Stay. Don't move, boy."

The guys almost laughed as both Rocketeer and Max stilled at Zach's command.

Max managed to lift his eyelids. His world didn't match. Instead of being outside under a rock outcropping, he was in a sterile, white room with his teammates all standing around him. Rather than hard-packed dirt, he lay on a semi-soft bed. "Hospital?" his cracked voice asked.

Jake grinned. "Yeah."

"Poster boy ain't as dumb as he looks. Got it in one," Finn quipped as relief surged through him. He reached for a plastic cup and brought it into Max's field of vision. "Water?"

Max gave a slight nod, and Finn moved the cup to his lips as Grant lifted his head. He wanted to drink greedily, but Finn only dribbled a few drops in. "More."

"Sorry, only a little. Your kidney is infected, so you only get enough to wet your whistle for now," Grant explained.

His throat now less dry, Max's voice came out more normal. "Infected, how?"

"As far as we can figure, your swim in the sewer with Massi caused this. Sorry I didn't let you explain on the plane. All this could've been avoided." Jake continued to hold Stirling's hand, and when the kid squeezed hard, he asked, "Need pain relief?"

"No, I'm fine," Max lied as his mind chewed on the fact Marshall apologized. Then wondered why Jake would ask if he needed meds until Max registered he gripped his team leader's hand. Releasing his hold, Max blushed, but lucky for him his already fever-flushed face concealed his embarrassment.

"Liar," Finn exclaimed gruffly. He, along with the rest, had not failed to spot Stirling's white-knuckled grasp on Jake's hand.

Max's gaze shifted to McBride. He owed the man his life, but he didn't know what to say or how to say it. So, he opted for cockiness. "Am not."

Finn turned to Grant. "Shoot him up with morphine. The kid's acting stupid and breaking rules one and six. He fucking hurts, but for some reason won't tell us."

Rocketeer yipped until he got Zach's attention. His front paws inched forward, trying to move nearer to Max. A grin lit Zach's face as he said, "Finn, Dave, move out of the way," and started to push Rocky's bed. The only way to settle his pup was to shift him closer to Stirling.

As Zach repositioned the bed, Grant chuckled at the thought the nurses would be none too happy. He headed out of the room in search of one to request painkillers for Max.

Finn lowered the bedrail on both beds before moving out from between them, and Zach finished pushing them together.

When Rocketeer lay his head near him, Max's hand reached out to pet the Malinois noting the dog's bandaged leg. "Is Rocky going to be alright?"

"Yeah, only a flesh wound. Couple of weeks and you both will be back in business," Zach answered, not sure who was happier with the new arrangement ... Rocky or Max.

His lids growing heavy, Max closed them as he fought the rising tide of pain on his right side. He hoped the painkillers arrived quick. He heard a gasp and chuckles, before the slight burn of medication entering his IV.

The guys snickered when the nurse gasped at her patient and the canine lying next to one another. Luckily, Max's IV port was on the opposite side of Rocky. She worked quickly to administer the morphine and left even faster.

Beginning to drift into a pain-free world, a cool cloth placed on his forehead caused Max to crack his eyes open again.

Jake wiped Max's fevered brow. "Rest now. We'll talk later."

A compassionate Marshall confused Max, but as Morpheus drew him into his arms, he gave up trying to comprehend.

Finn resumed his seat, hiding a grin as their hard-as-nails leader continued to wipe the kid's brow. Finn had never witnessed Jake treat any of them with such tenderness. The closest he had to measure the action by was when Jake's youngest son, Tommy, got sick on a camping trip last fall.

And now that Max had woken, spoken to them, and returned to a healing sleep, Finn noted the coiled tension appeared to ebb out of his fearless master chief. Unbidden, Duncan's words came back to him, and Finn conceded Jake might be a Papa Bear when it came to their cub.

After staring at the unruly, blond mop for a long moment, Finn shifted his gaze around the room, studying his brothers. Though he would never be accused of being the most sensitive, share-his-feelings type of guy, Finn did possess emotions, and he was not blind. What he perceived in their expressions led Finn to realize they were all affected by this young buck. Somehow, someway, with only one official mission under his belt, the cocky little shit got under their skin.

Analyzing things more thoroughly, Finn recognized Stirling earned their respect the day he risked his life to rescue Levi. Though they hadn't known him at the time, the bravery he displayed by running through the village and climbing to the roof to help an injured and trapped brother counted in their books.

And when he volunteered again, rushing to the weapons depot to save his, Axel's, and Babcox's asses combined with his outright refusal to leave his fallen brother, Tanner, was further proof Stirling had what it took to be on Zulu, despite his youthfulness.

Finn blinked, sleep wanting to pull him down as he returned his focus on Max. *Me, Dave, Grant, and Rocky … little brother has saved over half the team so far.* He let out a sigh and pulled his chair closer to the foot of the bed, and placed his crossed arms on the footboard.

Resting his chin on his forearm, Finn yawned. *We gotta keep a tight rein on this wild stallion, or we're liable to lose him too soon. Wonder if the kid gets the recklessness from his father?*

FOB – Detention Area

In the observation room, Nicole watched and listened as the CIA's interrogator questioned Nazeri. As much as she should pay attention, her mind wandered as she yawned. She kept circling back to Carlson's original plan and couldn't for the life of her make any sense out of it.

If three members of Charlie Team had not gotten ill and they executed the op as planned, there would be six flag-draped boxes waiting for a flight home. Master Chief Hanson's team would've run smack dab into Nazeri's force outside the village.

Several unanswered questions rolled in the lieutenant's head. *Is Carlson truly that bad at planning a mission? Why would Hanson agree to such an ill-conceived strategy? Personality aside, Hanson isn't an idiot. The honor of leading a top tier SEAL team is earned not given out like a prize in a box of caramel popcorn and peanuts.*

Unsettling thoughts crept in. *Why did Carlson tell the Canadians they wouldn't be going until next month? How ill are Hanson's men? Seems a bit convenient they became sick at the last minute. Is someone gunning for Zulu? If so, who and why?*

Nicole sighed. She conceded Zulu had a reputation in their world for being the best, yet most difficult team. Some of the top brass took issue with how they got things done, or rather that they did so despite orders that hindered them. Many times, the men of Zulu got creative to ensure a successful outcome but left senior officers with egg on their faces.

One mission, the rules of engagement prevented them from firing unless fired upon, so McBride loudly and proudly belted out God Bless America to instigate a firefight. The wild scheme created a diversion allowing Zulu to save everyone at the embassy. Still, Ambassador Bindell made it clear to Admiral Droit he was not pleased with McBride's 'antics' as he referred to the actions.

Another time, Marshall *'borrowed'* a Mexican cartel's cocaine to buy the freedom of five Americans held for ransom by a rival cartel. In the end, they rescued the tourists and put a massive dent in both cartel's operations when they blew up the drugs.

Nicole added two more names to the list of officers who didn't turn a kind eye towards Zulu. Air Force General Havershash and Captain Franckle. After both refused to authorize air support, they'd been shamed when the Canadian General Broderick and Colonel Sutton came to Zulu's aid.

Slumping in the chair, Nicole rubbed the back of her neck as her thoughts returned to Carlson. Something didn't add up, yet she didn't think she had all the pieces of the puzzle. Heck, she didn't even know if it was a puzzle.

There might be nothing more to this than poor strategy, crappy and incomplete intel, and a glory-seeking CIA agent who sought a promotion off the backs of others and didn't give a damn if any of the operators died in the process.

Nicole tuned in as Nazeri said a name she recognized. A smile formed. *Zulu did well bringing him in alive. Nazeri might give us details that will bring down the Hamood Network.*

Hospital – Max's Room

Three hours after visiting hours ended, Bryan entered the room and found his entire team asleep. The doctor called demanding he come order his men out. His smile grew as he gazed around.

Jake's head lay on the edge of the bed, and his hand covered the kid's. Zach slept on the far half of Rocketeer's bed, with the dog between him and Max. Rocky's head rested near Stirling's waist, and Max's hand draped over the canine's neck.

Dave's body sprawled across three chairs pushed together. Grant sat propped in a corner on the floor, his head supported by a blanket. Finn's strange position appeared a bit painful. He sat in one of the chairs, his upper body folded over the footboard with his head on his left arm and right hand holding Max's foot.

This scene, Bryan never expected. True, the men of Zulu might be considered closer than most teams. Still, if anyone told him or merely suggested all the guys would circle the wagons and defy authority to maintain a bedside vigil of their newest member, he wouldn't have believed them.

Yes, they visited injured brothers while in hospitals, but usually only Jake checked on his injured man or men, and then best buddies hung close. Jake for Dave, Grant for Zach, and vice versa for those four. Finn had always been somewhat of a loner, and though he would pop in, the Scottish cowboy never stayed long. Finn certainly never slept with a hand on a brother. The action made Bryan believe it stemmed from Finn's need to reassure himself Max's was still alive.

This is new … a change … something I must understand. Bryan stepped out and closed the door without waking them. When he turned, Dr. Bajwa stood in his path.

"About time you got here. They must leave, especially that dog. We are a hospital, not a kennel."

Incensed by the attitude, Bryan said, "They're not causing anyone any trouble. Leave my men be."

"But it is against our rules," Bajwa insisted.

"Screw your rules. They are staying. End of discussion." Bryan strode out, wearing a grin. For whatever reason, the gruff and hard-core SEALs he commanded deemed it necessary to remain with the kid, so he would fully support them.

Chapter Eleven

Five Days Later – Hospital – Max's Room

URGENT need to relieve himself awoke Max from a light slumber. He blinked, opening his eyes and found his room still empty, like the past five days. Wincing as he swung his legs off the side of the bed, Max prepared to walk to the head.

Grabbing the IV pole, as much for stability as for the fact the damned thing must go with him, Max slid off the mattress, gaining his balance. He peered at the distance to the toilet, only a few steps, but might as well be crossing the Sahara Desert.

The only positive to moving was the cool tiles under his feet. His fever stubbornly held on, and Max was sick to death of being uncomfortably hot. Though he spent days and weeks in scorching climates, for some reason, a simple fever made him more miserable than the midday sun beating down on him.

Shuffling forward, his healing flank twinging with each step, Max realized the fever might not be the cause of him feeling like an abandoned puppy or a cake left out in the rain. His dour mood had more to do with the strange dream he wished was real. Waking up with an entire team surrounding him had been so foreign, but something he desired more than he cared to admit.

But it was only a dream. *A compassionate Marshall ... ha! That is my first clue it isn't real. No way in hell would Master Chief Marshall wipe my fevered brow with a cool cloth.*

Nor would a hospital allow Rocky to be in my room, in my bed. And hell, the Mighty McBride would never, EVER, hold my foot or offer quiet words of reassurance. Waking with them all around me is as likely as Dad, Mom, or Grandma walking in here to hug me. Never would happen.

Reaching the toilet, Max took care of business and then leaned on the sink as he washed his hands. After shutting off the lukewarm water, he peered at his reflection. "Quit wishing for things that will never come to pass. Zulu is like every other team. No one visits you. Nobody gives a damn.

"You're on your own. You can do this. You've done it all your life. Suck it up and realize you're gonna be kicked off Zulu once they release you from the hospital. You were the weak link on your first mission. They'll replace you with someone they can count on not to screw up and ruin a crucial op."

As he turned to return to bed, Max wondered if he might be allowed to rejoin Red Team. Sure, Captain Ridgeway hated him, but Gabe Miller and the rest of the team accepted him. It was the first and only place he felt he belonged. He got his opportunity to touch the stars with Zulu, but like everything else in his life, it turned out to be wishful thinking.

This time Max couldn't blame anyone but himself. If he spoke in the mess tent and told Marshall he was not up to par, the op wouldn't have been screwed, and there wouldn't be a hole in his back. If he'd manned-up on the plane and made Marshall listen to him, perhaps he would've earned a bit of respect.

But he hadn't, and he didn't, so the consequences would be his to bear … alone, as usual. Nothing new to him. His whole life after his dad died when he was six had been nothing but loneliness and wishing for something he loved and lost … family.

Max gingerly lowered himself to his bed but remained sitting, not ready to give up the coolness on his bare feet. He snagged the plastic cup from the table and took a drink of tepid water. As he set it down, the door opened, and he hoped it was Nurse Karen because she would stay and talk a few minutes.

"Hey, Max."

As he stared at Rob Powers, Sierra One, he backtracked his previous thoughts. Red Team was not the only place he belonged. Rob and the guys of Sierra, except for Babcox, welcomed him. Hell, they went so far as to arrange housing for him when he was released from the hospital in Virginia after taking a nosedive off the cargo netting while training with them.

"Cat's got his tongue." Scott entered behind his team leader.

"How ya doing?" Devlin asked, coming into the room after Scott and plopping down on one of the chairs.

"Um … fine … I guess." Max continued to gape at the three as they made themselves comfortable in the various seats. Gathering himself, he asked, "How did you get here?"

"Flew … those things called planes are quite convenient." Devlin chuckled.

"I mean, why are you here?"

"Got spun up to help Zulu on several upcoming raids. They have been hitting it hot and heavy the past five days. Taking Nazeri alive was a real boon. Farris has a ton of targets for us to hit. Zulu's been doing two or three raids each day," Rob said.

Scott, Sierra's second-in-command and medic, snagged the chart on the wall and perused the details before turning to Stirling. "When we landed and found out you were stuck in here, we came to check on you before we grab a bit of shuteye." He waved the clipboard. "Things are improving. They'll likely boot you outta here soon."

"Yeah, they'll be giving me the boot, that's for sure." Max failed to keep the despondency out of his tone.

Rob shared a glance with Scott and Devlin. They heard it too. He moved in front of Max. "Something you want to share?"

Max sighed. "I screwed up my first mission. Marshall's pissed, and I'm sure they're gonna dump me as fast as they can." The burst of laughter caught Max by surprise. His protective shields started to rise, wondering if he misread their overtures and only assumed they were his friends.

Viewing the wariness in Max's expression, Rob settled as the other two still chuckled. "Hey, kid. You got it all wrong. Though with the high fever you experienced, I'm not surprised."

"Got what wrong?"

"Everything," Scott said as he also repositioned so he could look Max in the eye.

"Kid, without you, all of Zulu might be dead," Rob noted the continuing confusion. "I'll spell it out for you. Because you got sick, which no one blames you for, and then got injured, which could've happened to Grant or Finn if they entered that room first, the team discovered Nazeri's force outside the village.

"If not for you leaving early for exfil, Draper wouldn't have arranged for an extra drone, and the guys would've had no heads up and run right into fifty insurgents on their way to exfil. Sucks you ended up with an infection and hurt, but there is a silver lining. It saved your team."

When Rob paused, Scott added, "And you risked your life, saving Rocky's. I can tell you ... that action alone will keep your place on Zulu. Everyone loves Rocky."

"So that part was real? Is the pup hurt bad?" Max sagged on the bed.

"Flesh wound. Zach said he almost had to muzzle Rocky to get him to leave your room. The doctors were being assholes about Rocky being in here. Rocketeer's been in the kennels ever since. The keeper is pampering him while the team is out on raids. According to Draper, they're so wiped out when they return, they drop into their bunks." Rob took a seat and leaned back.

"Raids?"

Devlin nodded as he placed a baggie, containing twelve banana nut muffins he baked before leaving Virginia, on Max's table. "Yeah, a lot of them. They're dismantling the Hamood Network doing multiple ops every day. Nazeri's been a goldmine of info.

"Your team's been running with Echo Team for the last five days, but Echo's deployment is up, and they're returning stateside, so we got spun up to run with Zulu."

Max let those details roll around in his head as he stared at the package. Devlin, a closet baker and a damned good one, started doing it as a way to handle stress. Tempted, he reached for the bag, and after savoring a bite of the moist, flavorful treat, Max said, "So they've been busy. Is that why they haven't visited?"

Rob grinned, giving Max a nod. "Yes. According to Lockwood, all the guys and Rocky stayed with you the first night, but when Farris began identifying targets they had to leave."

So I didn't dream them being here? Or maybe I did … still can't see Marshall wiping my brow or apologizing. And McBride … Nah, no way he would be touchy-feely. Max blew out a long breath and decided it didn't matter if he dreamed of those actions or not. The team had been here, even if all they did was sit in a chair and sleep. That alone gave him hope he had not screwed everything up. Putting his thoughts away, Max grinned. "Thanks, these are great."

"Thought you might like something resembling food," Devlin said, and the tone of the room changed as he launched into a description of his latest attempt at making baklava, and all the trouble he had with the phyllo dough.

FOB – TOC

Jake reached for the coffee pot to pour a mug of much-needed caffeine. Afterward, he shuffled over to his chair at the table the men gathered around and lowered his aching body down. The last five days had been non-stop except for the few hours of sleep they managed between ops.

Yawning, he focused on the map Lieutenant Farris displayed on the monitor. When the door pulled open behind him, letting in a blast of hot air, he pivoted and grinned. "Rob, about time you got your sorry asses over here."

"Hi to you too." Rob entered, followed by his team. He redirected his gaze to Farris. "Sorry to interrupt. Go on."

Nicole allowed a slight smile to form, happy Sierra arrived.

Before Farris could continue, Grant asked Scott, "You stop by and check on the kid as I asked?"

"Yeah. Max is improving. Fever's only low grade now, so they must've found the right combination of antibiotics for him." Scott snagged a chair and straddled it, resting his forearms on the back.

Devlin leaned his hip against one of the wooden tables. "You need to be aware of something, though. With your continual, but inopportune absence, Max thought he'd be kicked off Zulu. We set him straight."

Jake grimaced as he nodded. He disliked not being able to visit and leaving things up in the air, but duty called, and he would always be a frogman first. Even his wife Valarie knew missions came first. Once he did have time to speak with Max, he would ensure the kid realized they had not abandoned him lightly.

Nicole cleared her throat, bringing everyone's attention back to her and the task at hand. "Tonight, you have three targets in one location." She pointed to the map as she said, "The first is Fahd el-Arif. He is one of Hamood's financiers. He rarely leaves his compound, but with the recent hits on their network, chatter indicates he's been summoned here to a high-level meeting.

"The second is Abuska Gul, a Pakistani national who also handles a lot of the network's financial affairs. The last," Nicole allowed a smile to bloom, "is Ameen Hamood himself. He is expected to be there too."

"Hot damn!" Finn slapped the table. If they snagged Hamood, they would have a break, and they could see the kid. It stuck in his craw to leave him alone for so long.

"My thoughts exactly," Nicole said, and then launched into all the details she gathered. When she finished, Nicole sat back as Zulu and Sierra planned the mission, glad this piece of intelligence came together so fast. In truth, she expected it to take much longer before she identified Hamood's whereabouts.

Lockwood settled next to Farris and grinned. "The boys will be happy for this to come to an end."

"They live for this stuff," Farris countered.

"True, but they're tired and need a break." Bryan yawned.

"We'll all deserve one after this." Nicole reached for her coffee.

Virginia – Jake's Home

Valarie pulled to a stop in their driveway and shut off the ignition. Her left hand still gripped the steering wheel with force as she tried to remain calm and level-headed. Ranting at Jamie wouldn't solve the problem, but oh boy, did she want to lay into him for his stupidity.

She inhaled to a count of four and exhaled the same as she turned to peer at her eldest son in the passenger seat. She couldn't help letting out a few words, but they came without venom, just disappointment. "Jamie, I don't know what you were thinking. We didn't raise you to be so irresponsible. Someone could've been killed. *You* could've died."

Jamie pulled the lever of the door. "I didn't. Nobody did. Not an issue." He pushed it open and started to get out, but a hand on his sleeve stopped him. "Let go!"

"Stop. We need to talk this through and figure things out."

"Nothin' ta talk bout." Jamie yanked out of his mom's grip and slammed the car door closed after exiting.

Val sighed. "Lord, grant me the strength to find a way to help my son before we lose him." Spotting her younger children at the front door, Val got out and plastered on a smile for them. Juggling the home front when Jake left at a moment's notice and was gone for an undetermined amount of time was never easy.

But she accepted the life of a frogman's wife and all that went with it when she married Jake. She'd always known Jake's dream and supported him. Though the movies about heroes always seemed to forget those at home and the sacrifices they made so their loved ones could save the world. In particular, the children who had no choice in what their parents did.

Though Val willingly chose this life, Jamie, Eve, and Tommy didn't. They loved their dad dearly, but by the time they turned eight, they understood someday he might not come home. Sure they were proud of what Jake and their honorary uncles did, even if they never knew details, but never knowing if their last goodbye might actually be the last one put a strain on everyone.

Lately, eighteen-year-old Jamie struggled more than ever. It didn't help that Jamie and his father butted heads whenever Jake came home. After what occurred today, Val feared things would blow up once her husband found out.

Sure, she hid trivial problems from him, so he didn't have distractions on the job. But there was no way Val would or could conceal the fact their son got arrested for underage drinking and driving while under the influence after crashing into a tree near the lake. Thankfully, he didn't hit another car. There would be lawyer bills and court dates to attend in the coming months.

"Mom, is Jamie alright?" fourteen-year-old Eve asked.

"He will be. He needs some rest. Bumped his head in the crash." Val didn't expound on the other bits.

Eve put her hands on her hips and eyed her mom. "Jamie was drunk when he crashed, wasn't he?"

"Let's go inside." Valarie motioned towards their door.

"He was. I swear he is so stupid sometimes. Didn't he listen to any of the school lectures on the dangers? He isn't twenty-one. Jamie shouldn't be drinking," Eve huffed out.

Tommy stared wide-eyed. "He drove drunk?" His gaze turned to where his older brother stormed up the stairs.

"Inside." Val gently marshaled her kids in the house. The last thing she wanted was to have this discussion with her children in front of the neighbors, especially judgey Mrs. Wooten, who had no clue Jake was a top-tier SEAL. She believed he worked in sanitation because he answered her inquiry about what he did with, *'I take out trash.'* At the time, Val found it funny, but over the years, their neighbor treated them all like they were beneath her.

Once inside, two sets of blue eyes stared at her. "Yes, Jamie drove after drinking. He will be facing the consequences."

"Dad's gonna be mad," Tommy said.

"A huge understatement. We might not have a brother after Dad's done with him." Eve shuddered.

Val only nodded. Jake would be furious, but he loved his son so they would work through this as a family.

Chapter Twelve

Zulu Aircraft

SQUINTING in the early morning sunlight, Max made his way to the plane. Sounds of people stowing gear wafted to him, and he caught a word or two from Finn as he razzed Devlin about becoming Bessy Cocker. He chuckled when Devlin let the entirely wrong name ride, and retorted it was better than turning into the Pillsbury doughboy, and Finn insisting he is not fat.

As Max approached the aircraft's ramp, Draper exited and flashed him a smile. "Thanks."

Kira halted upon spotting Max. "For what?"

"The clean uniform. Wearing a gown home or my smelly clothes. Not a pleasant idea. And for the drone too."

"All part of my job." She smiled, secretly wishing she could've glimpsed him in a hospital gown … from the rear. *These men are eye candy, especially Stirling, and no red-blooded woman wouldn't want a peek or two.*

"WHAT THE FUCK!" shouted from inside the aircraft garnered their attention.

Kira chuckled as Max joined her on the ramp and asked, "What's going on?"

"Oh, a bit of payback … I think." Kira turned away and hurried on her way to grab a few more boxes to be loaded.

Max slowly entered and found the guys all laughing at Stewart Babcox, who held a soaked backpack as he glared suspiciously at those around him.

"Who did this?" Stewart demanded.

Laying on his brogue, rather thickly, Finn assumed an innocent countenance as he said, "Keep the heid, wee scunner. Whit's fur ye'll no go past ye."

"What the hell did you say?" Babcox took a step towards McBride, suspecting he was the one who doused his rucksack in something that smelt like camel piss. Now he would have to wear his grimy uniform on the flight home.

"Ye heard me well enough."

"You poured some shit all over my bag, didn't you?"

"Yer bum's oot the windae!" Finn countered, enjoying the confusion on Babcox's face. After Scott confided to Grant that he believed Babcox purposely dumped the tray of drinks on the kid in the bar during their celebration, Finn figured the guy deserved a little comeuppance for his part in setting the stage for their assumption Max was drunk.

"Speak English!" Babcox yelled, but McBride ignored him, turned, and strode to the back of the plane.

"Poster boy, well ain't ye a sight for sore eyes," Finn said as he spotted Max.

Unsure what to expect as McBride approached, Max stiffened, but when Zulu Three pulled him into a hug and clapped his upper back, done with the best intentions Max believed, he couldn't stifle the moan.

"Oh shit! Sorry. Forgot your back." Finn released Max.

"Finn, you red-haired menace. You better not have done any damage," Grant chided as he strode forward. "Kid, you okay?"

"Yeah."

Grant eyed him. "Truth?"

Max nodded, but his gaze tracked to the webbed seating. Dressing and the ride over from the hospital wore him out. He would settle for sitting but really wanted to lie in his hammock.

Zach ambled up to them and reached for Max's bag. "Got your hammock set up next to mine. Rocky insisted. Once we're airborne, you can take a nap."

"Did the doc send any medications with you?" Grant asked.

"In my bag," Max answered, taken aback by the greeting and concern shown by three of his team. A little ember of hope flickered to life. *Perhaps Zulu will accept me too.*

His eyes sought out Marshall, wondering how he would react to his presence. He found Jake pacing with a phone to his ear and wearing an expression of barely concealed rage that made Max want to turn around and exit.

Zach followed Max's gaze and shook his head. "Not directed at you. Come on. You need to sit, and Finn can tell you all about how he snagged Hamood last night."

"You guys got Hamood?" Max gaped at McBride.

"Aye, and you wouldn't believe …"

Allowing Grant to draw him toward the seats near the front as Finn launched into the tale, with some exaggeration to be sure, Max glanced at Rob, who only smiled, nodded once, and joined the men of Sierra at the rear of the plane. Max also spied Babcox as he grumbled and tossed his wet bag on the floor before sinking into a seat and sulking.

Virginia – Naval Intelligence Office

Captain Richard Athole leaned back in his chair after reviewing the preliminary report Lieutenant Farris sent him. Mixed emotions swirled inside as he sorted through the details. Grabbing Hamood would be a feather in his cap and aid him in his next promotion, but there were two downsides to this whole affair.

The first, he expected Carlson to call in a favor to fix his stupidity. Though not happy about the jerk's lack of common sense, Richard would do whatever he could to salvage Carlson's job. Not because he cared one whit about the man. No, his reasoning hit closer to home. If Carlson believed his career ruined, he might begin talking about things he shouldn't.

Richard couldn't take a chance, particularly after learning his worthless nephew was now attached to Zulu, the second downside. He had been aware someone managed to pull strings to remove the brat from under Ridgeway's heel and place him in a support role within Kendrick's command. However, finding out Zulu Team selected Maxwell blew him away.

He believed Jake Marshall, and for that matter, Lieutenant Commander Lockwood would've rejected Stirling based on his jacket. He read every negative assessment and agreed with each one. Maxwell didn't belong on Zulu any more than Preston had. The pissant didn't deserve that honor.

Shifting forward, Richard flipped to the part of the initial report, which made him grin. Perhaps Marshall would recognize his error. Preston's spawn jeopardized the entire mission, and his actions during this op revealed him again unworthy of being a member of a top tier outfit.

Understanding he couldn't do anything overt, Richard began to scheme. He always preferred to work in the shadows and ensured nothing ever traced back to him … even indirectly. As an idea formed, Richard smiled. *Yes, it will take a great deal of planning and won't be instantaneous, but in the end, I'll kill two birds with one stone, and no one will be the wiser I had a hand in this.*

Opening his desk, he withdrew one of his burner phones and stood. He would place a call to an old friend in the CIA. If he chose his words carefully, she would be obligated to assist him with Carlson. His next call would be to Carlson to plant the seed, which would grow with the right nourishment.

As he exited his office, Captain Athole said, "Larro, I'm stepping out for an early lunch. If Farris arrives before I return, tell her we will debrief tomorrow."

"Yes, Sir, but um, with the time difference and flight time, the lieutenant won't arrive until late tonight."

"Quite right. Carry on." Richard strode out, allowing his plan to gel in his mind as he considered what he would say to Olivia.

Max's Apartment

Exhausted, Max struggled to insert the key in his lock and ended up dropping his keychain. He started to bend to retrieve it only to have a gruff voice tell him to "Stop." Max peered at McBride, still weirded out by him insisting on driving him home.

Hell, the solicitous actions of Finn, Grant, and Zach during the long flight still left him unsettled, but pleasantly for once. Jake and Dave kept their distance, but he learned Marshall was not upset with him, only dealing with a family issue. He didn't know what exactly, but whatever it was, had the man wanting to slug the fuselage, and it took Dave to calm his ass down.

Finn reached down and picked up the keys. "Wee Willie Wobbly, its time you hit the hay." He opened the door with a flourish and waited for Max to quit staring at him like he possessed three heads.

Having learned in the last hour that arguing with McBride was like slamming his head against a wall, Max sighed and strode into his place. He turned back to his teammate and said, "I'm home now. You can go."

"Whoa, nice place you got." Finn ignored Max and ambled to the island that separated the little kitchen from the sitting area. He set Stirling's rucksack on the stool and his bag of medications on the counter.

"Devlin found it for me," Max admitted, unsure how to make Finn leave. Although he slept almost the entire flight, all he wanted at the moment was his bed.

"He's just down the hall, right?" Finn pivoted to study the kid. "Yeah."

"Okay, well, hie yourself off to bed. I'll make myself comfortable on your couch.

"I can take care of myself. You don't need to stay." Max reached out for the wall, still far from his best.

"Grant's orders whether either of us likes it," Finn grumbled to cover the fact he and Grant drew straws for who would keep an eye on Max for tonight … and he won.

Giving up trying to win, at least this battle, Max turned and headed for his bedroom as he said, "Suit yourself. There's beer in the fridge."

He shut his door with a click and was half-tempted to lock it. Not bothering to turn on a light, Max shucked his boots, pants, and shirt before crawling under the covers. He let out a sigh, the cool sheets felt good, and he wished his fever would go away.

On the verge of sleep, Max cracked open his eyes as a rustling sounded near him. Finn stood in front of him with a glass of water in one hand as his other reached towards him. "What now?"

"Meds."

Max huffed as he shifted up, his back protesting the movement. He popped the pills and washed them down with water. "Anything else?"

Finn grinned and teased, "Not unless you want a bedtime story or lullaby."

Though it cost him a bit of pain, Max chucked his pillow at McBride as he said, "Get out. I don't need a mother-hen."

"Tsk, tsk. You need to be takin' better care of that body. You got McBride blood in your veins now."

Flopping his head down, Max mumbled, "Probably why I still have a fever … my body is rejecting the poison."

Finn laughed out loud. "Sleep, Kid. Need anything, holler." He set the half-full glass on the nightstand and started to leave. He stopped and turned back. "Ye ken, I'm sorry. If I watched out for you better, you wouldn't be in this condition."

Again in uncharted waters, Max didn't know how to respond. "Not your job. I'm self-sufficient. This is my fault. I let the guy get the drop on me, and I should've told Marshall I was not fit."

"That's where you're wrong. It is part of my job. Rookie wrangling is one of Three's responsibilities. Nite." Finn exited with the words 'self-sufficient' rolling in his mind, leaving his gut unsettled.

Max closed his eyes and realized McBride only brought him home out of obligation and duty … not friendship.

Dave's Home

Crawling into bed beside Cathy, Dave hovered over her a moment and inhaled as he gave thanks for his loving wife and sweet children. Coming home to them after each op solidified why he chose to be a SEAL ... to keep them safe. He settled his head on his pillow and draped an arm over Cathy.

"You're home," Cathy murmured.

"Sorry I woke you."

Cathy rolled over and peered at her husband. "I'm not." She kissed him lightly and lay a hand on his arm. "All the boys make it home safe?"

"Yeah. The new kid is a little banged up, but everyone's fine."

"Max, right? What happened?"

"Yeah, Max Stirling. He got sick ... actually from a previous op, but his symptoms showed during this one. Got hurt as we were clearing rooms. God works in mysterious ways. If not for him being ill and injured ... we, well, things might've gone quite differently, and I might not be laying here now."

Knowing not to pry, Dave shared the bits he could, Cathy smiled. "Thank God, you boys selected him. Want me to schedule the welcome BBQ with Val?"

"Um, not certain she's gonna have time."

"Why?"

"Jake talked to Val before we left. Jamie got himself in a world of trouble, and they'll need to focus on sorting things out."

"What did Jamie do?"

"Crashed while driving drunk."

"Oh, my." Cathy sighed. "Jamie's been a handful lately. I'm not sure where the sweet boy went."

Dave nodded.

"Well, then I'll just make all the arrangements, and we can have the BBQ here in a few days." Cathy paused. "How sick is Max? Will a couple of days be enough for him to be better?"

"He's still running a fever. I'll check with Grant tomorrow." When she nodded, Dave pulled Cathy close and closed his eyes.

Max's Apartment

Soft, mournful sounds brought Finn out of a light slumber. He shifted up on the couch and listened again, wondering if a stray cat was prowling outside, but then he recalled Max's place was on the second floor. Another quiet cry coming from the bedroom had Finn on his feet and moving.

He pushed open the door, the light from the hall throwing a thin beam into the room. "Max? You alright?" When he didn't receive an answer, Finn padded towards the bed, worry increasing as he found Max curled up. "Hey, kid."

Still not getting a response, Finn took a knee at the bedside and studied Max's face. It was not lax as in sleep … it was screwed up with what he would call fear. The pitifully small voice that emitted next pulled on Finn's heartstrings.

"No. Don't hit me. I'll be good. I promise. Not the belt, sir. Please. I'll clean up the mud … I'm sorry … I was just playing. Don't. No. Please … stop. Daddy, help me. Don't let him beat me again. Daddy, come home. Don't leave me with him."

Finn couldn't take anymore, and he reached out and shook Max's shoulder. "Hey. Wake up. Kid. Max."

Jerked from a dream of one of the many beatings he received at the hands of Uncle Athole, Max blinked and stared doe-eyed as McBride's face came into view. It took him a moment to recall his teammate brought him home before embarrassment kicked in as he realized he must've witnessed his nightmare.

"You good?" Finn asked.

"Yeah." Uncurling, Max drew in a sharp breath as his injured back didn't appreciate the movement and told him loudly.

Finn glanced at the clock as he stood. "Time for pain meds. I'll be right back." He hurried out, giving Max the space to pull himself together. When he returned, Max was sitting up on the edge of the mattress.

"Here." He offered the pills, and Max took them without a word. Finn noticed the slight shake to Max's hand as the kid picked up the water glass from the nightstand.

Max refused to meet Finn's gaze as he downed the medication and lowered the glass to his thigh.

An unknown force caused Finn to sit on the bed beside Max. Wholly out of character, he asked, "Want to talk about it?"

Max snorted. "No."

A desire from somewhere he didn't understand, made Finn dig a little deeper. "Who beat you with a belt?"

Rounded with shock, Max's eyes darted to McBride.

Finn didn't recognize the softness of his own voice as he spoke to Max, a burgeoning urge to protect this kid growing in the pit of his stomach. "You were begging someone not to hit you for playing in the mud, I think."

"Old history. Doesn't matter. He can't do it now." Max pushed up to his feet.

"Who?" Finn demanded.

"Gonna hit the head." Max ignored him and shuffled out of his room to the bathroom.

Finn stayed put, watching the kid go, as anger burned his gut. *What kind of father would allow someone to beat his kid and get away with it? Preston Stirling must've been as terrible a father as he was a team leader.*

When Max returned, he found Finn sitting in the same place. "If you want the bed, I'll take the couch."

Finn eyed Max and shoved the anger to the back, realizing now wasn't the time to push Stirling. He rose and grinned. "It is comfier, but the sofa is closer to the beer."

As Max passed Finn in the middle of his room, he said, "Why did you stay?"

Halting and turning around, Finn waited until Max sat before he replied, "It's what brothers do. You're part of Zulu. We take care of our own." He flashed another grin. "Being self-sufficient is fine when you're alone, but you got five big brothers to watch your back now."

Five brothers? Speechless, Max only stared as Finn pivoted and left. *Do they really consider me a brother?*

Chapter Thirteen

Dave's Home

MAX parked his Mustang a couple of houses down from the address Dave provided him. The past two weeks had been a trip through the Twilight Zone for him, and he was still trying to get a handle on his new team.

Finn stayed more than one night, and Max finally kicked him to the curb on the third day. The crazy Scottish cowboy turned out to be an alright guy, but intense and downright bossy at times. Max grinned as he recalled the two of them bantering about which football team was the best and his team slaughtering Finn's. He won a twenty from that bet.

Grant dropped by every day until his fever disappeared. After the medic checked his vitals and redressed his wound, they spent several hours discussing a variety of topics. His teammate also shared a bit of his past with him. Still too unsure of his place on the team, Max reciprocated with only a few minor details beyond he went to a military boarding school from the time he turned eight until he graduated and joined the Navy.

The second week, Zach began visiting and brought Rocky with him, carrying the pup up the stairs each time. When Zach spotted his chess set, he indicated he had not played in a long time since no one on Zulu played the game. They enjoyed several quiet hours engaged in chess matches as Rocky snoozed on his couch.

Dave stopped by a couple of times to check on him, and also told him his wife Cathy arranged a barbeque for him as soon as Grant deemed him well enough to be out and about. In Max's mind, that had been a week ago, but something came up with Jake, which resulted in the party being pushed another week.

He still didn't know what family issue his team leader had on his plate, but whatever it was, it must be time-consuming because he had not seen Jake ever since debrief on the day after they returned stateside.

Debrief had been an interesting affair in an of itself. Max learned the full details of what happened while he was incapacitated and how the Canadians helped. Captain Kendrick made an appearance to inform them the agency assured him Carlson wouldn't be working any future ops with them. The agent likely got banished to some basement, which he deserved.

A rap on his hood brought Max from his musings, and he found Finn at the front of his car.

"Gonna sit there all day?" Finn asked as he peered at Max.

"I'm coming." Max opened his door and climbed out.

"Awesome wheels. Prefer my Harley, though."

"Belonged to my dad." Max grinned.

"Whoa. It's in great condition. You store this for years?"

"No, my uncle sold it. Freak coincidence when I started searching for a car, this was for sale by the person who brought it from Uncle Asshole. Well, his wife … he died. I blurted out I would pay anything she wanted. Being a warmhearted lady, she sold the Mustang to me for much less than she should've."

In the short dialog, Finn logged a couple bits of information. Max referred to his uncle as an asshole, and he wanted the car his dad owned at any price. Although Finn wondered if the guy who beat Max as a child might be the uncle, he didn't comment.

He, Grant, and Zach each tried to learn more about their young enigma. They all recognized Max staunchly protected others, but the kid seemed to believe he was on his own. They needed to change his thinking. "Steak should be almost ready. Let's go."

As they entered the backyard, Max took stock of his environment. Dave and Cathy's home was not grand, but it wasn't shabby either. A middle-income home that reminded him of where he lived with his parents. The covered patio boasted a table filled with food and several chairs.

It appeared Dave, or some previous owner extended the patio with interlocking bricks and created a fire pit and grill station. Beyond was grass, two climbable trees, a sandbox, and a swing set with toddler seats attached. The swings were occupied with Dave's twins, and Jake's youngest son, Tommy, pushed them, much to their delight.

He appreciated Dave sharing photos of his and Marshall's families and telling him their names so he wouldn't be inundated, trying to remember a bunch of names and faces today. He nodded at Grant, who kicked back in a lounge chair next to a woman he didn't recognize. She hadn't been in any of the photos.

Max noted that several of Sierra were here too, Rob, Devlin, Scott, and Terrance. As Dave's wife approached him, Max smiled and said, "A pleasure to meet you, ma'am."

Cathy laughed. "Ma'am makes me sound like your mother. Please, call me Cathy." Her gaze moved to Finn. "Where are your manners? Why doesn't Max have a drink?"

"Well, maaaa'am," Finn drawled out the term, "seein' as he just arrived, I didn't get a chance yet."

Max's gaze bounced between them, not certain of the dynamic.

Cathy linked her arm in Max's. "I'm only teasing him. Come with me. What's your pleasure, beer or wine?"

Shooting Grant a glance, Max replied, "Best if I stick to ice tea or water."

"Oh, my gosh, I forgot. Kidney infection, no alcohol for you." Cathy flashed him a smile. "At least not today. I hope you like beer, 'cause you're certainly gonna be supplying these boys with a bunch, and it would be a shame if you couldn't partake."

Max chuckled as he let Cathy pull him towards the table and several coolers. Finn made him aware of the Zulu tradition.

Two hours later, having grabbed a bottled water, made the rounds of introductions, filled his plate with a boatload of delectable foods, and consumed way more than he should, Max relaxed in a padded patio chair placed under the shade of one of the trees. He found the afternoon to be idyllic, and his desire to belong to a family might be within reach.

The only sticking point, he needed to speak with Jake. Though the rest of the team appeared to accept him, Max's insecurity, borne from a childhood of neglect, required Marshall's stamp of approval and acknowledgment he still wanted him on Zulu.

As Finn approached, carrying a massive piece of cake, Max said, "I'm stuffed."

"This ain't for you. You want cake? You got two feet." Finn grinned as he leaned against the tree trunk and shoveled an enormous bite into his mouth.

Content, for the most part, Max broached a topic he thought about for the last two weeks. The night Finn took him home and apologized. He wanted to ensure their burgeoning friendship was not tainted with misplaced guilt. "The hole in my back and ruptured hematoma isn't your fault."

Pulled from contemplations fueled by food and friendship, Finn cocked an eye at the kid. "What?"

"I don't blame you. I'm the one who lost my footing. Would've ruptured when I fell. Thanks for carrying me."

"Jake, carried you," Finn deliberately deflected.

"I might've been a bit out of it, but I know for a fact Jake didn't carry me to the rock outcropping." Max pinned Finn with a direct gaze.

"Yeah, well, couldn't leave your scrawny ass lying there. Though, I could've maybe let Rocketeer drag you up the hill by the scruff of your neck." A grin played on his face as Finn thoroughly enjoyed their banter.

Max chuckled and shook his head. "Well, thanks anyway."

In a flippant tone, Finn said, "Least I could do since you saved my ass in Algeria."

"So, we're even?"

"Yeah, Kid. So no gettin' more holes in you, doing something stupid like wasting your life, or someone else is hauling your ass out," Finn gruffed to cover sentiments he never experienced for a teammate before.

Every member of Zulu was a brother to him, and he took to heart the SEAL brotherhood and would defend any one of them without hesitation, but something about this blond colt burrowed under his skin and got him in the feels.

Being around the rookie brought to the forefront a protective streak Finn didn't expect. He thought perhaps it might be Stirling's age … or maybe they were like blood brothers … a blood bond with a little brother. Whatever this was, it was intense, and Finn couldn't shake the need to look after the kid … and tease the hell out of him too. 'Cause what older brother worth his salt didn't give his younger brother a ration of shit.

When Jake approached, Finn pushed off the tree and groused, "About damned time someone came to babysit the cub." *Also about time Papa Bear talked with the kid. Damned glad we picked Max. Though we'll never know what to expect with him, I like the idea of having a wee brother.*

As Finn strolled away, Jake grinned, set the folding chair he brought with him on the ground and held out a cold beer. "Grant says one is okay."

"I'll stick with water."

"Okay." Jake settled into the chair, opened his beer, and studied Stirling for a few moments. Being direct would be the best way to handle the issue. "I owe you an apology. I should've allowed you to explain on the aircraft. It was a break of faith and a mistake I won't make again. I'm sorry my actions and lack of judgment put your life in jeopardy."

The apology wholly unanticipated yet appreciated, Max nodded. "Trust is a two-way street. I should've informed you I wasn't up to par before we left. I put the mission and team at risk. Sorry."

They sat in silence for several minutes, their gazes locked, attempting to read one another, before Jake asked, "We good?"

"Yeah, we're good, Boss." Max's worry rolled off his back, and he relaxed. *Damned glad Zulu selected me. Having brothers is an unexpected benefit.*

Jake leaned back and stretched out his legs. He closed his eyes, enjoying the shade and a moment of peace. The past two weeks had been nothing but contentious to the point he almost kicked Jamie out of the house.

Upon Val's urging, they met with a family therapist, not that he wanted to go to psychotherapy, but he was willing to do anything to figure out why Jamie went off the rails. So far, after two sessions, nothing had been revealed or resolved.

He wished he could have a conversation with Jamie like he just had with Stirling. *Confront the issue. Solve the problem. Move on. Done and dusted.* His daughter's sweet voice brought him to the present, and he opened his eyes.

Eve beamed as she held a plate with a slice of cake. "I thought you might like a piece of the chocolate cake I baked before Uncle Finn eats it all."

Jake gaped. *No! No! HELL NO!* Eve was not offering the cake to him, and he recognized her ga-ga expression, the one she reserved for members of insipid boy bands. She now directed it at his blond, good-looking rookie ... his twenty-four-year-old, rookie ... a man ten years older than Eve.

"Don't mind if I do." Jake grabbed the plate.

"DAD!"

"What?"

"That is for Max." She set her hands on her hips.

Max struggled to hide his grin. Though no stranger to being considered eye candy by many lovely females, he was no dummy, and he would never cross certain lines. Being the object of a fourteen-year-old girl's crush, especially when her father was his team leader, a SEAL well-versed in killing, and capable of making people disappear, put him in Jake's crosshairs.

Jake took a forkful. "Delicious. Thanks, honey. Now run along and play with Tommy."

Max barely held in the snort of laughter at the enraged expression on Eve Marshall. Her eyes appeared almost as deadly as Jake's. He didn't want to be around when the sparks flew but decided to attempt to de-escalate the situation. "Appreciate the offer, but I'm stuffed. I actually fed the last part of my steak to Rocky."

Eve turned back to Max, her gaze softening. "You gave Rocky some steak."

"He deserved a treat." Max caught Jake's flash of steel-blue eyes, warning him he swam in dangerous waters. Hoping to ease Jake's worry and let Eve down easy, he said. "If it isn't too much trouble, maybe you can wrap me up a slice to go, and I can eat it when I come back from visiting my girlfriend."

Eve deflated. "You have a girlfriend?"

"Yes. Cali's special. She likes to bake too. You two would probably have a lot to talk about." Max flicked a glance at Jake and inwardly sighed with relief when he gave him a slight nod. *Whew, I'll live another day.*

Trying not to reveal how much she hated that Max had a *special* girlfriend, Eve forced a smile. "I'll wrap up a piece for you."

"Thanks." Max leaned back and closed his eyes.

After Eve left, Jake asked, "So, this Cali, is it serious?"

Max lifted his lids and peered at Marshall, wondering why he asked. "We've been out a few times."

"If you get jacked up, you know she won't be notified if she's not next of kin."

"Not at that stage—"

Jake cut him off, "But if you want her added to the wives and girlfriends network, give Val or Cathy her number. We watch out for our own, and that includes extended family."

"Okay. Thanks. I'll think about it, but like I said—"

"Not at that stage," Jake finished for Max as he stood. He turned to Max and added, "You tell Cali about this injury?"

"No. Haven't called her since we got back."

Nodding, Jake switched topics again. "Thanks for being kind to Eve."

"Welcome."

Jake chuckled, but there was a glint of steel in his eyes as he said, "I won't rest easy until she starts calling you Uncle Max."

"Copy, Lima Charlie," Max said before Jake strode away.

As the afternoon turned into evening, Max found himself fully relaxed as he chatted with the entire team, their spouses, and family. The unidentified woman from earlier turned out to be Grant's sister Paula who made a stopover in Virginia to visit with him on a business trip.

Dave's three-year-old twins were a riot, and he enjoyed watching them running around. He also thought their names were clever. Aidan and Nadia spelled backward resulted in the other twin's name. The party appeared to be wrapping up with several people leaving, but Max was content to stay in his lounge chair for a bit longer.

Kira sauntered up to Max, happy to find him doing better than the last time she saw him. The flight back had been exhausting for him. He could only lay in the hammock for so long before his back hurt too much. Mostly the pain had come from where the rounds slammed into his vest. She suspected he was still black and blue from them.

She knew each of the guys had had chats with Max, trying to smooth over their mistake of assuming the worst about their new teammate without allowing him to set things straight. Kira needed to apologize too. She sat in the chair Jake set here several hours ago and smiled at Max.

"Hey, Draper."

"Hey."

Max sighed, noticing her contrite expression. "Not you too. Like I told everyone else, none of this is your fault."

"Nice of you to say, but not true. We are a team. Someone should've noticed or said something. I should've, and I'm sorry."

"I didn't even know I was sick in the beginning, so how could you?" Max challenged.

"Didn't the boys tell you?"

"Tell me what?"

"I'm clairvoyant." Kira chuckled.

Max eyed Draper. "As in a psychic or fortune-teller?"

"Nah, as in someone who takes the time to observe and take action. But I let a misperception cloud my ability this time. I won't in the future." Kira held out her hand. "Give me your phone."

"Why?"

"I'll enter my contact info. And while you have time on your hands, you can think about your wish list of equipment and send me a text. That way, you'll have everything you need when you are ready to operate again."

Max dug in his pocket and handed over his cell. He spotted Jake rounding up Eve and Tommy as Val said goodbye to Cathy. "I didn't meet Jake's oldest."

"No. Jamie didn't come. He's in a bit of trouble. Jamie's the reason Jake was about to explode on the flight back. He found out Jamie crashed while intoxicated ... and he's only eighteen."

"Wow. Anyone hurt?"

"Thankfully, no, but Jake's at his wits end with the boy. Jamie's a good kid, but lately, he's been off the rails, and no one can figure out why." Kira finished entering her details and gave Max's phone back and smiled. "Welcome to our band of misfits we call a family. Don't forget to text me your list."

"Will do. Thanks."

Kira rose with a nod and strolled over to patio to bid the others goodnight.

Deeming it was about time for him to go too, Max stood and grinned as he surveyed his teammates. *Family ... are these guys truly my new family?*

Chapter Fourteen

Curry Cove Restaurant

INHALING the exotic aromas as he waited for his order, Max leaned on the counter of a hole-in-the-wall restaurant Devlin swore served the best chicken tikka masala. Devlin insisted he would fall in love with the grilled chicken dish with a thick, creamy gravy made with a tomato-yogurt sauce spiced with ginger, chili, garlic, and garam masala.

After several weeks of his limited cooking, Max was ready to try something new. Going stir-crazy with nothing to do, he also needed a break from his apartment. It had been four weeks since his injury, and a week since the barbeque. He wanted to return to work, but Dr. Irving had other ideas and refused to clear him for another two weeks.

At least beginning tomorrow, he would be allowed on base to observe Zulu while they trained. He hated being sidelined, but the opportunity to watch his teammates in action, and to learn their rhythm would be better than nothing.

"Bahut dhanyavaad," Max grinned as he thanked his server in her native Hindi as the woman handed him a plastic bag containing his food. The lady told him to enjoy and to come back again soon before he turned to leave. His stomach rumbled, eager to partake in his meal. Exiting, Max strolled down the well-lit sidewalk to his car.

Outside Curry Cove

Sounds of a struggle came to Max as he approached a narrow side street. When someone groaned, and another person said, "Hit him again," Max hurried forward. He rounded the corner to find five men. Two rough-looking men held a thin, wiry guy, pinning his arms while a burly man landed a blow. The fifth stood off to the side, giving orders.

"Is there a problem here?" Max asked, interjecting himself into the scene.

"Get lost. This has nothing to do with you," one man barked.

Max tried to make eye contact with the guy being assaulted, but his head hung down, and the other two mostly held him up. "Beg to differ. This party appears to be a bit unfair. Let him go, and I'll let you walk away … unharmed."

The four men laughed as their boss smirked. "Unharmed. You don't stand a chance … four against one."

"I'll grant you the odds aren't good … for you." Max allowed his cockiness free rein as he sized up the men.

"I warned you. Boys, teach him a lesson not to stick his nose in where he isn't wanted."

Encumbered, Max dropped his bag as three came at him, leaving their victim to collapse to the ground without their unwanted and painful support. He ducked the first punch and blocked the second. Max rammed the heel of his hand into the nose of the third guy, resulting in the man screaming in pain and dropping to his knees as blood rushed from his broken nose.

The two remaining minions ramped up their attack, angry they failed to land a single strike. After several blocked hits and more misses, both men came at him together. Max spun at the last second and delivered a kick to the back of the largest man, sending him headfirst into the brick wall and knocking him unconscious.

Dancing backward, Max grinned at their boss. "Told you. Two down, two to go, unless you walk away now."

Furious, the bossman ran toward the interloper, ready to make him pay. A moment later, he lay on his back, blinking away stars.

Freaked out how fast, hard, and effortlessly the blond put his boss down, the final thug backed off. "I'm done. You win, dude."

Max nodded, and stepped over the still dazed leader to the victim. He gently gripped the young man's bicep and pulled him to his feet as he said, "Let's go before they decide they want a bit more punishment." The beaten guy kept his head down but allowed him to lead him out. Max halted briefly to scoop up his dinner and then guided the guy towards his car.

Once there, Max said, "I can call the police if you want to press charges on them."

"No." Lifting his head for the first time, he viewed his savior. "Thanks, but no." He started to leave, wanting to get as far away as fast as he could, but stopped when the stranger spoke again.

Surprise lit Max's eyes. "You're James Marshall."

Staring at the unknown guy, Jamie asked, "I never met you. How do you know my name?"

Still somewhat shocked, Max answered, "Dave Katz showed me your photo before the barbeque."

"Who are you?"

"Max Stirling. I recently joined your father's team."

Jamie groaned. "Damn, I can't catch a break. Bet you're gonna blab this to him."

Noises of the attackers coming around prompted Max to take action. He opened the passenger side door and said, "Slide in."

"No."

"I said, in! Do it, or I'll do it for you." Max pinned a hardened gaze on James.

The leader stumbled out and yelled, "You're gunna pay for this, Marshall. I'll find you, and you'll wish you were dead."

"Wish I was already," Jamie mumbled, doing as Max directed, knowing full-well, even if he had not seen him in action, that any member of his dad's team would have no problem shoving him into the car.

Max turned to the thug. "If you value your life, forget you ever met Marshall."

Max's Apartment Complex – Parking Lot

When the Mustang came to a halt, though not ready to face the music, Jamie opened his eyes. He glanced around in confusion. "We're not at my house. Where are we?"

"My place."

"Why?"

Max met the kid's gaze head-on, noting the swelling around his eye and his split lip. "Well, for one, I have no clue where you live. And two, I figured you would rather clean up a bit before facing your parents."

"I'm not going home."

"Never said you had to. Come in, wash up, and then I'll take you anywhere you want to go." Max opened the door, snagged his food, and got out. "Coming?"

With no plans at the moment, Jamie sighed, exited, and trailed after Max. He studied the man's back, surprised he talked to him like an adult and left the choice up to him. Any of his uncles would've treated him like a child and dragged him home without question.

Max's mind continued to whirl, trying to determine the best way to deal with James. Although they were strangers and he was flying blind, Jake's son needed help. According to Kira, he was a good kid but appeared to be spiraling out of control.

That he understood all too well, perhaps he could use his life experience to help James with whatever he was dealing with. Drinking was usually a symptom of an underlying problem, not the problem itself, especially in a teenager. Max maintained his silence, planning his strategy as James followed him into the complex and up the stairs.

Max's Apartment

After entering, Max placed his dinner on the counter and continued into the kitchen. He grinned when James shut the door and took a seat on one of his stools.

Grabbing a bag of frozen corn and a dish towel, he tossed them to James before turning to go to his bathroom for his first aid kit.

"What do I do with these?"

Max halted. "Wrap the bag in the towel and ice your shiner."

"Why corn? Don't you have instant cold packs?"

"Cheaper, molds easier, and doesn't get mushy like peas after repeated use. Back in a minute." Max disappeared down his hall.

James rolled the frozen package in the cloth, then gingerly pressed it to his eye and hissed. *Damn, that hurts.* He gazed around the room, noting its sparseness. He guessed it was similar to Uncle Finn's place, though a lot cleaner, and there was no Zulu flag on the wall. The couch looked to be in better shape, but Finn had a bigger TV and every game console made.

Returning, Max set his kit on the countertop and opened it. "We can do this one of two ways, your choice. I can clean and dress the abrasions now, or you can take a shower, and I'll put antibiotic ointment on the few that require it after."

"I don't have anything to wear."

"You can borrow a pair of shorts and a t-shirt. Our waists are about the same, and I got a few older shirts that are smaller."

"Why are you doing this?" James lowered the ice pack.

Max shrugged. "Wouldn't you do it for someone in need?"

"Sure, but …" James stopped before putting his foot in his mouth.

"Shower?"

"Yeah, thanks."

"Okay. Let me grab a clean towel for you and the clothes." Max pivoted and went to his bedroom as James made his way to the bathroom.

While James showered, Max whipped up a batch of minute rice so he could share his chicken dinner with the teen. He set out two plates, utensils, and bottled water for both of them then waited for him to finish. Max began picking at his portion of the dish after twenty minutes passed. He rarely took more than five minutes in the shower, so in his book, James was taking an eternity.

Max realized James had not grown up in a military boarding school where the luxury of long showers didn't exist. There were a lot of things most teens took for granted that Max didn't have, but the only thing he ever wished for was not a thing ... it was his mom and dad. He would've given up every material item to have one more day with them.

When the tap shut off, Max turned on the microwave to reheat James's portion. He was switching plates to heat his when James schlepped out wearing the shorts and t-shirt he provided. "Not sure you like Indian food, but the chicken tikka is supposed to be delicious."

"This is your dinner. I can't—"

"Yes, you can. There's more than enough for both. Let me put the ointment on while mine reheats." Max moved forward and inspected the cuts, none of them deep or requiring steri-strips or stitches. He smeared a bit of antibiotic cream on a few before the kid dug into his meal.

Max retrieved his reheated food and sat beside James. After taking a bite of chicken, he said, "Mmm, Devlin is right, the spiced tomato-yogurt sauce is tasty."

"Yeah, it's good."

They ate in silence, and Max grinned when James finished every scrap on his plate. He stood and picked up both plates, moving them to the sink.

"I can wash up ... to repay you."

"Sure. Need to change my dressing anyway." Max grabbed his kit and walked towards his bathroom.

James watched Max as he finally realized this was the new guy he overheard his dad talking about. He got injured on the mission, and Dad was pissed. Dad never took it well when one of the team got hurt, but he'd never heard him rant about it quite like that to his mom before.

A snort emitted from James as he started to wash the plates. *No wonder Dad treats me like a child, he called Max, a SEAL in a top tier team, a kid.* James sighed. *I guess I'll never measure up.*

Max returned and found James sitting on the couch with the corn ice pack on his eye. He lowered himself in a chair facing James, considered his words carefully, and decided to come at this indirectly. "So, I got to meet everyone at the barbeque except you. Got any questions for me?"

"Huh?" Expecting to be grilled, James blinked.

"Well, everyone seemed to be curious ... some more so than others. Let's see, your brother Tommy asked me if I ever killed anyone. Your mother shushed him. The answer is yes. Your sister wanted to know how old I am ... twenty-four. Um, well, other things, but do you have any for me?"

James stared with only one eye. "You're only twenty-four? I wondered why Dad called you kid."

Max laughed. "I've been called worse."

"How did you make it to Zulu so young?"

"Perseverance, drive, and a bit of luck. Helped I knew exactly what I would strive to be since I turned five."

"And your family supported you?" James leaned forward.

Max exhaled heavily. "No. My uncle did everything in his power to make me believe I would never reach my goal. I'm sure he threw in some roadblocks along the way."

Jamie's shoulders sagged. "Yeah, that must've sucked."

Reading the body language, Max added, "But I never let him crater my dreams. What about you, you're what, eighteen ... what are your dreams?"

"Doesn't matter."

"Why?"

"Just doesn't."

"Sure, it does. Everyone's dreams matter."

Jamie puffed out a breath. "Not mine. I'm just a waste of space and will never measure up to what my dad thinks is important or manly. I'll never save the world like him." His volume dropped to a whisper, "Not that I even want to."

Max didn't miss the soft words. "What do you want?"

"If I tell you, you'll laugh."

"I won't. I promise."

Jamie hesitated, unsure whether to tell him. "I want to be a fashion designer. Not men's clothes … women's. I took a sewing class in tenth grade because the elective I wanted was full, and I, well, I can't explain, but something about creating clothing spoke to me. Though I never told anyone, I made my girlfriend's prom dress. She kept my secret because everyone thought she bought it from one of the high-end design houses."

Max nodded.

"So, you see … I can't tell the mighty Jake Marshall, the man's man, a badass SEAL, that I want to make dresses for a living."

"Why not?"

Jamie choked out a laugh. "Serious?"

"Yeah, serious. He's your dad. He loves you. He would support you. And your mother would too."

"You honestly don't know my parents. I would be such a disappointment to them."

"What makes you think that?"

"'Cause it's a sissy profession."

Max snorted. "I doubt you believe what you said."

"No, but they would."

"I think you are selling them short." Max let the silence hang for several minutes and then asked, "Is this why you are drinking so much? Maybe thinking if you lower their estimation of you, they might accept you when you tell them you want to be a designer?"

"No," Jamie forcefully answered.

"So why the drinking?"

Jamie shrugged, and his gaze dropped to his lap before he confessed, "Tried hanging out with some new guys. Those who like to drink and do macho stuff. Thought maybe they would rub off on me, and I might find something more acceptable to my mom and dad. Something more masculine. But things got out of hand."

He lifted his eye to Max. "Hell, I don't even like the taste of beer. It is gross. Tastes like piss. I like wine, though."

Max shook his head and grinned. "Oh, man, the stupid shit we do when we think people won't accept us for who we are. Been there, done that, got the scars to prove it."

"Really?"

"Yeah. The hole in my back for one. I underestimated your father, and it nearly cost me my life. Had I been upfront with him from the beginning, I could've saved myself and others a whole boatload of trouble."

Jamie nodded. "Trouble … yeah, I got that too."

"Who were those guys pounding on you?"

Wincing as he sucked in his split lower lip, Jamie debated whether to tell Max and decided to come clean. "The guy giving the orders is Seth, one of the guys I hung out with lately. Didn't realize he deals drugs."

"Okay? So why was he beating the crap out of you?"

"When I found out, I told him if he didn't stop dealing to kids at the high school, I would tell the cops. He didn't like that much."

"When did you find out?" Max had a hunch, and it might make things better for James in the long run.

Jamie sighed. "The night I so-called crashed while driving drunk. I was down by the lake drinking and saw him selling crap to some kids from my school.

"I confronted him, and one of Seth's goons slammed my head into the trunk of my car. It dazed me, and they shoved me in the front seat. Seth got in and drove a bit. I recall him revving the engine before he jumped out. The next thing I know, the police are there, and they're arresting me for DUI, and my car's smashed into a tree. I can't prove it, so I never said anything, and I thought that would keep Seth from trying to kill me."

Max nodded. "I understand proving the truth without evidence is difficult."

"Yeah. Tell me about it." Jamie sighed and dropped the cold corn on the couch. "I hate my life. Everything is so screwed up. I can't figure out how to fix things."

Leaning forward, Max grinned. "That's why you have family."

Chapter Fifteen

Jake's Home

NERVOUS, Jamie fidgeted in Max's car as they pulled up to his house. It was now quite late, well past eleven, but it took him that long to work up the courage to come home and talk to his parents. He appreciated how Max discussed things with him and didn't tell him what to think or do, but offered him some examples from his own life.

What Max shared made his own life seem like he lived in a country club with a perfect family. Jamie couldn't imagine losing both parents and his grandmother at such a young age and having to go live with an uncle who despised him.

After he pulled his head out of his ass, Jamie recognized his mom and dad cared about him. Their actions after the crash were shining examples, but looking back at his entire life, he found a plethora of evidence they wanted only the best for him.

"Ready?" Max asked.

"Not sure."

"You can sit here for as long as you need, James."

Jamie grinned at the use of an adult name. Max treated him as an equal and put the ball squarely in his court, which with their six-year gap, felt good. He liked to think of Max as an older brother rather than another honorary uncle. Drawing in a breath, Jamie turned to Max. "Would you go in with me?"

Still uncertain about his place on Zulu, Max didn't like the prospect of getting between his team leader and his son. Jake might view this as overstepping, but the pleading in James's expression indicated the teen required support.

When he was eighteen, and out of his depth, he wished someone would've offered to assist him. Although this might be a colossal mistake, he would never leave someone in need hanging, so Max manned-up and said, "If you want."

"Yeah. I should do this alone ... but—"

"No explanation needed." Max moved his hand to the door handle. "Now?"

Jamie nodded, opened the door, and got out. He marched up the front walk, hoping against the odds his mom and dad would understand and help him sort out the mess he made of his life.

Entering the house, he found most of the lights off. His siblings were likely in bed asleep, but he overheard his parents talking in the kitchen. Before he chickened out, Jamie said, "Mom, Dad, I'm home. I brought someone with me too."

Max followed Jamie through the entry and living room, taking in the furnishings and decorations. The details he observed spoke of a well-tended home. One wall with a collage of family photos, a bunch of smiling kids and parents, made him sigh with envy. He halted behind Jamie when Jake barked, "Where the hell have you been all night?"

Val reacted differently as she spotted her son's contused face. "Oh, my goodness! What happened? Are you alright?"

"Yeah, Mom. I'm okay ... thanks to Max." Jamie stepped to the side, revealing his new friend-brother.

Jake's brows scrunched together as he spotted his rookie, and questions flooded his mind. "Max?"

"Dad." Jamie inhaled and released a rush of air. "I want to talk with you and Mom. If you can hold your questions until I finish, I would appreciate it. What I need to say isn't easy, and I'm only here now because," he glanced back at Max before returning his gaze to his dad, "Max helped me put my head on straight."

"Alright. I'm listening."

Val said, "Jamie, please sit down, and—"

"Mom, please call me James. I'm not a little boy anymore. I'm an adult, and it's time I started acting my age."

"Okay, James." Val glanced at Jake, both noting the change in their son appeared to be significant. Her gaze moved to Max. "Please have a seat too. I believe this will be a long discussion."

Uncomfortable, but unwilling to abandon James, Max nodded and chose a chair on the opposite side. His position allowed him to be out of the way, and for James to sit between his parents.

Jamie launched into his tale. He revealed how Max saved him from Seth and his goons, the car crash, and the reason he started drinking. Jamie concluded with, "I messed up big-time, all because I was afraid you would be disappointed in me if I told you I wanted to design women's clothing for a living."

Speechless for a moment, Jake stared at his son, wondering how he created an environment where his child feared to be himself. "Jamie … um, James, son, all I ever wanted for you was to be happy and safe. You've always been creative," he grinned, "and you'll be successful at anything you go after."

Val reached out and grasped Jamie's hand. "Lizzy's prom dress? You made that amazing gown?"

Blushing, Jamie nodded. He peered at Max, and with heartfelt sincerity said, "Thank you for giving me courage to talk to them. You were right … I sold them short."

"The courage is all yours, buddy, but I'm glad I could help." Shifting his focus to Jake, Max asked, "About the crash. Did they take pictures of James's injury?"

"Yes, why?" Val answered.

Max smiled. "Because I think there might be a way to prove James's version of events. If the airbag deployed—"

"It did," Jake said, and added, "James couldn't have struck his head on the dash, and there would be DNA on the bag if he were driving. The steering wheel might have Seth's DNA too." He turned to his son. "Where were you when the police arrived?"

"Um, the front passenger seat, sorta half on the floor."

Jake grinned. "I'll call the lawyer in the morning. That is … if you are willing to press charges against Seth for both assaults?"

"Yes." A weight lifting from his shoulders, Jamie never thought something so simple might prove his innocence.

Val squeezed Jamie's hand as she beamed. "And while that is getting all sorted out, you and I can start searching for a fashion design school. It might be a little late to gain entry for the coming year, but you could work on a portfolio of designs and maybe take a class or two at the community college."

Jamie stood, pulled his mom to him, and hugged her. "Thanks, you're the best mom ever." He released her and pivoted to face his father. He only waited a beat before his dad rose and embraced him. "You're always in my corner, and I should've known that. Sorry for being so stupid. I love you, Dad."

As Val joined the father-son hug, Max turned his head and swiftly swiped at his damp eyes. He sucked in a breath, and blinked a few times, figuring he should leave now. Max stood and inched toward the archway, not wanting to disturb the family moment.

"Max?"

He halted when Jake called his name and met his boss's eyes.

"Thank you."

Giving a slight nod, unsure how to respond, Max repeated the words Jake said to him at the barbeque. "We watch out for our own, which includes extended family." Still uncomfortable, he grinned and resorted to humor to cover his unease. "I should be going. Early morning. Don't want to be late, or my hard-as-nails team leader will be upset and make me run the hills."

Jake stifled a chuckle as he retorted, "Damned right. See you tomorrow, Kid. And don't forget the beer."

"Bye, Max. And thanks again," Jamie said.

"I add my thanks as well. Goodnight, Max, Drive carefully." Val winked and said, "I have a lot of pull with that CO of yours, so if you're a tad late, don't worry about running hills."

Grinning, Max exited, happy his help didn't backfire on him.

Zulu Equipment Cages

Max lugged in what would be the first of many cases of beer, at least according to Finn. The room was empty, so he set today's tribute on the tall table in the middle and turned towards his cage. His eyes rounded, and jaw dropped before a broad grin bloomed. Like a kid in a candy shop, he raced forward, unlocked, and swung open the door.

His fingers ghosted over the scope, and he almost drooled. Never in his wildest imagination did he think when he put this on the list he sent to Draper he would actually receive this scope. He turned when he heard Jake and Dave entering.

Dave laughed outright. "Damn, the kid's expression is exactly like Aidan's on Christmas morning."

Unsure if this was a prank, Max's voice annoyingly came out tentative as he asked, "Is this truly for me or—"

"Yours!" Jake stated. "Top-tier means we can acquire and test all the latest toys. Draper did tell you to make a list, and she'd procure everything, right?"

"Yeah, but I didn't … I never … Christ, if I asked for extra batteries on my previous teams, I had to wait months and ended up buying them myself."

"You aren't on those teams anymore. You're Zulu," Dave said as he leaned against the wire. "We should hit the range today and let you play a bit."

Max sighed. "Doc hasn't cleared me yet."

"For ops and heavy training. Nothing keeping you from the gun range." Jake started to move to open his cage but stopped to study Stirling. "The fact you are early, tells me you didn't believe Val last night."

"Oh, no, I believed her." Max grinned. "Just saving the chit for when I might genuinely need her help."

Jake laughed.

"What's so funny?" Finn asked as he strode in and spotted the beer. "Rookie's here." He turned to Max. "Damned good thing you brought the right kind, or else you'd be bathing in it."

Max grimaced. "Think I've had enough of beer bathing."

"Damn straight!" Grant said as he entered and overheard his teammates. He smiled, noting the pile of new gear in Max's cage. "Draper's been busy."

The last to arrive, Zach held the door open as Rocketeer trotted in. He grinned as he reported, "The vet gave Rocky the all-clear this morning."

Jake crouched, and Rocky padded over for a pet. "Who's a good boy? You are. Welcome back, Rocky." He ruffled the pup's fur, then stood and laughed as he spotted Finn tousling Max's hair as he repeated his words to their rookie.

Max shoved Finn back. "I'm not a dog or a boy."

"I remember what you look like without that scraggly beard. Yer just a wee laddie," Finn teased again.

"Nas fheàrr na a bhith na seann ghobhar," Max retorted.

"What'd ya call me?" Finn scrunched his brows.

Max laughed as he recalled Babcox's confusion on the flight, "You don't know Scots Gaelic?"

"No, not really. Only phrases my Nana and Gramps used," Finn admitted. "So, what did you say?"

Max shifted closer to the exit as he answered, "Better than being an old goat."

"Why you!" Finn lurched forward to grab the kid.

Max darted out of the room, his laughter peeling down the hall as Finn raced after him.

Sighing, Dave shook his head. "Life's gonna be interesting with those two."

"Yep." Jake sat on his camp chair and grinned.

"What's got you all happy today?" Dave asked as he moved to put his bag in his cage.

"Things are going to work out with Jamie." He peered at the guys. "From now on, please call him James."

"Okay. What happened?" Dave halted and turned to Jake, as did Zach and Grant.

"The kid happened."

"Huh?" Zach questioned.

"I don't follow you," Dave said.

Jake spent the next fifteen minutes explaining what occurred last night and Stirling's role in helping James.

Grant grinned. "Never thought James would be one for the military. I wish him well in his endeavors."

"So, does your lawyer think he can get the charges dropped?" Zach asked.

"Yeah, he's fairly confident. Most likely will take a week or so to do the DNA matching. Fortunately, Seth's DNA is already on record due to a previous bout with the law. The lawyer is also searching for possible witnesses at the lake to corroborate James's claim they slammed his head into the car's trunk, put him in the passenger seat, and Seth drove."

"Awesome." Dave grabbed his gear and glanced around. "Think we should go find the children?"

"Nah, let them play a bit longer. Max has been pulling at the reins and needs to work off some energy," Grant suggested.

"And Finn could do with working off some fluff. He ate too many of Devlin's muffins," Zach added.

Jake nodded. When he selected Max, Jake worried he made a mistake, but now realized the kid fit perfectly with them. He was glad he didn't allow Max's lineage to stop him from choosing him. Jake comprehended he and his son James were vastly different and now suspected Maxwell was different from Preston. He also conceded the kid might make a decent team leader years down the road with the right training.

Max's Apartment

The rapping on his door made Max grin as the strode to answer it. He glanced back at his island and the place settings, then swept his gaze around his room to make sure nothing like an errant pair of boxers or something equally embarrassing was lying around.

He opened the door, and his smile grew. "Welcome to my humble abode."

Cali stepped inside, her stomach aflutter at seeing Max again.

Max shut the door and turned to Cali. "Lasagna should be ready in a few minutes. Can I grab you something to drink?"

Holding out the bottle of wine, Cali said, "I brought this. Thought it would pair well with dinner."

"Perfect." Max took the wine and headed for the kitchen to procure his opener, glad he bought one during his hasty shopping trip this afternoon.

"Did you make the lasagna yourself?" Cali scanned Max's place, small like hers, but sufficient for one or two people.

Max chuckled. "My culinary skills stop at reheating stuff in the oven and boiling water for ramen or minute rice. Hope you like Mama Mia's frozen lasagna."

"Well, as long as it isn't frozen when we eat it, I'll be fine. I'm not all that picky. Remember, I'm one of seven kids, and five were boys. We ate whatever Mom cooked. Though I must say, my mom is a whiz at making the most mundane stuff taste wonderful."

Cali sauntered over to the island and smiled as she teased, "I didn't take you for a cloth napkin and candlelight sort of guy."

"Ugg, me caveman, like cloth. Fire good ... cook meat ... yum." Max laughed as he made Cali giggle. When the cork popped, he said, "Don't have wine glasses. Tumblers should suffice."

Leaning in like she was revealing a huge secret, Cali whispered, "Don't tell anyone, but I don't either. I still use plastic cups."

Morphing his expression into fake shock, Max gasped. "Wow. Plastic. Oh, the horror. I'm telling your colleagues."

Giggling again, Cali sat on one of the stools. "You think they would stop inviting me to their posh parties if they knew?"

"Nah, you're too gorgeous. You could drink straight from a bottle, and they'd think you were perfection."

"You sure know how to flatter a girl."

"Woman. I don't date girls."

"So would that make me your womanfriend instead of girlfriend?" Cali joked.

"I'll make an exception for that word."

"Um, is something burning?"

"Oh shit." Max set down the bottle before rushing to the oven. A billow of smoke came out when he opened it. Grabbing the hot pads, Max pulled out the foil pan. "Dang, the cheese on top is all brown and crispy."

"Yum."

Max dropped the pan to the stovetop and peered at Cali. "Are you serious?"

"Absolutely. The best part. Used to fight Gabe over the crunchy pieces." She preened as she poured the red wine for them. "I always won. He's such a pushover for a pout."

After serving up portions of overdone lasagna and a mixed greens salad, which Max confessed to buying pre-packaged, he set their plates on the counter and took the other seat. He raised his glass and said, "To a lovely lady who graciously forgave me for not calling her in the last four weeks."

Cali arched a brow. "I should be mad you didn't call, but I'll give you this one time since you said you were ill and still feverish when you returned."

Max sighed, recalling the razzing his teammates gave him when Jake told them he hadn't bothered to tell his girlfriend he returned. When he explained he didn't want to contact her until his back fully healed, Dave gave him an earful.

His 2IC told him he wouldn't be able to hide the injury from her since there would be a scar. And if he thought Cali might one day be wife material, it would be better to be upfront with her when he was injured. Dave said if he kept things from her, she might question his truthfulness in other areas. As a team guy, their inability to share certain things with their significant others was a hurdle they all had to overcome.

Deciding it was time to own up to most of it, choosing to leave out taking four rounds in the vest shielding Rocky, Max said, "I didn't only have a kidney infection. I got injured."

Cali blanched. "What happened?"

"Can't share details, but got a little puncture wound."

"Where? I mean on your body?"

"Right flank. The guys took care of me. It's nearly healed."

Cali inhaled slow and released gradually. "As they should."

"I'm sorry I didn't tell you, but for you to worry over something trivial—"

"Trivial?" Cali interrupted. "You get knifed, and you think that is trivial?"

"I wasn't knifed."

Cali shook her head and drew her brows together, endeavoring to hold back her disbelief and concern. "Then, how?"

Max chuckled, trying to change the tone of their exchange. "Fell on a stupid pointed pyramid. Real graceful for my first mission with the team. Made me wonder if they would keep me or send me packing."

"Pfft. According to Gabe, you're one of the best operators he's ever commanded. If Zulu got rid of you for a fall, then they don't deserve you."

Max grinned at the way Cali defended him. "Well, they didn't. Had fun training with them today. I was not allowed to participate in most of the drills, but learning how they move and operate together was useful."

He leaned in and kissed her cheek. "But I'm going to enjoy my night with you much more."

Cali smiled at the incorrigible expression. "What do you have in mind beyond burnt frozen lasagna and pre-packaged salad?"

With that, dinner was forgotten as the two ended up kissing, and moving into Max's bedroom for several rounds of vigorous bedsport.

Chapter Sixteen

Four Weeks Later – Training Grounds

PARTNERED with Zach, Max ran up the hill in the wooded area. People might think him crazy, but he enjoyed the last two weeks of non-stop, hard-hitting, down-in-the-dirt training. He never trained harder or been quite so wiped out when he dropped into his bed each night.

Back in top form, Max wouldn't wish away a single moment of his time with Zulu. Though his count of cases of beer owed for firsts climbed to an ungodly number, and he began to think the rookie tax might exceed his federal taxes, he found a few ways to subtract cases here and there. His brothers liked to bet, and he had an uncanny ability to win said wagers.

He would win this one too. Max and Zach only needed to capture one more flag to be victorious. They managed to snag a second flag only moments ago, and while Dave and Jake were still mired in the trap they set, he and Zulu Five would reach the crest of this hill and grab their third flag.

His grin grew as they got closer. A win would knock off ten cases from his tab. Digging deep into his reserves, Max poured on a spurt of speed, pulling away from Zach. His eyes on the prize, only fifty yards away now Max wanted to chortle, but a rumbling sound behind him and a yelp made him spin around. Max gaped as Zach tumbled down the steep incline.

Ass over tea kettle, Zach careened downward, the rocks, twigs, and general crap on the forest floor bit into his unprotected face since tactical gear, including gloves, protected the rest of his body. In the seconds he rolled, Zach chided himself for his misstep. His partner would be pissed if they lost on account of him. The kid placed a hefty bet on this game of capture the flag.

Coming to a sudden halt, Zach's trouble went from a five to one hundred in a blink of an eye. He froze as he came face-to-face with a pissed off canebrake rattlesnake. The coiled serpent shook its rattles menacingly and swayed, preparing to strike.

Things would've been interesting if time slowed down as in the movies. Zach could've experienced all the details of slow-motion action, but this was real life, and that didn't happen. Instead, one moment he stared into the face of a venomous creature poised to inject a potentially lethal dose with sharp fangs, and the next, the space before him was empty.

He must've blinked, and for a moment, Zach thought he might've only imagined the pit viper, but his gaze shifted. Pinned to the ground, not more than six inches from him, a tactical knife through its head, lay a dead rattler. Sounds rushed in, making Zach aware his world had been eerily silent as he faced off with the serpent.

"Five, sitrep?" Stirling's voice rang in his ears, causing Zach to look up the hill.

"I'm good," Zach called out. His eyes turned back to the snake and stared at the knife before peering back up to Max. *How did he do that from that distance?*

Max descended the incline, sending a shower of loose pebbles and dirt towards Zach. He reached Zulu Five and crouched beside him, worried his brother had not moved. "You get bit or are you injured?" came out a bit breathless, not from exertion, but from the jolt of spotting the rattlesnake threatening Zach.

He would've shot the rattler, but for this exercise, they carried paintball guns, leaving him with one choice, his knife. His heart rapidly thudded once he sent it sailing, hoping to hit the mark.

Gathering his wits, Zach shifted to his butt and blew out a breath. "Not bitten. Close. Too close." As he focused on the dead snake, Zach asked, "How the hell did you hit it?"

Max let out a half snort, half chuckle. "Several summers spent at an outdoors, backwoods camp. One of my favorite activities was knife throwing."

Holding out a hand, Max said, "If you're not hurt, let's grab the last flag."

Taking hold, Zach allowed Max to help haul him to his feet. He tested his legs and found nothing amiss, other than a couple of sore spots, which would likely be black and blue in a few days. He reached down and selected a large rock. "Grab your knife, and I'll smash its head so the damned thing can't inject venom if someone happens to stumble upon the carcass."

Max retrieved his blade and waited for Zach to crush the snake's head and fangs before pivoting and sprinting up the hill. Ten yards from victory, Max groaned as Jake's voice came over the comms. "Final flag captured. One and Two win. Ten more cases added to the kid's tab."

The Barnacle

Miserable and damned grumpy, Finn used a straw to suck up his beer because when he tried to drink from the mug, too much dribbled down his chin. "Wolen ips an tong, uck," he grumbled, almost incoherently, attempting to speak with a swollen tongue and lips.

The guys, all except Grant, laughed at Finn. He was a sorry sight. Actually, both Grant and Finn were. One side of Finn's face resembled a balloon blown up to its capacity, almost making his left eye invisible. Grant's hands had the same puffiness to them.

"That's what happens when you tangle with a hornet's nest," Dave said with a smirk.

"But the flag was in the tree," Grant protested.

"We bypassed that one," Zach said. "Not worth the risk."

"Same here," Jake raised his mug and took a sip.

"o uts, no ory," Finn mumbled.

Max snickered at Finn's attempt to say no guts, no glory. "Yeah, but no stupidity, no stings."

Finn gave Max the stink eye, with only one functioning orb as he held up all his digits and said, "Id owes en mor ases."

Sighing, Max peered at Jake. "If you recall, we fought a war based on taxation without representation. This rookie tax is getting excessive. I might need to start a revolution."

"You believe this is a tax?" Jake asked.

"Yeah, and I'm going broke." Max hid his grin. "Been eating ramen for a week now to afford all the beer."

Zach sighed but stepped up to do the right thing. "Us losing is my fault. I'll pick up the tab on the ten cases."

"Twenty." Max eyed him, struggling hard not to laugh at Zach's confused expression.

"Twenty?"

"Wager deducted ten or added ten … so my total increased by twenty."

"Yeah, okay. Better than dealing with a snake bite. Twenty it is," Zach groused.

"It isn't a tax." Dave popped a peanut in his mouth.

"What would you call it?" Max asked.

"Team dues."

"Taxation if I'm the only one paying membership tariffs," Max argued, wanting to see where he could take this conversation.

Jake watched the new guy, recognizing he was enjoying the banter, but the kid had a point, and it was time to equalize things. He leaned forward, garnering everyone's attention when he cleared his throat. "I think our accounting is a little off."

"Nnu, ee ows irty asses," Finn interjected.

They all laughed as Finn struggled to speak coherently. At this rate, they might need to resort to pen and paper for him to communicate anything recognizable.

"By my accounting, some deductions are outstanding," Jake said.

Intrigued, Max asked, "What deductions?"

"Well, as Dave pointed out, this is not taxation, but not team dues either. Yes, you gotta pay for firsts, but others owe for things as well, and when it concerns you, it serves as a credit or deduction from your balance."

"Still sounds like taxation to me. So, what kind of credits and deductions?" Max relaxed as he lifted his mug.

Jake rubbed the back of his neck. "Let's see. One case subtracted for rescuing Levi."

"Hey, Max was not on the team then. Doesn't count." Zach recalled almost going broke for two months, and believed their new guy, as much as he liked him, and he did like Max a lot, deserved the same level of initiation.

"Sure, it does. Zulu owes him for saving a brother," Dave supported Jake's line of thought. "Which means cases come off for covering Finn, Axel, and saving my ass too."

Finn grumbled something, but the guys ignored him.

"Kept me from getting stabbed, so one for that too." Grant flexed his swollen fingers. He got stung as he tried to bat the hornets away from Finn's face. The angry hornets attacked with a vengeance when Finn accidentally broke open their nest while grabbing their first flag. They didn't care about the game from that point on, too preoccupied running away from the swarm.

Dave grinned at Zach, who appeared to be pouting. "Another for taking four rounds to save Rocky."

Max piped up, "No, that one doesn't count. The Rockstar took one while protecting me. We're even."

Zach grinned at a new nickname for Rocketeer and decided he would play this game too. "Deduct one for saving me today."

"But you're already covering the twenty," Max countered.

"My screw up, my bill."

"Ad ne fo aruing his ass," Finn slurred, wishing his tongue worked.

"Don't know what the hell you said, but okay, we'll take off one more," Jake said.

"Add on, ot subact" Finn managed to say somewhat clearly.

"For what?" Max reached for a handful of peanuts.

Jake chuckled, having lost count and came up with a solution. "Bring a keg to the annual picnic on Saturday, and we'll call it even."

"I can do that. Does the beer tax end?"

"Hell, no!" Zach declared as the others shook their heads.

Max groaned. "I'm still gonna be buying a boatload of cases, aren't I?"

Grinning, Zach nodded. "Perils of being Six." He rubbed his hands together like an evil villain. "There are so many firsts for you to experience."

"But things like saving your asses will offset what I owe?" Max asked.

Jake and Dave both gave the kid a nod.

Ballfield on Base

Cali peered around at the vast number of people, young and old, as she strolled towards one of about twenty tables set up around a massive wall-less tent. Under the canopy, several more tables stood, all laden with various dishes and beverages. "I thought you said this was a team picnic."

Max grinned. "It is."

"Okay, Zulu's bigger than you let on."

"No, not just Zulu. According to Jake, several of the teams that work together often and the support personnel combine the event and also play a single-elimination baseball tournament."

"Who can play?"

"Anyone eighteen and above. They instituted that rule a few years ago after someone's thirteen-year-old daughter got beaned by an errant ball. Knocked out two of her teeth, and the team ended up in a brawl when one of the guys accused the pitcher of doing it on purpose. Lockwood decided keeping it to adults would help prevent a reoccurrence. You want to play?"

"No, thanks. I like my teeth where they are. How about you?"

Max grinned and chuckled at her humor. "Yeah, I'm participating, but don't worry, I got excellent dental coverage."

Cathy spotted Zulu's newest member and made a beeline to him and the woman she assumed to be his girlfriend. Coming to a stop, she smiled. "Max, I'm so glad you came today."

"Hi, Cathy. I'd like to introduce you to Cali Miller. Cali, this is Cathy Katz, Dave's wife."

"Pleasure to meet you," both women said simultaneously.

"I brought chocolate cupcakes." Cali lifted the box she carried.

"Wonderful. Come with me. I'll show you where to put them."

"Cali, you want a beer?" Max asked.

"Sure."

They separated, Cali following Cathy, and Max walking to where the chilled keg he arranged to be delivered had been set up. He filled two red plastic tumblers and chuckled as he recalled their banter about wine glasses and Cali's confession that she still used plastic cups. He decided a set of stemless wine goblets would be the perfect gift for her birthday next week.

As he turned to locate Cali, he faced three unknown bearded men, which clued him in to them being team guys.

"You must be Zulu's new pin-up girl." Dominic said.

Spying the flash of annoyance in the blond man's eyes, Wade stepped in before his rookie started something he shouldn't. "Don't mind Dom. He's not housebroken yet." He held out a hand. "I'm Wade Dunn."

Holding two cups, Max put one cup between his forearm and chest so that he could grasp the outstretched hand. "Max Stirling. You're Delta One, right?"

"Yep."

Delta's rookie extended his hand and grinned. "I'm Dominic Martill, most people call me Dom."

"Or Dumb," Wade snickered, razzing his teammate as Max shook hands. "I hear we have you to thank for the beer today."

"Yeah. The keg cleared the slate." Max grinned as he turned and offered his hand to the last man. "And you are?"

"Connor Reid, Wade's 2IC," the third man introduced himself before adding, "Slate won't stay clear for long."

"Yeah, I'm aware." Max spied Cali and didn't want to leave her hanging alone too long. "If you'll excuse me, my date's waiting."

The three guys all nodded and turned. Dom let out a low whistle. "Man, she's gorgeous."

"She's out of your league," Connor said before pouring himself a beer.

Max joined Cali, and he made the rounds, introducing her to the guys and their family members. Glad he explained to Cali the situation he needed to avoid with Eve, he breathed easier when Cali started a conversation with Jake's daughter about baking. The two appeared to hit it off, as he went to join his team for their first game.

"Hey, Max," James called out. "I brought you a mitt. I hope my old glove fits."

"I'm sure it will. Thanks." Max accepted the glove and slipped his hand inside. "Works."

"Got great news yesterday." James's eyes flashed with glee.

"What?"

"My record is officially expunged, and the prosecutor believes he got enough evidence to put Seth away for several years. But the best part is, I got accepted to the Valley Design Institute. I'm going to be staying with my aunt Leslie in Phoenix, at least until I can find an apartment of my own."

"Cool."

Jake interrupted the chat. "We're up. We want to win the trophy again this year, so everyone bring your A-game." Jake trotted over to the umpire to determine who would bat first.

About an hour later, at the bottom of the ninth, with one out left and down two points with the tying runs on base, Max strode to the batter's box. Although Barry, a Delta support team member who played college ball, threw a wicked-fast curveball, Max remained confident he would knock the ball out of the park to secure Zulu's win and move them forward in the tournament.

With Zach on second and Dave on first, Max tested his swing as he eyed Barry, and prepared. He resisted swinging at the first pitch, which was a little outside the box. Balls two and three quickly followed ball one.

Barry appeared to be struggling, and Max overheard the guys speculating earlier that the shoulder he dinged in Delta's last op might be bothering him. Setting up for the fourth pitch, Max grinned as Zulu cheered behind him, although Cali's supportive voice overrode everyone else's as Barry let the baseball fly.

Blinking, it took a moment for Max to orient himself. A cacophony of sounds rushed in as did pain on the left side of his face. He lifted a hand to his stinging eye. Blurry images came through his watery eye, while crisp ones registered in his right one.

Jake knelt beside Cali, both reaching Max only moments after he hit the dirt. Waving his hand near Stirling's face with his thumb holding the pinky, Jake asked, "How many fingers?"

"Three." Max started to push himself up, realizing the fastball struck him, though he attempted to dodge it.

Barry stood off to the side, appearing remorseful. "Sorry, dude. The ball got away from me. Didn't mean to bean ya."

"Are you alright?" Cali's expression filled with concern.

"Yeah, I'm fine." Taking Jake's offered hand, Max stood and brushed the dust from his shorts. His left eye continued to water and hurt, but he wiped it and chose to present his tough-guy persona in front of all the guys.

The umpire roved over him with an assessing eye. "Take your base."

"Nah, I'll bat." Max glanced at Draper, who was up next, and he didn't want her anywhere near the batter's box if Barry couldn't control his pitches.

Jake shook his head. Whether Max owned up to it or not, they all comprehended getting beaned with one of Barry's fastballs hurt like hell. "Nope. Ball four, you take first."

Dunn patted Barry's back. "Go ice your shoulder. I'll take over as pitcher."

When Barry nodded, Max complied with Jake's bidding and jogged to first as Dave trotted to second and Zach to third.

With bases loaded, Kira readied to hit. Her grip on the bat firm, she held it over her right shoulder. She swung, connected, and a huge grin plastered her face as she dashed for first base, then second, third, and slid into home, ensuring Zulu's seven to five win over Delta, and advancing them to the next bracket.

Kira laughed as Finn smothered her in a bear hug. The big lug sometimes forgot his strength. She followed the boisterous Zulu team to the tents as they grabbed ice-cold beers to celebrate their win and relax before their second game.

However, no one took more than one sip before the phones of all Zulu, Sierra, and Delta members started buzzing and ringing with messages. In less than two minutes, they bid loved ones goodbye, and several arranged to hitch rides with teammates, leaving their vehicles for wives or girlfriends.

Watching Max jog to Jake's truck, Cali sighed as she clutched the key to his Mustang. She realized her life would never be the same. Max would answer the call for some dangerous mission without hesitation, and she might never see him again. Though wanting their relationship to work, Cali remained uncertain she possessed the fortitude to be a SEAL's wife … that is if they progressed in that direction.

Val and Cathy flanked Cali, and Val said, "Max provided me your number. If anything happens to him, I'll call you."

Drawing in a shaky breath, Cali nodded. "Thanks." She turned to Valarie. "Does this ever get any easier?"

"Truthfully, no. But you can count on each one of those men to do everything in their power to ensure they and all their brothers come home. I often believe their bonds are stronger and deeper than blood bonds."

Chapter Seventeen

Team Room

LOWERING himself into a chair, Max strove not to touch his throbbing eye. Part of him wanted to ice it, but now was not the time, he needed to focus on the briefing for the mission that required not only Zulu but also Delta and Sierra.

Draper dropped an instant cold pack on the table in front of Stirling as she moved to her place. "You're gonna need to see out of that eye, so put that on now."

Still surprised how Draper magically conjured the items he required, Max somewhat believed their logistics specialist might possess powers of an oracle, soothsayer, or at least an uncanny sixth sense. Not wanting to appear incapacitated, Max eschewed her offering.

"Gonna be a beauty of a shiner there, Bat Boy," Finn chimed in as he swiveled his seat to study Max. He didn't much like the fact the kid was starting his second mission with them already a little banged up.

The comment drew Jake's attention, the message clear in his stern gaze. Reluctantly, Max placed the gel pack against his left eye, and his action appeased Marshall, who returned his focus to Farris.

Nicole stood at the head of the table. "Sorry to ruin your day, boys, but we received word a group of modern-day pirates led by August Baxter—"

"Isn't that the guy who is responsible for hi-jacking an oil tanker in the Gulf of Mexico?" Dave asked.

"Yes, the same. He got away and is now targeting an offshore drilling rig in Brazil. The gas and oil platform," Nicole flashed a photo on the monitor, "is owned by the American company Biopetrol. They recently won the deep-water drilling rights in some of the richest oil fields of the Western Hemisphere.

"When they took over the rig last week, the company placed a crew of ten men on board to perform an initial assessment of maintenance before ramping up production. Today, Biopetrol's CEO received a demand for twenty-five million dollars from Baxter, indicating he will blow up the platform along with the crew. According to Biopetrol, that rig possesses the potential of producing five billion barrels.

"The CEO said the board of directors considered paying, but with Baxter's reputation, they fear even if they pay the ransom, he might detonate the bombs."

"So our mission is to save ten hostages and stop Baxter from creating an ecological disaster," Jake said.

"You got it," Lockwood responded. "Courtesy of Biopetrol, we have full schematics of this platform, and their engineers determined the most vulnerable locations for explosives."

Draper pulled up the files and displayed them on one screen as she connected to a satellite to provide the team with current imagery over the target to assist them in their planning session.

"Dave, what are you thinking for infil?" Jake asked.

Viewing a copy of the blueprints, Dave rubbed his beard as he considered options. "Since we're not sure where the hostages are, we need a quiet approach, so helos are out."

Looking to gain points in the eyes of Zulu, Stewart Babcox, Sierra Seven, suggested, "HALO in."

Max shook his head. "Full moon. We'd be sitting ducks for the hostiles if they spotted us."

Babcox frowned, when Jake said, "Good point. HALO out."

"How about a fishing trawler," Babcox tried again.

"Platform is outside of known fishing lanes, would be a dead give-away," Max countered.

"You don't know that," Babcox barked, still miffed that Marshall selected Stirling to fill the spot on Zulu. He fully believed Preston Stirling's son didn't deserve to be on the elite team.

"Stirling is right." Kira pulled a commercial fishing map and highlighted the Biopetrol platform location, indicating it was too far outside the zone.

Finn snorted. "Stirling two, Babcox zero."

Getting them back on track, Dave asked, "What U.S. ships are in the area?"

Kira's fingers flew on her keyboard. "The USS Buckley." She sent the imagery of USS Buckley's current position relative to their target, to the monitor for the guys to view.

Dave studied the image. "If we land in Rio De Janeiro, and catch a helo to the Buckley—"

"We could take rubber raiding crafts halfway to Biopetrol's rig, and swim the remainder of the way to keep our approach stealthy," Jake finished, his mind working in tandem with Dave's.

"Exactly." Dave shot a glance at Finn. He noted the scowl but gave McBride props for not voicing any complaints. Dave never quite understood why a guy who hated swimming in the ocean chose to be a SEAL.

"I like," Wade Dunn, Delta One, agreed. "What about on-site? How do we want to tackle the bombs and the hostages?"

Having given that some thought, Jake said, "The number of hostiles remains unknown, so I'm thinking we use a two-pronged approach. Dunn, your team, will focus on locating and rescuing the crew, while my guys deal with the guards on deck and defuse the explosives."

Jake turned his gaze to Rob. "Sierra will wait close-by, in boats, ready to swoop in to extract everyone."

"Works for me," Sierra One answered.

Lockwood interjected, "Given the potential for damage, I arranged for an explosive ordnance disposal technician."

Jake nodded. "Can we get two more? Based on the vulnerable locations, the engineers determined, probably best to break my team into three, and have an EOD with each of us."

"We'll contact the Buckley's captain, and make arrangements for both EODs and the assault crafts." Lockwood glanced at Draper, who nodded and set to work.

With their basic plan settled, the guys began to discuss the finer details. Thirty minutes later, as they left the room to gather their gear, Finn chuckled and patted Max's back. "Case of beer for first time swimming."

Max shook his head. "Been swimming lots of times."

"Not with us," Zach said.

"What's his count now?" Dave asked.

"Well, that would be one since he brought a keg to the picnic," Jake replied.

"Hey, hey, he owes one for the first time getting a black eye too," Finn quipped.

"And one for the first time he tried Cathy's blueberry pie," Dave added.

"Another for my baked beans." Grant got in on the fun.

Delta Six said, "How about one for his first run with Delta?"

"Dom, that's one for you ... first time running with Zulu," Connor, Delta Two, interjected, causing their rookie to frown and everyone else to chuckle.

Zulu rattled off more firsts as they strode down the hall. Things like, the first time in the South Atlantic Ocean, in Brazil, in Rio De Janeiro, on a destroyer, and the list continued to grow. By the time they reached the equipment cages, Max was up to twelve more cases.

"So much for the keg keeping me from going broke," Max muttered, to the laughter of his teammates.

The only one not laughing was Babcox. After the debacle of Stirling's first op, Babcox firmly believed Marshall should've booted the idiot from Zulu. But here he was joking with them as if he belonged. Babcox hoped Stirling did go broke buying beer.

South Atlantic Ocean – USS Buckley

Both teams suited up and checked their scuba gear. As Max pulled his mask on his face and settled it into place to check the seal, he winced at the pressure on his bruised cheek.

Grant eyed him carefully. "The swelling isn't inhibiting your seal, is it?"

"No," Max answered truthfully, having learned from the first mission he must be honest. He refused to put the op or his team in jeopardy again. If he were not fit for the swim or task, he would tell Jake and swap with one of Sierra.

Like now, Grant hovered a bit during the flight, checking him several times for signs of a delayed concussion or vision problems. However, besides the tenderness and slight swelling, which he could handle, Max experienced no side effects.

Lifting the mask, Max spied Draper handing Finn something. "What's that?"

Dave chuckled. "Finn's anti-shark device."

"His what?"

"He fears swimming almost as much as the jungle," Grant teased.

"He's scared of swimming?" Max gazed at McBride with an incredulous expression.

"Not afraid," Finn groused as the others chuckled. "Another case of beer for the rookie."

"Why?" Max inquired, wondering what else might be a first for this mission.

"First time in shark-infested waters." Finn grinned as he clamped on his magnetic wristband.

"Great, nothing like owing thirteen cases before an op. Nothing can go wrong with that number," Max muttered under his breath.

Jake overheard and broke out into a grin. "Kid owes one more case for being superstitious."

Max gaped at Marshall, then smiled. "That is one case I won't mind buying. Even fourteen."

Patting his rookie's shoulder, Jake said, "Got your back, kid."

All chatter ceased as they boarded the rubber assault crafts, which would take them to the location where they would begin their long swim to the oil rig.

In the TOC set up on the destroyer, Draper crossed off Blue from the mission board. Next up would be Hammerhead when they arrived at the target. Kira smiled as she recalled Finn's shudders as they named the steps of the operation for all the possible sharks in the region.

Biopetrol Oil Platform

Coming up from the depths under cover of the platform, the teams waited for comms to relink before Jake spoke in a soft tone, "TOC, Zulu One, Hammerhead. Any update on the number and location of hostiles we're facing?"

Lockwood relayed, "Five hostiles seen on the main platform. Two on the helo pad. No sign of the hostages."

"Copy," Jake signed off.

Fifteen men began their climb up the framework on opposite sides. Upon reaching the top, they concealed themselves and prepared for the assault. Jake paired with Max, Dave with Grant, Finn with Zach, and each pair took an EOD tech with them.

Moving with stealth, they went in different directions to neutralize the hostiles and investigate the most likely locations for explosives. At the same time, Delta headed towards the three-story tower where they believed the rig's crew would be held.

With suppressors attached to their assault rifles, Max and Jake moved towards two men as Draper guided each team to targets. Jake dropped one man with a clean shot while Max dusted the second, neither man managed to fire their weapon, so they maintained a quiet upper hand for the moment.

Silence didn't last long as Finn and Zach engaged three and took return fire. Dozens of armed men spilled out of the tower building on each of the three levels, more than any of them had honestly expected.

An intense firefight started as Delta breached the building's interior and began searching for the prisoners. After six minutes and plowing through five men, Dave and Grant made it to the landing pad with their technician. Zulu Two took up a sniper position, providing overwatch for the others while Grant and their EOD searched for a bomb. Dave picked off two more men sneaking up on the backside of Jake.

Jake and Max heard the thuds near them and pivoted, spotting two bodies laid out on the metal grating not far behind them. Both moved to protect Senior EOD Technician Bob Bailey.

"Zulu One, I don't have a clear shot on a third to your northeast," Dave called out.

"Copy." Jake glanced at Stirling.

"Got it." Max ducked around a pylon, preparing to cover their six while Jake motioned to Bob to continue to their targeted location. If a plastique charge existed on the main pipe and it exploded, the structure would experience successive crippling blasts, making the collapse of the entire platform a possibility.

One man swiftly turned into four then grew by two more, so Max laid down cover fire as Jake moved Bailey to a more secure position. Although Bailey was armed and capable of firing, his primary purpose was to defuse the explosives, and as such, they needed him alive and unharmed.

Taking out three of six, Max spotted one more drop, most likely sent to hell by Dave. Stirling shifted positions to deal with the remaining two.

As they rounded a corner, Bailey halted, tapped Marshall's shoulder, and pointed. "Found the bomb."

"Zulu One to TOC. A device with a significant amount of Semtex located on the central pipeline."

Finn reported, "EOD Three indicates our bomb contains enough C-4 to wipe out the whole south structure."

Grimacing as he stared at the massive bomb, Grant conveyed, "Another found on the helo pad as well."

USS Buckley – TOC

Lockwood turned to Farris. "This doesn't feel right. There are too many men to evacuate effectively, and those bombs are over-kill. They don't fit Baxter's profile."

Nicole sucked in her lower lip, considering the possibilities.

"I'm thinking some sort of setup." Draper glanced at them before returning her gaze to the monitor. "Zulu Two, ten more converging on Zulu One's location."

Nicole paced as she thought. "You're right."

"What do we know about Biopetrol?" Lockwood asked.

"Not as much as I should. I'll rectify that now." Nicole pulled out her phone and dialed.

Biopetrol Oil Platform

Max took out three more adversaries, providing cover for Jake and Bailey. Within a hair's breadth, a barrage of bullets began hitting metal all around him, causing Max to dive for cover. A burning sensation streaked across his left bicep.

He ignored the pain as he poked his rifle around the corner and fired several more shots. Ducking back, he switched out his clip. "Zulu Two, this is Six, I'm pinned. Do you have targets in sight?" He moved to the other side and picked off another man.

"Negative. No joy." Dave adjusted a little, attempting to find a useful angle. He couldn't move positions, needing to provide overwatch for Grant and the tech as well as for Finn's team.

"I need higher ground." Max scanned for a solution.

"Zulu Six, there is rigging to your right. If Zulu Two can lay down cover fire, you can gain height," Draper reported as she watched the heat signatures and prayed the boys made it out of this one alive.

"Copy," both Max and Dave said.

"Six, haul ass on my mark. Three, two, one, go," Dave ordered, as he opened up on the area between the kid and at least fifteen enemy combatants.

Max sprinted; glad his shoes didn't slip on the water-soaked metal. He reached the skeleton rigging and started to climb. His arm throbbed, but he couldn't waste time thinking about the injury, and luckily adrenaline helped mask the pain.

Attaining a position, he linked one leg around the gridwork and stabilized his rifle. Now with a clear visual on them and somewhat protected by the girding, Max began picking off adversaries. *Like shooting fish in a barrel.*

Delta One's report sent a damper through all the men. "Hostages located. All ten dead. Shot execution-style. By the stench and rigor, they've been dead several days."

The sound of boots slamming on metal accompanied EOD Three's frantic voice shouting, "No time. Outta the building now!"

Only moments before the platform violently shook with an explosion, Delta used the safest and fastest exits available, jumping out of windows, and plummeting several stories to the ocean. In the moonlit night, Connor surfaced and began taking stock of his team. He found Wade unconscious and floating face-down.

"Zulu Three, Delta One, status!" Jake regained his feet after being knocked to the ground as he glanced upward, finding his rookie still in the girder and apparently unharmed.

Connor flipped his team leader over and held him as he trod water. Dom swam over, checked Wade's airway and gave him a thumbs-up, Wade still lived and breathed. "All Delta elements accounted for, but Delta One is down. We're in the water."

As he ran like a bat out of hell, Finn had been picked up and thrown by the blast. His body slammed into a row of metal pipes bringing him to a dead stop. Like a rag doll, Finn limply crumpled to the grating with his left sleeve on fire.

Zach, who had been shielded in his position as he guarded Finn and their strap, rushed toward his buddy. Witnessing the young EOD's charred, dismembered body land near him, turned Zach's stomach, and he fought off a bout of nausea. Unfortunately, he couldn't do anything for the dead sailor, but McBride might still be alive.

Skidding to a halt and dropping to his knees, Zach used his gloved hands to pat out the flames before using his teeth to tear off one glove. He reached for Finn's neck, hoping to find him alive as he peered down at the still form. "Zulu Three down, his pulse is thready. EOD Three KIA."

As bullets began to fly around him, Zach seized McBride's vest at the shoulders and dragged him to cover. "Taking fire. A little help over here."

"Gotcha covered," Max shouted, picking off several targets as their heads popped out from behind cover.

Lockwood got on the comms, "Delta, be advised, Sierra moving in. Boats are six mics out."

"TOC, explosive on helo pad diffused," Grant reported, then glanced at Dave seeking permission to go to Zach and Finn's location to render aid. Getting the nod of approval, he darted off as both Dave and Max covered him.

"Zulu Five, Zulu Four is on his way to your pos," Dave informed Zach.

USS Buckley – TOC

Fuming after checking with several sources, Nicole urged Lockwood, "The guys need to be off that platform now. One of my trusted sources did some digging for me and discovered Biopetrol's representative bribed Brazilian officials to obtain the winning bid. The company will lose their earnest money and the contract once the investigators press charges later next week.

"She found evidence Biopetrol's Chief Financial Officer is involved. The rig is insured, and if it is destroyed in the act of piracy or terrorism, they'll recoup all the funds paid out so far, plus more. She also learned the maintenance crew members were all demolitions experts. There are likely more than three bombs. Our guys are standing on a death trap, one set up for financial gain." Nicole shifted her gaze to the monitors, her gut seizing.

Unwilling to lose his men, Lockwood ordered, "All Zulu elements, abort, abort, abort. Get off that rig now!"

Chapter Eighteen

Biopetrol Oil Platform

BAILEY'S eyes widened as he studied the device before him, and the lieutenant commander's orders rang in his ears. The EOD tech stood, pivoted to Marshall, and declared, "He's right. I can't defuse this one. We need to move. NOW!"

Marshall's commanding voice shouted, "All Zulu elements, dive, dive, dive!" He grabbed Bailey and shoved him in the direction of the platform's edge. "Run. Go!" Once Jake ensured the tech jumped, he turned to check on Stirling's descent, refusing to bail until the kid reached him.

Dave pushed EOD Two to the side of the rig. "Ditch the helmet and weapon. Jump feet first. When you surface, swim away as fast as you can." Before following the young sailor, Dave glanced in Jake's direction and tracked his gaze upward.

"Shit!" Dave noted their kid dangled upside down as he tugged on something. In his peripheral vision, Dave caught Jake's body jerking backward and dropping. "Six is stuck, and One is down!" Aware he couldn't save both, his gut twisted.

Though the decision stabbed him through the heart, Jake was closer and incapacitated—he wouldn't make it off this deathtrap on his own. Max, at least, still had a chance if he cut himself loose. Dave started for Jake, worried his friend might already be dead, but would willingly risk his life to bring him home.

Registering Dave's words and knowing he had to reach Jake, Max used his knife to slash the rifle strap tangled in the rigging. He reached for the structure but missed. His six-foot fall came to an abrupt end as Max's back and left shoulder slammed into the unforgiving surface.

Adrenaline pumping fast and furious through his veins, Max scrambled to his feet, failing to register his injured joint as he sprinted for Marshall. Much closer than Dave, by more than triple the distance, Max shouted, "I got him!"

As bullets pinged metal around him, he tried to move his left arm, only then, when it failed to respond, did Max realize he dislocated his shoulder. With no time to spare, he grabbed Jake's vest one-handed and dragged him behind cover near the edge.

Relief flooded Dave. Max would ensure Jake got off this wretched platform. He adjusted his course, ready to make his multi-story swan dive. Before jumping, Dave dropped his weapon and helmet in the ocean and sighted where Jake would likely land. Determined to help Max with Jake after surfacing, he would swim over instead of following the instructions he gave to the EOD to get the hell away from this damned thing.

Max released his grasp on the vest. With adrenaline no longer covering his excruciating pain, Max understood he must reseat the joint, or he wouldn't be able to lift or maintain hold of Jake. Though it would hurt like hell, he had to perform a self-traction technique before they could escape.

On his knees, Max gritted his teeth as he grabbed his left wrist. Cussing a blue streak, he gradually and firmly pulled his arm forward and straight in front of him to guide the ball of the bone back into the socket. Max panted heavily after popping it in and wished he had time to rest, but getting their asses off this powder keg remained his priority.

Peering down, Max realized from this height he would likely lose his grip on Jake when they hit the water. Breathing through the fiery agony moving his shoulder caused, he cut Jake's gun strap and used the length of material to tie their vests together.

He removed both their helmets and tossed them over the side along with their weapons. Next, Max crouched, and though his injured shoulder screamed bloody murder, with brute force, he lifted Marshall and held him tight.

As Max prepared to jump, the concussive wave from a massive explosion blew him off his feet, propelling him outward away from the rig. Heat kissed his backside for only a moment before he plunged feet-first into the ocean. His training prevented him from reflexively sucking in a breath with the initial ice-cold impact.

Down and down he went with Jake. Once his descent stopped, Max struggled to kick upward, towing Jake up with him. Breaking the surface, Max noted secondary and tertiary explosions as the entire platform groaned and erupted in flames.

Rolling to his back, Max positioned Jake on his chest. Marshall's unconscious state meant he wouldn't have been able to control his breathing when they submerged, and if he sucked in too much water, he would drown. Placing his hand near Jake's nose and mouth, relief surged in Max when he felt an exhale followed by several weak coughs and an inhale.

As waves crashed over his head, Max flipped Marshall on his back to keep his leader's face out of the water and ready to assist if necessary. Wrapping his injured arm around Jake's chest, he gripped Jake's vest and hugged him to his torso.

Though he attempted to swim away from the wreckage before anything toppled down on them, Max made scant headway using scissor kicks and his one functioning arm. He hoped Sierra would drag them both out of the drink before his strength gave out.

TOC Onboard USS Buckley

The heat and smoke from the burning platform impeding the visibility of the drone overhead, Draper noted the assigned signals denoting each team member as blips began appearing on her other screen. "Locators active. I have beacons. All Delta. Zulu Three, Four, and Five. EOD One and Two." She bit her lip, waiting. *Come on, boys, turn on your locators.*

Nicole tapped the screen. "There. Who is that?"

"Zulu Two."

His gaze on the platform monitor, Bryan noted several more explosions shown as bright white spots on the thermal imaging. Due to the smoke, they had not been able to tell if Jake or Max got off before the second explosion. Bryan ran a hand across his jaw as he asked, "One or Six showing yet?"

Kira shifted her gaze to the lieutenant commander. "No." Voicing her hope, she said, "Six did take a substantial fall, and his locator may be damaged." She didn't mention Jake's locator because they all saw him jerk, drop, and being dragged by Max … and he might be dead.

"My medical team is standing by. We'll be ready for your men when they arrive," the ship's captain said.

"Thank you, sir." Lockwood focused on the twelve blips, silently willing two more to show up.

South Atlantic Ocean – East of Platform

Zach held Finn, giving Grant a break. After jumping into the ocean with their unconscious teammate, Grant had to do mouth to mouth while treading water until Finn thankfully coughed up what he inhaled. Unable to fully assess Finn's injuries, Grant indicated he was not out of the woods yet, though he now breathed on his own.

As they bobbed with the waves, Delta Team managed to swim to them. Both McBride and Dunn required medical care, as did several Delta members. They suffered lacerations and various injuries from leaping out windows or from debris raining down on them after each blast.

Sharing a glance with Grant, Zach wondered if their other teammates made it off the hellish oil rig or had been blown to bits. His thoughts shifted in the next instant as he pointed to a tell-tale dorsal fin. "Shark."

"Must've smelled blood. Boats would be good now." Grant pulled out his sidearm and prepared to fire if necessary.

"Guess Finn's shark bracelet is bogus," Zach quipped as he shifted McBride in his arms to grab his gun too.

As Grant notified TOC of their situation, the remainder of Delta formed a protective circle surrounding him, Zach, Finn, Connor, and Wade. Each man hoped the boats reached them before they became shark food.

South Atlantic Ocean – West of Platform

Struggling to keep Jake afloat, his entire shoulder throbbing, Max dug deep, refusing to let go. To disassociate his active mind from his pain, Max thought about his father. He created a world where they were at the beach, but he was no longer five. They were equals, both fit and strong SEALs engaged in a friendly wager to determine who could tread water longer.

When his dad called his name, Max turned towards him, but the illusion of Preston now appeared further away and slowly dissipated. In his dad's place came the image of Dave. His imaginary world dissolved as reality snapped back in, along with the pain when Dave shouted, "MAX. JAKE."

"HERE! OVER HERE!" Max yelled.

The rookie's voice carried over the cacophony of follow-on explosions, and groaning metal as pieces of the platform twisted and buckled. Dave spun toward the sound and spotted two heads in the water. Relief replaced doubt and fear as he realized he headed in the right direction, and both teammates breached the surface after the plunge. Recognizing they might need help, Dave swam hard and fast to reach his brothers.

Coughing, trying to clear the little water he inhaled, Max watched as Dave plowed towards them.

"Damn glad I found you, brother," Dave breathed out as he noted Jake to be unconscious. "What are his injuries?"

"Don't know. Didn't have time to check. Still breathing."

"Here, let me take him." Dave started to pull Max's arm away to gain a hold on Jake but halted at a strangled cry.

"You hurt?" Dave spied Max's grimace in the moonlight.

"Shoulder dislocated in my fall, put it back before jumping. Moving my arm still hurts like a mother."

"Okay. Okay. Take it slow." Holding Jake, Dave waited for Max to release his grip and move his arm.

"He's tied to me. So I wouldn't lose him."

"Smart. Got you both." As another blast from the oil rig sent more debris in their direction, he said, "Let's move." Dave grasped the back of Jake's vest and pulled him along with Max trailing. He kept checking on Max and observed him flagging as the gap the leashing allowed between them grew. After reaching a relatively safe distance, Dave stopped. "Boats will find us here."

Realizing he failed to activate his locator, using his right hand, Max reached for the device, only to find it missing. "My locator is gone. Forgot to turn on Jake's."

Despite their situation, Dave chuckled. "Think you had more important tasks on your mind." He reached around and switched on Jake's rescue beacon.

"Your comms working?" Max asked.

"Nope. Fried. Not sending or receiving. What about yours?"

"Headset missing. Either lost in my fall or splashdown." The pain, cold water, and exertion all taking a toll, Max breathed heavy, wishing one of Sierra would reach them soon. He laid back, attempting to float to conserve his energy.

"Hey, Max. Stay with me," Dave urged as the kid's head slipped beneath the waves. He tugged on the material connecting Max to Jake. "Come here. Rest on my shoulder a moment."

"Thanks." Max appreciated the assist. With a bit of a breather, he would be able to hold his own again. Closing his eyes, Max focused inward, trying to ignore his misery and exhaustion.

"Got you, brother." Another chuckle emitted from Dave. "Saving the team leader has got to be worth a case of beer."

"More like ten," Jake murmured then inhaled water as a wave crashed over his head. Coughing sent ripples of pain through his chest. Although somewhat disoriented, his mind registered Dave's voice as he roused.

As the coughing fit subsided, Dave asked, "Jake, you with me?"

Saltwater splashing his face stung Jake's eyes as they fluttered open. "Yeah."

Relief surged through Dave as Jake spoke to him. "Where do you hurt?"

"Chest, head." His thinking clearing a bit, he asked, "The kid?"

"Right beside you. Max hauled your ass off that platform. Sprinted like the wind to you after falling six feet. Tied you to him before jumping. Kept you afloat until I reached you."

"Others?"

"No idea. My comm unit is malfunctioning, and Max is missing a headset."

"Locat—" Jake lost his breath and coughed, hissing in pain, recognizing he probably sported at least one broken rib.

"Beacons on. They'll scoop us out of the drink soon. Shouldn't be long now."

Becoming aware Max remained quiet, Jake turned, and his blurred vision found the closed eyes of the rookie. "Kid injured?"

"Separated my shoulder, but I'm okay," Max answered and opened his eyes. "Ten case deduction, huh? My total is four."

Jake snorted, causing himself pain. "That was ten for Dave … not a cocky rookie who got tangled up in rigging."

When Grant's voice sounded in his ear, Jake realized his earpiece was still in place, and his comms worked. "Shit. Sharks are circling the others. Boats are one mike out from them."

"Which means they're about three to us," Dave said.

Pressing the comms button, Jake said, "TOC," his words were interrupted by coughing, "Zulu One."

"Damned glad to hear your voice. Boats inbound to your pos. Got a signal on everyone except Zulu Six," Bryan shared.

"Kid's with me."

A huge smile broke out on Bryan's face. "Copy. Shouldn't be much longer before we have you out of the water."

The distance sound of approaching boats cut their chatter, all three more than ready to be picked up.

Max's relief was short-lived as something huge bumped into his leg. He pulled back, kicked out, and his boot slammed into something hard. His action alerted his teammates, and they all realized they were in danger.

Grabbing for his sidearm, Max said, "Dave, cut the tether between Jake and me."

After slicing the material, Dave tightened his hold on and pulled Jake closer. As he scanned for a dorsal fin, a sinking realization formed—a shark would attack unseen from below.

Though struggling for air as Dave's embrace increased, Jake keyed his comms. "TOC … this … is … One, … sharks … in … our …" The oxygen required to speak exceeded his ability to draw in a breath. He grimaced with pain as pressure in his chest amplified, and his head lolled to the side.

"Jake?" Dave shifted his friend to view his face. A predator lurking beneath them took a backseat to this new crisis. "Breathe. Jake, breathe."

As the night air rent with distant blood-curdling screams and gunfire, Max turned his attention to Dave and Jake. "Why isn't he breathing?"

"Bruised or collapsed lung, maybe. Shit, this isn't good." Dave adjusted his grip, reducing pressure from Jake's chest. When Jake made a slight gasping sound, Dave prayed for his brother's life. A split second later, his prayer altered to include all their lives.

Something rammed into Max's abdomen and propelled him away from the others with speed. Powerless to stop the motion, he began firing in front of him when he spotted a dorsal fin.

Fire ignited his thigh when something sharp dragged across it. He bobbed on the surface as the locomotive appeared to veer off. Waiting for the next attack, expecting to be yanked under at any moment, Max murmured, "Dad, help me." Seconds later, a boat roared into view, causing Max to grin despite the dire circumstances.

Piloting the craft, Babcox headed to the beacon's coordinates and came to a halt near Zulu One and Two.

Dave grabbed the side as he yelled, "Pull Jake in. He's having trouble breathing."

Babcox seized Jake's vest at the shoulders and hauled him into the rubber boat. Once he situated him against one side, he turned to assist Dave. Aware his actions tonight would put him in good stead with the Zulu leaders he hid his hatred of Stirling as he asked, "Where's Six?"

Dave pointed after scrambling in. "There. Hurry. Shark. Give me your weapon."

Turning, Babcox spotted the interloper about thirty yards away. After handing over his weapon, he moved back to the boat's controls. Though he wanted to hesitate, since his problems would be solved if a shark killed or maimed Stirling, he didn't. The urgency in Dave's voice told him if he didn't act with haste, any chance of making Zulu would be forfeited.

Babcox barely turned the boat in Stirling's direction when gunfire erupted. With Dave's attention directed at the rookie, Stewart allowed a slight smile to break out on his face. *No way we'll reach Stirling in time. The spot on Zulu will be mine now.*

Jake roused and took in his new location. Drawing in a ragged breath, his gaze landed on Sierra Seven and wondered why he was smiling. When Dave aimed the weapon outward, Jake struggled to rise, and the sight he beheld twisted his gut.

Max gave thanks Dave and Jake were safely aboard, but when a fin appeared and rapidly came in his direction, he accepted his time was up. In a last act of defiance, Max emptied his mag in the path on the oncoming shark.

The sound of rounds from an HK 416 joined with his 9mm pistol, but his impending death continued straight for him. Max took one last breath and gazed up at the stars. *At least I attained my goal, and my brothers are safe.*

What happened next would become a legend within the teams. So improbable to be considered a myth or a tall tale by most who would later be told the story. Though for the four sailors witnessing the event, they would know the truth.

An enormous black-and-white apex predator breached the surface only a couple of feet from Max. Clamped in the orca's jaws was a twelve-foot bull shark. In the next instant, the wolf of the sea splashed down and disappeared into the ocean's depths, leaving only a wake in its path.

Max coughed as he swallowed water caused by the killer whale's waves. His heart pounded and adrenaline flowed as he continued to dumbly stare at the spot until Dave's hands grabbed the shoulders of his vest and hauled him into the craft.

His gaze met Dave's. "Did you see that?"

"Yeah, brother. God works in mysterious ways."

"Where's … blood … coming … from?" Jake gasped as the water around him turned red.

"Shit!" Dave's eyes moved to Max's thigh. "It got you." His hands wrapped around the profusely bleeding wound, applying pressure.

Becoming lightheaded, Max began fading, not hearing Dave yelling at Babcox to get them moving. Thoroughly spent and in extreme pain, Max's lashes lowered, and he welcomed the cloak of blackness enveloping him.

Chapter Nineteen

ORGANIZED chaos greeted them upon returning to the destroyer over an hour ago, leaving three of Zulu in uncertain territory, and three others worried and relegated to the ship's mess along with most of Delta and Sierra.

With the onboard medical team dealing with the most critically injured, the teams' medics, Grant, Scott, and Dominic, set up a triage in the mess to treat the minor wounds of not only their teammates but several of the pirates who jumped from the platform after the second explosion.

Dave discovered the horrific screams didn't come from any SEALs. It unsettled his stomach to think how seven hostiles met their end—eaten in a shark feeding frenzy. A fate that could've been Max's too if not for the orca. Thankfully, Sierra plucked all their men out of the water before they became shark chum.

Abnormally anxious, Dave paced while the last three detainees had their wounds stitched and burns bandaged. The Buckley's Master at Arms waited in the wings to take the men to a holding cell. Dave expected Nicole would be interrogating them soon, and hopefully, determine how the Navy got sucked into this fiasco.

Zach halted near Dave and handed him a cup of coffee. "Before Lockwood left, he said the kitchen crew is coming in earlier than their normal shift to prepare a hot meal for us."

"Thanks." Dave turned as Kira, and several sailors entered, all carrying bags. She headed straight for him with three packs.

"Brought you a change of clothes." Kira held out two bags to Zach and one to Dave. "Any word yet on the boys?"

Zach took his and Grant's backpacks from her. "No, but Lockwood was called to the infirmary about ten minutes ago. So we're hoping to find out soon."

Kira nodded. "Arranged for you to take showers too. Seaman Chavez will show you where."

"Delta and Sierra can go first." Dave tossed his bag on a seat.

"I'll tell Rob and Connor." Zach pivoted and strode over to Sierra One and Delta Two.

Puffing out a breath that made her bangs flutter, Kira studied Dave. "Are you alright?"

"Yeah."

"You sure?"

"Why do you ask?" Dave took another sip of hot coffee.

"You seem, I don't know … antsy, disjointed … not like your normal self."

Dave chuckled and sat on the table near him. "Well, can't pull the wool over your eyes."

"I realize Jake is hurt—"

"No, that isn't it."

Kira waited, hoping for him to explain, but anything he might've shared halted as a commotion behind her drew their attention.

Having ignored the doctor's advice, Jake made his way to the ship's mess where the remainder of his guys were located. Lockwood trailed behind him, Dr. Burgess called for his CO, attempting to keep him in bed, not realizing Bryan would side with his need to reassure the others. With the infirmary too small to accommodate the guys, they gathered here.

Spotting Connor as he entered, Jake strode to Delta Two and halted. "Dunn woke. He's concussed, but the doc says Wade's got one helluva thick skull, and he'll be fine in a few weeks."

Connor released a held breath. "Thanks for the info." He hurried over to the coffee urn to relay the news to his men.

His movements slow with one arm around his torso, Jake moved to the table where Zulu and Sierra sat, and lowered himself into a seat. "I'm fine. Bruised, not broken ribs." He breathed in and clenched a hidden fist at the pain. *Sure as hell feels like broken, though.* "Also, no concussion."

Jake left out that he had not told the doctor how long he was unconscious because he was unsure. He also omitted the bruised lung, categorizing it as need-to-know, and they didn't. He would heal before Lockwood sent his team on another mission.

Though Grant suspected more damage based on Dave's account, he allowed Jake to downplay his injuries. Dr. Irving would ensure Marshall took the requisite time off to heal properly. Instead, he asked, "How is Finn?"

"What I know so far is he suffered a concussion, a couple of busted ribs, a second-degree burn on his forearm, and water inhalation. He woke briefly and recognized me, so no brain damage." Winded, Jake took a moment to catch his breath.

Relieved they didn't find any internal hemorrhaging, Zach chuckled and quipped, "He is already brain-damaged."

"Well, nothing additional," Jake responded with a grin, aware of the need for a little humor to release the tension.

"And the kid?" Dave asked.

"Max is sleeping. They strapped the kid's shoulder, and when we return stateside, he needs a scan to determine if he tore any ligaments. They cleaned the graze on his right arm and stitched the lacerations on his thigh. They're tanking him up on fluids."

"He could've met a horrific end." Dave swallowed hard as he peered at Jake, recalling firing at the shark as it went for Max. "If I hadn't cut the tether, you both might've been shark food."

Rob grinned with relief at the positive report. "Perhaps, but I think this is a sign you picked the right guy for Zulu. I mean, your mascot is an orca, and one shows up out of the blue and saves Max from certain death."

Scott agreed with his team leader. "If that's not an omen, I don't know what is."

Devlin, who also listened to Dave's incredible account earlier, chuckled. "I'm not certain I believe your tale, but at the minimum, Jake owes Max a case of beer for getting him off the platform."

Grant nodded. "I think his bravery wipes the fourteen cases off the books."

Recalling Jake's words to Max in the water, Dave now agreed deducting too many cases might encourage Max to take risks. "Nah, that would give the cocky kid a swollen head. Give him the wrong idea of how to save a few dollars."

The men nodded as Kira changed topics. "Who's gonna tell McBride his shark repellant thingy doesn't work?" All the guys shook their heads. "Okay, so the story you're going with is that because he wore the magnet, the big bad sharks stayed away from him." They all grinned in agreement, causing Kira to chuckle.

USS Buckley – Infirmary

Dr. Anthony Burgess approached the young SEAL who currently occupied one of the beds. Though tired and not having tended this many injured in a long time, he had been glad he ran a tight ship, and all his staff performed their duties admirably.

He halted and studied the current vitals on the monitors. Stirling's pulse and blood pressure indicated, like the other two SEAL patients, he possessed a body of a finely tuned athlete. When his patient blinked open his eyes, he inquired, "Are you comfortable? Is the medication adequately relieving your pain?"

"Yes, sir." Max glanced over to where Jake had been before he nodded off and noted the empty bed before shifting his gaze to Finn, who appeared to be still sleeping. "How are my teammates?"

"Both doing well, though one is being more cooperative. Marshall insisted on leaving to update your other teammates."

Max nodded.

Anthony reached in his pocket and withdrew a small plastic bag. "Thought you might like a souvenir."

Max took the bag and peered at the one-inch long shark tooth with serrations along the entire blade.

"Found the tooth embedded in your thigh."

"Really?"

"Yep." Burgess glanced around, making sure they were alone before speaking. "Can I ask you a personal question?"

"Okay." Max gave a slight nod.

"Are you Preston Stirling's son?"

Max stiffened. "Why do you want to know?"

Noting the reaction, Anthony said, "You remind me of the first sailor I treated after receiving my commission. A shark bit him. You possess the same facial features as Preston, but his eyes were paler blue and his hair a little darker blond. The young man left quite a positive impression on me. Always wondered if he passed BUDs and achieved his dream of becoming a SEAL."

"You treated my dad for a shark bite? Where did he get bit?"

Anthony chuckled. "His buttocks."

Max snorted and grinned. "How in the world did it chomp on his ass?"

Anthony smiled. "We were both stationed in Hawaii. Preston and a buddy went swimming near the reefs and horsed around to attract the attention of a flaxen-haired beauty. His friend pushed him into the coral reef, and something pierced his backside."

Chucking, Anthony continued, "He landed on a reef shark, and the poor little thing bit in self-defense. Preston did, however, end up winning a date with the lovely lady. I think her name was Louise or something close."

"Lois?"

"Might've been. Why?"

"My mom's name is Lois. She passed away when I was five, and my dad died about a year later."

"I'm really sorry to hear that."

Noting the sincere expression, Max said with pride, "My father achieved his dream. He became one of the best SEALs ever. I chose to follow his path."

"I'm certain the man I met back then would be proud of you." He smiled and said, "I need to check on my other patients. If you're pain increases, tell the nurse. We want to ensure you are well managed before your flight out."

"Thanks, I will." Max shut his eyes as the doctor moved on. He grinned and allowed his imagination to create a beach scene with his dad meeting his mom—a new memory to cherish since he had no real recollection of how his parents met. Drifting back into a drug-induced slumber, Max's thoughts shifted, wondering if his call for his dad's help brought forth the orca.

USS Buckley – Mess

Choosing to sit alone, sick of his teammates lauding Stirling's actions, Babcox shoveled in another forkful of eggs. Some of the sailors who came to the mess for breakfast overheard Delta and Sierra members praising the asshat for saving Marshall. However, Stewart viewed the whole affair differently.

If Stirling had not been clumsy enough to become tangled up on the girder, then Marshall wouldn't have waited, and wouldn't have taken the two rounds to the vest that necessitated Marshall's rescue. Everyone seemed to discount the fact Mr. Silver Spoon was the cause in the first place.

All they focused on was he reset his dislocated shoulder by himself, picked up Marshall, and kept him afloat until Katz found them. The crew of the Buckley talked like Stirling was some kind of superhero, particularly after the story of the shark and orca made the rounds.

Stewart also couldn't comprehend Zulu turned a blind eye to the facts again. This was Stirling's second mission and the second—no, the third debacle if he counted the Massi operation where Turner died because the glory seeker Stirling rushed to the munitions depot after Chase and McBride went down.

In his mind, if Zulu had selected him instead of Axel Chase after Levi was medically retired, then the undeserving usurper wouldn't be being talked about like he was some sort of legend.

The seats around him filled with crew members who came in for a meal. Their chatter inevitably turned to the latest hot topic, since not much ever happened aboard ship, and having three SEAL teams on board was juicy. Babcox held back a growl when a baby-faced seaman dared to speak to him.

"Hey, you're one of the SEALs, right?"

Babcox only glared, hoping his silence would deter the little shit, but it didn't.

"What's it like to work with a legend? I mean, he's gotta be one badass SEAL to kill a bull shark with his bare hands."

The admiration and hero-worship in the teen's voice made Stewart want to gag. "He's no badass. He didn't kill the shark. He only got lucky a killer whale was hungry."

"But I heard—"

"You heard wrong. He's nothing special. Don't believe everything people say. He screwed up, and his team leader almost paid with his life." Babcox stood and walked away, leaving his tray half-eaten. He needed air before he punched the gullible sheep.

The seaman turned to his buddies and chuckled. "I think he's only jealous." They all nodded, and their conversation returned to recounting the things they overheard. The tale morphed as it would during a game of telephone to an unrecognizable accounting where a severely injured SEAL single-handedly saved his teammates from sharks and an orca.

USS Buckley – Infirmary

Resettled in his bed, Jake drew in a shallow breath and reluctantly accepted the pain medication from the nurse as Dave gave him the stink-eye. After he ate a light meal, Lockwood ordered him to return and rest for the next several hours as they waited for transport back to Rio De Janeiro.

"You have a bruised lung, don't you?" Dave said as he crossed his arm, none too pleased to learn Jake defied doctor's orders to come to the mess to update them. Lockwood could've done the same, and Jake could've gotten the rest he required.

"What of it?" Jake pulled the blanket up to his chest and closed his eyes to avoid the righteous indignation in Dave's eyes.

"You shouldn't have left this bed. How do you think the kid would feel if, after all his effort, you did something stupid and ended up in worse shape?"

Jake snorted and grimaced as his ribs protested the movement. "Me! What about him? The kid damned-near killed himself when he cut the strap to reach me."

"We'll need to ask him how he got tangled up in the first place." Dave sat on the empty bed beside Jake's and glanced over at Stirling.

"I already know."

"You do?" Dave turned back to Jake.

"Yep. Wasn't his fault. He was taking fire and moving fast to come down. Saw what happened right before they tagged me. Sparks flew as bullets hit the metal around the kid. One of the bars gave way under his foot about twelve feet up. He twisted in the air, trying to grab hold, and came to an abrupt halt when his strap caught on a piece sticking out."

Dave shook his head. "Kid must have a lucky horseshoe up his ass. A drop from that height would've done more damage than a dislocated shoulder."

"True ... we both might not be here." Jake lifted his lids and peered at his best friend. "Kid did good tonight, but we need to instill some self-preservation in him."

Nodding, Dave lowered his volume. "Given his rocky past, it will take some time, but I do believe once we earn his trust, we'll make headway. And speaking of that, with a gimpy leg and limited use of his left arm, he's gonna need some help when we return. Do you think his girlfriend is up to the task?"

Jake considered the question a long while. "I'm not certain. Her brother is a SEAL, but I'm not sure she's had true exposure to the dangers of our work. Although Max added her to the wives and girlfriends list, their relationship is new, and it might be a bit early to put the pressure on her."

"You have a point. Finn's gonna buck at having someone around, but he's going to need help too. Wonder if we should put them together and rotate me, Grant, and Zach stopping by."

"Could work, but I'll be going over also."

"No, you won't. Val will put you on house arrest." Dave snickered. "If not bed arrest. Either way, she won't be letting you step foot out that door unless it is for a doctor's appointment."

Jake groaned, not from pain, but because Dave was right. Though Jake loved Val with all his heart, she could be overbearing when he came back with more than a minor injury.

Dave chuckled. "Think of it as having quality time with James before he leaves for design school."

"There's that." Jake shifted his gaze to Stirling. "Still can't believe Jamie opened up to him and vice versa."

"I can. Max is closer to James's age than he is to ours. Hell, the kid is young enough to be your son. And although there is a vast difference in their worldly experience, James would view Max as his equal, and Max treated him as such. The rest of us behaved towards James as though he was still a child."

Dave's words hit home with Jake, especially the part about Max being of an age to be one of his kids. The strange sensation he had when he viewed the kid in the Argentina hospital bed resurged. This time he understood the meaning, but he wasn't sure what to do with the knowledge.

Never before had he viewed a teammate as anything other than a friend or brother-in-arms. This feeling hit too close to the heart and left Jake questioning whether he would be an effective leader to a man who brought out a fatherly concern in him. Dave's next comment pulled him out of his musings.

"From what you shared with me about what James found out, Max has been on his own since he was six. He needs a family who cares about him, not an asshole uncle. We need to show him Zulu is now his family. Might be the best way to curb his risk-taking."

Dave noted Jake fading due to the meds and stood. "Get some rest, brother. We'll sort things out once we're stateside."

Chapter Twenty

Two Days Later – Virginia – Naval Medical Center

WANTING to argue, but finding Zach's logic to be sound and his reasons to be weak at best, Max stared at Zach, who stood beside his bed with a wheelchair. He wanted to go home, but to do so, he would need to find someone with access to Zulu's equipment cage to retrieve his spare keys since he gave his other set to Cali so she could drive home when they got spun up.

He almost called her but remembered she left on a business trip to Europe the day after the picnic, so she wouldn't return for another two weeks. He considered kicking his door open, but the building's maintenance man wouldn't be too keen on replacing a door, and his pocketbook, diminished by his beer tax, wouldn't support paying for one anyway.

Remaining patient, to a point, Zach waited for Max to accept he was going home with him. Although Dr. Irving didn't find any ligament tears in the rookie's shoulder, the team doc ordered Max's arm to be immobilized in the sling for several weeks to ensure the injury healed properly.

After a short discussion with Dave and Grant, he got Max, while Grant took Finn. Zach lucked out because Finn was an infamously cranky patient. But with Finn's more severe injuries, they decided Grant would be better equipped to handle him.

"You ready to go?"

Max huffed, "Yeah, alright. You win."

"Thought you would see things my way. Besides, Rocky will be happy to have another hand to pet him."

Halting mid-rise, Max peered at Zach. "Rocky lives with you? Thought all service dogs stayed on base in the kennels when not on missions."

"For the most part, that's true. But when I joined Zulu, I was offered base housing with a fenced back yard, so he could live with me since we can be spun up at a moment's notice. If, like our last mission, it isn't feasible for Rocky to be with us, he stays in the base kennels."

The idea of spending time with Rocky made this situation more tolerable, so Max shifted into an unnecessary conveyance. Though his leg ached a little, he certainly could walk on his own, but hospital policy required him to play the invalid to the exit.

As Zach wheeled him down the hall, Max asked, "When is Finn being released?"

"Today. We're actually carpooling with Grant since hopping up into my truck might be a bit much given your leg and strapped wing. They'll meet us downstairs."

"So, am I sleeping on a couch?"

"Nope got a two-bedroom place with a covered back porch and comfy patio chairs. After Grant drops us off, I'll run to the store to stock up on a few things. I'm going to grill burgers tonight. Anything, in particular, you prefer for breakfast?"

"No, whatever you like. I'm not picky, but let me contribute. Gotta pay my share."

Zach pursed his lips, considering how to respond. Part of him wanted to say, no friggin' way, this is what we do as a team. But on the other hand, in the short time he'd known Max, he noticed an independent streak. He decided now was not the time to pick a battle and simply said, "Okay," leaving the details undiscussed.

Parking Max near the entrance and not spying Grant or Finn yet, he said, "Gotta hit the head. Don't go anywhere."

Max rolled his eyes, and Zach laughed as he trotted off.

Alone, Max took a moment to reflect on the past few days. On the flight home, they learned Lieutenant Farris stayed on the Buckley and would be flying with the detainees to Gitmo to continue questioning them. There was something fishy about the op, and she determined to find out what.

Although Farris seemed like a good person, he wondered about her track record, since the intel she provided for several missions appeared shoddy or incomplete. Before he joined, Zulu had been lured into a trap by Sayed Massi and sent on a mission to capture Anwar Massi, but the guy turned out to be an impostor who planned to break Sayed out of Gitmo. And Max would never forget his first unofficial mission with Zulu in Argentina. He had a scar on his ass to remember the psycho Arcilla who drugged and hunted him.

Either Farris didn't delve deep enough into the details leaving the team blindsided, or she didn't have a choice in the assignments given to Zulu. The thought crossed his mind that his uncle might somehow be messing around in his life again. If that was the case, he needed to do something because he refused to allow Uncle Asshole to injure or kill his new team.

But Max had no clue how to proceed. How would he prove an officer in good standing had a dark, murderous side, without proof? To accuse without evidence would crater his career, not Athole's.

"Hey, Shark Boy!"

Max turned at Finn's voice, and he put away his thoughts as he retorted, "What, Lava Girl?"

"Whoa, hold on there, young buck, no name callin'."

"You started it."

"Behave, you two," Grant groused. "I'll go grab the car." Noting Max was alone, he asked, "Where's Zach?"

"Pitstop."

"Ah, okay. Be right back. You both better still be sitting when I return." He strode two paces before turning back and directing his steely gaze at McBride. "No wheelchair racing!"

Affecting an innocent mien, Finn said, "Who? Me?"

"Yeah, you. The kid can use only one arm so it wouldn't be fair … and you're not to overexert due to your busted ribs."

Finn shot a glance at Max and laughed heartily. "He'd go in circles one-handed."

Rolling his eyes again, Max shook his head. This comradery is something he craved but still felt foreign to him.

"So, Shark Boy, I hear your stayin' with Zach. You got the better deal. Grant can be a pain in the ass." Finn pushed up out of his wheelchair, stifling a groan as his ribs protested, but not managing to prevent the grimace.

"Grant told you to stay seated," Max said.

"As I said, he's an overbearing PITA. Nothing wrong with my legs. Unlike yours. If you'd been wearing a magnetic band, the shark would've left you alone."

"Those things are only placebos."

"What?"

"You know, placebo, as in something that calms someone but has no true effect."

"I'm aware of what a placebo is, but my band worked. Nothing placebotic about that."

"That's right," Zach said as he sauntered up. "Worked real well, Finn."

Max peered at Zach, wondering why he agreed with McBride when he was aware several sharks circled them, and no one got bit because Sierra showed up in time to pull them all from the water. Later, when alone with Zach, he would probe, but for now, he let the subject drop.

Naval Intelligence Office

Nicole didn't bother to go home, though she required a decent night's rest, she had too much work to do. For the past six months, things had been off-kilter. Wrong or lacking intel put Zulu in several precarious situations. She didn't like operating this way. Their lives depended on her ability to vet the details.

She glanced at Captain Athole's closed door. Though not paranoid, Nicole did possess a potent dose of suspicion. A trait that served her well for many years in her position. Her ingrained sense of skepticism drove her to dig deeper and ferret out the truth as she prepared target packages.

Everything she learned from Baxter's men and her CIA contact about this past mission led her to a disturbing conclusion. Athole had accepted the operation and assigned Zulu without doing due diligence on vetting the situation.

Her gaze shifted to Larro. The petty officer had been in this office much longer than anyone in his rank typically would. The man appeared content not to move up or change positions, which was strange in and of itself. The man also had an unnatural admiration of Athole, so Nicole believed it would be fruitless trying to pry information out of him to support her theory.

Sighing, Nicole leaned back, and her eyes dropped to her laptop. As theories go, hers was half-baked with no evidence. She only had a gut instinct something was afoot, and Captain Athole might not be the stellar man his reputation purported.

The interview of every detainee followed the same path, netting identical stories. To her, that meant they had been coached or given a script to memorize if captured. They all said Baxter promised them a huge haul for taking the hostages.

One honest reaction she noted, each man revealed shock upon learning the crew had been killed execution-style. That had not been part of the plan as far as they knew. The whereabouts of Baxter remained unknown, though they each claimed he would've been in the building and assumed he died in the blast.

She arranged for a crime scene investigation team to be sent to the oil platform after a hotshot crew put out the flames. Once they sorted through the wreckage and conducted DNA testing on all the body pieces, they might determine if Baxter was among the dead. If they didn't find physical evidence of the notorious pirate, Baxter's fate would be uncertain. Not something Farris liked hanging over her head.

Nor did she like the lingering questions of why Athole handed this mission to a premiere team without validating the basic details. Her faith in her CO shaken, Nicole reflected on Athole's behavior towards her, especially when she questioned elements of the target packages he provided to her.

She might be a frog who jumped into a cold pot and failed to realize someone turned on the burner. *Could the captain truly be targeting Zulu or me? What about his nephew? By all accounts, Athole hates Stirling and doesn't believe him worthy. Could this be an attempt to get rid of the young man?*

Nicole let her mind sort through things a bit longer, and she concluded that these bad missions began well before Maxwell Stirling joined Zulu, so whatever was going on was directed at her or the team in general. The best way to figure out the truth was to begin digging. She flipped open her laptop and set forth on her task with renewed vigor.

Zach's Home

Relaxing in a comfy chair with a burger in hand, Max watched Rocky race after the tennis ball again and grinned. "Never knew they made hands-free ball toss things."

Zach refilled their ice teas as Rocketeer brought the ball back and dropped it into the catcher before trotting back into the grass as the mechanism rotated and prepared to launch again. "Saves my arm. He can play fetch for hours."

"Always wanted a puppy when I was a child. My dad said when I was old enough to take care of one, we would adopt one from the no-kill shelter. He died about a month later. I never got a dog. My uncle hates them." Max took another bite of his burger, surprised he shared so much.

Rather than dig for information, Zach shared too. "I was seven when we adopted our first dog. Mom took my two older sisters and me to the shelter to pick one out. They went ga-ga over all the little yappy ones. I headed straight for the big dogs. I searched for a bull mastiff, but they didn't have any."

Zach laughed. "Mom was thrilled they didn't, but I was crushed. We ended up with a teacup chihuahua. When Dad got home, he took one look at Tina and declared the rat wasn't a real dog. Much to my mother's initial dismay, the next day, Dad brought an Australian Shepard puppy home.

"We named him Blue, and he's the first pup I ever trained. He lived for eighteen years. The last couple of years of his life, I tried to make it home more often, and as sad as it was, fortunately, I made it back a few days before he passed away."

"Where's home?"

"Oregon, a small town near the border with Washington. My parents still live there. Dad owns an auto shop, and Mom is an elementary school librarian. My oldest sister Madison is married, and her husband works with my dad. They have two kids, both girls. My sister Audrey isn't interested in marrying, more focused on career. She now lives in Portland."

"Sounds like you have a nice family."

Zach noted the slight wistfulness in Max's tone. "Yeah. I counted myself lucky. Some of my childhood friends grew up with all kinds of drama in their life when their parents divorced and used them as weapons against the other parent."

Popping a fresh strawberry in his mouth, Max only nodded.

Taking a chance Max might open up with him too, Zach said, "Must not have been fun growing up at a military academy."

Max snorted. "No. But a hell of a lot better than living under Uncle Asshole's roof."

"Your uncle is Captain Athole?"

"Yeah, why?"

"To be honest, when we select a new teammate, we are allowed to review the personnel jackets. Saw Richard Athole listed as your next of kin."

"Although he is my mother's brother, Dick Asshole isn't any kin I would claim."

"If you feel that way, why did you list him on your CACO form?" Zach sipped his tea, hoping Max would answer.

Max stared out into the yard as images of his mom, dad, grandma, and Lacey came to mind. He sighed. "No one left to give a damn, but they required a name. After Lacey died, I listed him."

"Who is Lacey?"

Sensing a change in mood, Rocky dropped his tennis ball on the patio and trotted to his new boy. Carefully, he laid his head on his packmate's thigh, offering comfort. He succeeded when Max's hand stroked his fur.

"She was my fiancée. She passed away unexpectedly a week before I left for Green Team."

"I'm sorry."

"It's in the past. Should stay there." Max reached for his burger and took a huge bite, effectively ending the conversation.

Zach quietly ate, noting Rocky stayed close to Max, lying on the ground next to his feet. His pup took a liking to the rookie from the get-go, and he trusted Rocketeer's instincts. Despite what Preston may have done, the infamous Zulu Team leader's son turned out to be a decent guy and an excellent SEAL.

Orphaned at six, and having lived with a despised uncle for two years before being shipped off to a military boarding school, the kid needed family after surviving a childhood no one should have to endure. Regardless of his past, Max would find a family with Zulu if he chose. Bonds of brotherhood didn't require blood—they were forged, tested, and strengthened in battle.

Finn's Apartment

"NO! GET YOUR ASS BACK IN YOUR BED." Grant pointed to Finn's room, wearing an exasperated expression.

"Been in bed for three whole days. Need a little distraction."

"You cannot and will not go to Glitter Girls. Next week is the earliest you are gonna be stuffing their thongs with bills."

"Watch me." Finn feinted one way and moved the other.

Grant stopped him with three words. "I'm calling Jake."

"Damn, you wouldn't dare?" Finn deflated at Grant's reply.

"Watch me!" Grant grinned as he repeated Finn's words.

Chapter Twenty-One

Two Weeks Later – Jake's Home

VALARIE slipped her arms into her little black dress, pulled it up over her shoulders, and turned her back to Jake. Peering at him via the mirror, she smiled at the figure he cut in slacks and a dress shirt. Not often did he wear anything other than casual attire and his uniform. "Zip me, please."

Before reaching for the zipper, Jake leaned down and peppered Val's neck with kisses. "Perhaps we should skip dinner and go straight to dessert."

Softly chuckling, Val shook her head. "You owe me a night out, and besides, you've been itching to leave the house for two full weeks. This is your chance."

Jake finished zipping up Val's dress and spun her in his arms, so they faced one another. "You're beautiful." He captured her lips for a sensual kiss, hoping he could entice her to stay in, and perhaps order pizza after satisfying his carnal needs.

Pulling back, Val's eyes were alight with desire. "Dinner first, sailor."

Bested, Jake let go and grinned. "So, where am I taking my lovely wife for dinner?"

"Harborview."

"Mmmmmm steak."

Val laughed. "I'm ready if you are."

Max's Apartment

Shifting as Cali adjusted the annoying tie, Max thought about last night. Things went better than he expected when he told Cali about his latest injuries. Though her hands shook a little as she traced the new scar on his thigh, and shuddered when he explained a shark's tooth raked across it, she handled the news well.

"Hold still," Cali said as her boyfriend kept moving.

"Do I have to wear one?" Max groused.

"Yes. Harborview is an upscale dining establishment, and you can't appear as a heathen," Cali intoned haughtily then giggled.

"All my friends are heathens."

"That may be so, but you do clean up nicely." Cali gave him a peck on the cheek. "Let me help you with your sling."

"No. Grant said I don't need to use it any longer, but to be careful not to strain my shoulder. So, would you drive tonight?"

Her eyes lit with mischief. "Ooo driving the Mustang."

"Never realized you were into muscle cars."

"Absolutely. The faster and louder, the better."

"Since today is your birthday, you can drive my Mustang."

Cali shook her head. "Nah, only teasing. I prefer my RAV 4. The ride will be smoother … and quieter too. Are you sure you don't want to wear the sling? It's only been two weeks."

"I'm sure. I'm sick of it. Staying with Zach for a few weeks was okay, but I'm happy to be back at my place."

Giving Max's tush a slight squeeze, Cali flashed him a wanton expression. "Glad you are here too. I liked my welcome home present last night. And I'm not talking about the wine goblets."

"Tonight, will be an encore," Max promised. Cali was his equal in bed, and they enjoyed their romp. With his arm still hampered, she chose to ride him … and he didn't mind being her stud.

When Cali leaned in close and whispered the erotic things she wished to do tonight after they got home, Max found himself hardening at her words. "We should be going, or we might not leave the apartment."

Cali giggled as she strode out of the bedroom to grab her purse.

Harborview Steakhouse

Seated in the bar section, Richard downed his third whiskey sour. Though he ordered a meal, he let the food lie on the plate in favor of his alcohol. The perfect way to rid the world of the cocky little shit had not gone the way he desired. He almost danced a jig when the ready-made situation crossed his desk, but now he wanted to get sloshed.

Preston's spawn managed to survive, and in the process saved Jake Marshall, and started a fucking legend. An orca saving him of all damned things. Richard wished he had successfully drowned the pissant, but sea life intervened that time too. *Damned dolphins.*

He waved to his waiter, indicating he needed another drink. Not only did he have to figure out how to exterminate his sister's worthless excretion, but he must also ramp up his efforts to discredit Lieutenant Farris. The uppity bitch needed to be brought down several pegs.

In the past year, he hand-picked the packages assigned to her. Ones with tight deadlines and uncertain vetting, but juicy enough to grab the bitch's attention. His ass was covered since Farris was responsible for finalizing details before sending a team out.

Richard snickered into his empty glass as he thought about how he would word her annual review. *Lieutenant Farris's ambition, coupled with her lack of diligence, and impatience resulted in multiple failures, putting valuable resources in jeopardy.*

Soon he might be able to add a few more lines. *Her incompetence is directly related to the death of Petty Officer Stirling. It is my opinion she should be charged with Article 114 for recklessly endangering the lives of several tier-one assets, and Article 118 as her failures reveal a wanton disregard for human life.*

As the server set down his fourth whiskey, Richard shifted his thoughts to his conversation with Olivia. She agreed to cushion Carlson's fall from grace. The agent would end up with an out of the way position, from where he could climb again. The short chat with Carlson had been fruitful too, he stoked the already burning embers of hatred for Zulu, and specifically Stirling.

At the front door, the cheerful hostess asked, "Name?"

"Marshall."

"Reservation for two." The hostess picked up two menus and smiled. "Please follow me."

Jake and Val trailed the woman. It often required calling a week in advance to obtain a reservation, unless you were willing to eat in the bar. He liked this steakhouse for the high-backed private booths and dim lighting, which provided a sense of intimacy. Val deserved a bit of romance, and he earned a great steak ... so this place suited both.

After they sat, he ordered wine for Val, a beer for himself, and Val's favorite starter of fried garlic-pepper zucchini. Jake glanced around, not thrilled with their location near the bathrooms, but seeing as Val called only this afternoon, he couldn't complain. Here was better than being in their bar.

He quickly dismissed his surroundings and focused on the woman who put up with all his shit. She was a wonder, and Jake loved her dearly. In his line of work, both he and Dave were unicorns. They were in the tenth percentile when it came to their marriages. Most relationships didn't survive the rigors and uncertainty of the SEAL life.

Tonight would be date night, with no talking about work or kids. Just two lovers, enjoying each other. Something he valued more after realizing how close he came to dying in the last mission. If not for his rookie ... Jake halted his thoughts, shoving them to the background.

He leaned in close to Val and whispered the pickup line he used almost twenty years ago. "For some reason, I was feeling a little off today. But when you came along, you definitely turned me on."

Val laughed. "Still as cheesy as ever."

"You wouldn't want me to change now, would you?" Jake stole a kiss and draped his arm around Val, hiding the grimace when his bruised ribs protested.

"No. I love my hard-headed, mule-brained, frogman." Val pressed against Jake, careful of his ribs but enjoying the moment.

Outside Harborview Steakhouse

Cali pulled into a parking space and switched off the ignition. She glanced at the passenger seat and contemplated skipping dinner and taking Max back home. His eyes were closed and his breathing regular, indicating he nodded off.

She wondered if last night wore him out since he was still recovering from a significant injury. Cali drew in a ragged breath as the image of his fresh scars flashed in her mind's eye. A bullet grazed his arm, he dislocated his left shoulder in a fall, and he had almost been blown up and eaten by a shark.

Max's job appeared to be much more dangerous than Gabe's, or else her brother never told her about his brushes with death. Although she really liked Max, and perhaps might love him one day, Cali was not sure the life of a frogman's wife would suit her. She wanted stability.

Growing up with a druggie mother and her biological father unidentified had been rough. When the Millers adopted her, she learned what a real family was like, and Cali craved to recreate that for her future. Max's line of work came with a ton of uncertainty. She never knew when Max would leave, how long he would be gone, or if he would come home.

But there was something about him, beyond his handsome face and hot-body that attracted her to him. Part of it was the sincerity in his eyes, and his conviction to do something to make the world a better place for everyone. Though they had not shared their innermost thoughts, she got the sense he wanted to create a stable, loving family too.

Max roused and turned his head to Cali. He blinked a couple of times. "Wow, sorry. Didn't mean to nod off."

"No worries. It gave me time to ogle you," Cali quipped.

"Like what you see?" Max grinned.

"Yeah."

"So do I."

"Conceited much?" Cali purposely misinterpreted his meaning to get a reaction.

Max chuckled. "You know what I meant, beautiful. Ready to go in?"

"Starving, so yeah." Cali hopped out as Max did. They met at the rear of the vehicle and joined hands as they strolled to the entrance. "How did you manage to obtain a table on such short notice?"

Another chuckle came out before Max admitted, "I was not sure when we would be able to make it for a birthday dinner, so I made reservations under several names for the whole week."

Smiling, Cali asked, "So who are you tonight?"

With a twinkle in his eye, Max said, "Mr. Heathen."

Cali laughed.

Harborview Steakhouse

As Cali spooned up a bite of the chocolate lava cake and vanilla ice cream, Max leaned back and smiled. Tonight had been enjoyable. Cali regaled him with details of her trip, making him laugh at some of her antics. She was fun and lighthearted, in much the same way Lacey had been.

Though the two ladies' physical appearance was different, he concluded he had a type based on non-visual traits. Women who knew their minds, followed their dreams, possessed a sense of humor, and had compassion for others were downright sexy.

If he allowed himself, Max could easily fall madly in love with Cali. But an underlying fear of losing her like he did Lacey, kept him in check. Max was uncertain he would survive the loss of another love—Lacey's untimely death ripped his heart to shreds. For now, he vowed to simply enjoy the moment and let the future worry about itself.

"Aren't you going to have any?" Cali scooped up a huge piece and held the spoon out for Max.

"It's your birthday cake."

"Alright, but I want to share … that's what birthdays are all about."

"If you say so." Max allowed her to shovel in the cake.

She smiled as Max struggled to chew the enormous mouthful in a dignified way. "So, do you think you can come to the gallery showing?"

Muffled by cake, Max teased, "Do I haveta?"

Cali's eyes rolled. "No, but I would love for you to come. I want to show you the statues that I arranged to be on loan. They're gorgeous."

As his girlfriend rattled on about the details of the marble statues, Max managed to swallow. He rinsed it down with a gulp of water as she finished and asked him again. "For you, I would do almost anything. Are your professor friends going to be attending the party?"

"Yes, why?"

"Oh goodie, another night of insults."

She lightly jabbed him in the right bicep, steering clear of his injured arm. "Not nice. Frank and Morgan aren't that bad."

"If you say so."

"Well, at least the art and the food will be fantastic. My boss, Mr. Flanagan, is pulling out all the stops." She leaned forward and whispered, "He's even ordering beer."

Max chuckled. "Well, in that case, count me in." He shifted and said, "Excuse me. I need to use the restroom."

Cali nodded and took another bite of her cake. Tonight had been fun so far, and she looked forward to the rest when they got back to Max's place.

Jake relaxed as Val sipped her wine. He indulged more than he should by ordering the fourteen-ounce steak smothered in sautéed mushrooms. His eyes were bigger than his stomach when he ordered desert, which should be here at any moment. He needed to ask for a doggie bag, which would delight Tommy.

His son would eat it for breakfast as Eve harped on him about the value of consuming nutritious meals. His daughter acted like an avenger when something caught her attention. As the waiter delivered the treat, Jake spotted Stirling entering the restrooms. *Wonder if he is here with Cali. Might be getting serious about her.*

After taking care of business, Max exited the men's room and halted abruptly two steps outside as he came face-to-face with Captain Athole. The smell of whiskey strong, he realized his uncle had been drinking. Nothing good ever happened when Asshole came home tanked-up.

"Get the hell out of my way, pissant!" With an open hand, Richard targeted Maxwell's left shoulder and shoved him with a fair amount of power.

Wincing at the blow, Max moved to a defensive posture, unsure if another hit would follow. No longer a frightened and defenseless child who suffered from Athole's abuse, Max chose to remain composed, though he desired to ram his fist into Asshole's face. "Sir, officers are not allowed to strike enlisted men."

His face florid with excessive alcohol, Richard spoke louder than necessary or wise. "Don't sass me, boy. Or I'll whip your ass as I did before, you worthless piece of shit. You're not fit to wear the uniform just like your asshole father. The best thing he ever did was die."

Seething, barely maintaining control, Max's voice came out sharp-edged. "I overheard your conversation. I know what happened. One day, I'm going to prove it."

Richard sneered. "No one will ever believe the whiny tale of a delusional child."

Squaring his shoulders, Max ignored the burn still coursing through his left one. "We'll see. Already proved you wrong once. I'm on Zulu, despite every roadblock you put in my way."

"Why, you little shit." Athole balled up his fist, and started to pull back, but halted as a commanding voice intervened.

"Is there a problem here?" Jake's glare landed on the captain. He witnessed and overheard the entire exchange. Though he had never spoken with Captain Athole, he had seen him around the base multiple times.

Richard returned a glare and scowled. Though surprised to find Marshall here, he went on the offensive. "This doesn't concern you, Master Chief. You will leave now."

"Anything associated with my men concerns me. Particularly when an inebriated officer lays hands on an injured enlisted sailor and threatens him with bodily harm."

Aware of the power his uncle wielded and the damage he could do to Jake's career, Max shook his head. "This is a family affair, not a Navy one." He stepped to the side, clearing the way to the bathroom.

Recognizing Marshall had Lockwood and, to some extent, Captain Kendrick in his back pocket, Richard decided retreat would be in his best interest at the moment. He brushed past Maxwell, vowing to do whatever it took to bring the cocky bastard down … and keep his involvement secret.

After the door shut, Jake studied Max. "You okay?"

"I'm good. I need to get back to my date." Max resisted the urge to rub his shoulder.

"Alright." As Max started to leave, Jake added, "Grant will be by tomorrow to check your shoulder."

"Yeah, okay." Max hurried back to Cali, wanting to put distance between him and both his team leader and Asshole.

When Jake returned to the table, Val eyed him with a searching expression and asked, "What was all that about?"

Jake sighed. "I'm not sure, but I'm going to find out." He smiled at his wife. "I need a day pass tomorrow."

"Nope. Invite Max to our home for dinner tomorrow."

"Okay. Might be better that way." Jake offered his hand as Val scooted out of the booth, and then he picked up his boxed desert.

Val ran her hand down Jake's arm, causing him to meet her gaze. "He really is young, isn't he?"

"Yes, and I believe he needs some help. What we witnessed is disturbing in many ways. Part of me wants to report this to Lockwood, but Max's reaction makes me hesitate. Might cause more problems for the kid given Athole's reputation and resources."

Smiling, Val nodded. "I trust you'll do the right thing."

Chapter Twenty-Two

GRANT eyed Max, trying to discern if the kid was truthful with him about his pain level. Deciding to give him the benefit of the doubt, he nodded. "Okay. But I want you to use your sling for a couple more days, and ice it again tonight after you get back from Jake's."

Max nodded as he eased his left arm through the sleeve of his t-shirt. After tugging the material over his head and down, he asked, "When can I start physical therapy?"

"Doc said he would be scheduling you, Jake, and Finn, for the same time beginning next week. Don't worry about finding a ride. Jake's going to be driving both Finn and you."

"Okay." Max slipped the sling on and settled his arm in place. Though he didn't share with Grant, he'd been wearing it all day to help reduce the aching in his joint.

When he got home last night, Cali asked him what caused the pain, and insisted he ice his sore shoulder. He was uncomfortable sharing with her what happened, so he said he bumped it on something coming out of the restroom. Not a complete lie, but certainly not the whole truth either.

Uncle Asshole pretty much ruined the rest of his evening because he ended up falling asleep with a bag of frozen corn on his shoulder instead of having sex with Cali.

"You ready to go?"

"Yeah, sure. Thanks for checking my shoulder and giving me a ride to Jake's."

Grant grinned. "No problem. Just don't be running your shoulder into any more doors."

Max appreciated Jake didn't tell Grant the real reason, but dinner at the boss's house meant he would be fielding many unwanted questions. Marshall would want an explanation, and Max was unsure if he should say anything. Grabbing his wallet, he shoved it into his back pocket then picked up his keys as Grant headed for his door.

Though his anxiety grew, Max decided to play tonight by ear. He would reveal as little as possible to sate his master chief's curiosity, yet not enough to put Jake's career in jeopardy fighting a battle that was not his to fight.

Jake's Home

After being ushered into the house by Jake's youngest son, Max stood in the living room while Tommy raced off to inform his parents he arrived. His eyes sought the wall of photos, lingering on one of Jake's entire family. James, Eve, and Tommy might never realize how lucky they were to grow up in a loving home.

His attention so focused on the picture, "Eeeee," was the only warning Max got before a blur descended on and wrapped him in a hug. He stiffened with dread, realizing Eve clung to him at the same time he spotted Jake in the archway. As she kissed his cheek, Max simultaneously blushed and cringed. *I'm a dead man.*

After kissing Max a second time, Eve released him, and her youthful exuberance exploded in words. "Uncle Max. Thank you so much. I can't tell you how happy you made me. Jamie's Jamie again all because you talked him into telling Mom and Dad what he wanted to do. He promised to design some dresses for me."

Eve swirled, her eyes bright with glee, showing off the sundress she wore. "Jamie made this one yesterday. He's so talented. I can't wait for him to make me more. My friends will be so jealous."

Jake broke out in a broad grin. At first, he thought his daughter lost her mind, hugging and kissing Stirling. And he thought he might have to kill the kid, but she addressed Max with the uncle moniker, so everything was right in his world.

Linking her arm on his right, Eve pulled Max toward the kitchen. "Come on—no need to stand here. You're one of the family now. Mom's almost got dinner on the table."

Bewildered, perhaps a bit overwhelmed, Max didn't resist, and his gaze landed on Jake, who wore a Cheshire cat grin. *Did I just enter the Twilight Zone?*

Val smiled as Eve brought Max in. "Hello again. I'm so glad you came for supper. I hope you like spaghetti and meatballs."

"Yes, ma'am. Thank you for inviting me." He disengaged his arm from Eve as the teen went to help her mother.

Jake strode to the fridge and grabbed two beers. Opening one bottle, he handed it to Max since he was wearing the sling again. "What did Grant say about your arm?"

"No additional damage, but to rest it until I start PT." Max accepted the beer and took a sip. "Thanks."

The back door opened, and James entered with a smile. "Max, you're here. When we're done eating, I want to show you some of the designs I've been working on."

"Sure. When do you leave for Phoenix?"

"Next week. It will give me time to settle in with my aunt and find a part-time job before classes start."

"Sounds like you have a plan."

"Uncle Max, you can sit by me," Tommy said as Val indicated everyone should take their seats.

For the next hour, easy conversation flew between the family members, and Max relaxed. Though eating spaghetti one-handed proved a bit challenging, he managed not to drop any pasta or sauce on his shirt. He offered to help clear the table, but Val told him to stay put, so he did. James ran upstairs and grabbed his designs, and for a half-hour, Max listened as the young man prattled on about the clothing.

James halted, realizing Max might not be as interested in his topic as he appeared. "Sorry. I bet this doesn't float your boat. You being a sniper and all."

"Don't be too sure. Any sniper worth his salt must be able to sew a ghillie suit."

"Really?" James peered at his dad. "Does Uncle Dave sew?"

Jake snorted. "No. He tried once … it was a mess. Draper orders him what he needs now."

The evening passed in a weird semblance of a dream Max once had, of spending time with a huge family playing a game of trivia, laughing, eating popcorn, and drinking soda. About ten o'clock, as the kids said goodnight, Max didn't want it to end. He considered asking to play one more game and offering to come up with wrong answers so someone else could win, but didn't.

When Val rose, picked up the empty bowls, and told Jake she would be heading up to bed to read, Max's idyllic night came to a close. "Val, thanks for dinner and everything."

Smiling, she lay a hand lightly on Max's shoulder. "You are welcome here any time." Val leaned down and whispered in his ear, "Thank you for rescuing Jake and Jamie." As she straightened up, the temptation to ruffle his hair as she would do to Tommy was strong, but Val refrained. "Goodnight."

"Night," Jake said as Valarie headed into the kitchen. Silence descended on the room as he studied Max. He watched as a bit of tension re-entered the kid's body. He decided to start slow and build to the questions he wanted answered. "How'd you get so good at trivia?"

Max held in a sigh. *Yep, knew this was coming.* He met Jake's gaze. "Read a lot as a kid. Whatever books the library at Fairwinds offered."

"That's the academy you went to, right?

"Yeah."

"Eight's kind of young to be sent to a boarding school."

Max dropped his eyes to his lap. "Wasn't so bad. I received a decent education. Mr. Hartrum taught me a bunch of languages."

Jake nodded. "Your unique ability with languages is one of the reasons we selected you."

Max glanced up. "Really?"

"Yes. Among other things."

Resisting the urge to ask what, Max waited for Jake's next question.

Leaning forward, resting his forearms on his thighs, Jake clasped his hands and kept a steady gaze on Max. "Look, I could beat around the bush, but I'm more comfortable with the direct approach. What Captain Athole did in the restaurant isn't right. You have every right to press charges for conduct unbecoming an officer for assaulting you and public drunkenness.

"I won't report this to Lockwood if you are willing to talk to me. I overheard the entire exchange, and I can truthfully say, I wanted to pound my fist into the man. He's wrong, you earned your position on Zulu, and you deserve to wear your trident. You know that, right?"

"Yeah." Max clenched a fist as long-buried uncontrolled rage threatened to rise, but he took a cleansing breath and brought himself under control. As much as he was no longer the frightened child, he was also not the quick to anger teen.

Jake noted the flash of fury and how Stirling controlled his emotions. Another sign they had chosen the right man for Zulu Six. Though young, Max appeared to possess a level of maturity some men never achieved.

"What do you want to know?" Max asked, realizing if he talked, he might be able to save Jake's career because Dick Asshole would go after Marshall if he reported the indiscretion to the lieutenant commander. Max might also be protecting Lockwood's job since he was a lower rank than Athole.

"From what he said, I take it Athole was not on good terms with your father."

"Correct."

"Was that before or after Preston led the raid that got six men killed." Jake caught another flame of rage, swiftly banked.

Max fisted his hand again and refrained from blurting out his dad was not at fault for the team's demise. "Before. Uncle Asshole despised his sister and loathed the man she married. He's been a dick his entire life. The deaths of my mom, grandma, and dad allowed him to turn all his hatred on me."

Jake nodded and took a stab in the dark, but one that made sense to him. "He beat you as a child, but something caused him to put you in a boarding school away from him. I'm thinking for his sake, not yours." The brief doleful expression told Jake he hit a home run. "Will you tell me what happened?"

Max hung his head, and his fist tightened. When he finally raised his eyes to Jake's, his voice came out shaky with rage. "Yeah. Athole beat the shit out of me for the smallest infraction or perceived slight. Locked me in my room for days without food. Destroyed or sold everything that belonged to my parents."

Surging up out of the chair, Max paced, trying to rein in his emotions. The urge to tell someone his secret hammering away at the iron box he kept it locked up in made his chest hurt. He halted and stared at Jake. *Should I take a chance? Do I dare?*

Jake remained still. He struck a nerve with the kid, and anyone except a blind man could tell by Max's body language he wrestled with something weighty. He wanted to help but felt almost as powerless as he did when Jamie went off the rails. That thought gave him a possible solution.

Rising slow, Jake moved to Max, never breaking their gaze. He settled a hand on his right shoulder and gave it a slight squeeze. "When I offered you the Zulu Six patch, I told you the choice is yours. What were the first words out of your mouth?"

Max would never forget that day or any detail of the entire encounter. He sucked in a ragged breath, striving for calm. "Once Zulu always Zulu."

"Exactly. Lone wolves perish. You're part of Zulu's family now, and there's strength in the pack. You have brothers who will always have your back. The option is still yours. I won't force you to share, but I want you to understand, you're not alone."

Jake paused and added, "When James struggled with his problem and couldn't figure out how to proceed, what did you tell him?"

"That's why you have family."

"Uh-huh. And does that apply to you?" When Max's shoulders sagged and his head dropped, Jake allowed the fatherly side to come out, overriding the more standoffish team leader role. He drew Max to him and held him close until the kid pulled away. Jake counted it as a win because the embrace lasted almost a minute instead of him jerking back instantly.

Pivoting away from Jake, Max fought hard against the prickle of heat in his eyes. He swiped at the liquid pooling in them, still thrown by Marshall hugging him. Family ... all he ever wanted might be within his reach. But if he opened up and told Jake, Athole might rip them away from him.

Losing the people he cared about, fucking hurt. He was strong, but he would rather die for them than be left again with a shattered heart. And he was under no illusions ... Athole possessed power and position.

Keeping his voice soft, Jake said, "Max, this is an open offer. If you're not ready now, I understand. I broke faith with you the first mission and must earn back the trust I lost. But I promise you. Whatever is eating at you, it will be easier to face with your brothers at your side."

Turning to face Jake, eyes still glistening with unshed tears, Max choked out, "He might kill you too. I can't have that on my conscience. Val and your kids need you. I won't be the reason a family is destroyed." He shook his head and started for the front door at a rushed pace.

It took Jake a moment to process the words before his feet moved to catch Max. "Wait!" Without thinking, he reached for the kid to stop him from leaving, and his grasp landed on Max's left shoulder. At the hiss, Jake released. "Sorry. Please wait."

Facing the door, Max stood still. "What?"

"Who did Athole kill?"

The straightforward question caused Max to groan. He said more than intended and figured Jake would connect the dots in short order. Squaring his shoulders, he turned and once again faced his team leader. His stance rigid, Max said, "Zulu Team."

Jake reeled and took several steps back. "Your father's team?"

"Yes."

"How? Why? What do you know?" So many questions flew through Jake's mind.

"I overheard him talking with two people when I was eight. When I confronted him and told him I would tell the police, he laughed and said no one would believe a child. After the man and woman left, he beat the ever-living shit out of me and locked me in my room for three days.

"I survived because, after two years of abuse, I learned to hide bits of food and water in my room. He told the school I was ill and kept me home until the welts and discoloration faded."

Max inhaled and blew the air out with force. "A few weeks later he took me to the beach, said he was sorry. I didn't believe him. Asshole never regretted anything he did to me. He forced me to swim out far into the surf. My uncle tried to drown me."

He snorted and shook his head. "You probably won't believe this either, but bottle-nosed dolphins saved me. I'm a little fuzzy on the exact circumstances, but somehow, they got me to the surface and the shore. Asshole is a consummate actor. He had everyone there believing he was relieved I survived.

"Stupid me threatened to tell the police again. Asshole beat me senseless again, and when the bruises disappeared, he enrolled me at Fairwinds. Every school break, he would use me as his punching bag and threaten to kill me most painfully if I ever spoke of what I overheard.

"He also made it clear to any adults who would listen that I was a troublemaker, and he sent me to the academy for discipline. Scared and defenseless against a monster, I kept quiet. He made my life hell until I turned fifteen." Max paused and took several breaths as the memories replayed in his mind.

"I coldcocked him and sought emancipation. He must've realized if he fought me in the courts, the story of his abuse would come out. He relinquished his guardianship, but ever since I believe he's worked in the shadows to put roadblocks in my path to prevent me from attaining my goals."

Spilling his guts, Max added, "When Lacey passed away, I thought for sure Athole had a hand in it. But the doctors confirmed she suffered a brain aneurism."

Jake reeled, taking in all the details, and he didn't want to interrupt, but the last bit caused him to ask, "Who was Lacey?"

"My fiancée. She died right before I went to Green Team." Max raked a hand through his hair. "I don't have any proof of what Athole and the others did. Accusing him without evidence will get people killed. I can't live with the thought of him killing any of you. So, I need to keep my mouth shut."

Jake probed, "Do you know who he was talking to?"

Max shook his head.

"Truly, or are you keeping the detail to yourself?"

"Honestly. If I did, I would've dug around to find something that would corroborate my story. It is a dead-end. Everyone accepts Preston Stirling was a cocky SOB, who disregarded intel and got himself and his men killed."

Max sagged against the door; his eyes sad. "I miss him. He was an honorable man and the best dad ever. He didn't want to go on that mission. After Mom and Grandma died, he requested a stand down. Dad loved being a SEAL and a team leader, but he loved me more. He willingly gave up his dream for me."

When Jake moved forward and hugged him again, Max allowed it. Baring his soul and almost all his secrets lifted a bit of the weight Max carried for sixteen years.

Jake released Max but left his hand on his shoulder. "I believe you. I also agree accusations can't be made without proof. I'm willing to help you find some and then nail Athole's ass to the wall. And if we never do, you'll know, one person believes you."

Surprise lit Max's eyes.

Chapter Twenty-Three

Zulu Equipment Cage

DAVE perused the assortment of weapons and gear Draper placed on the table in the middle of their room. New helmets, night optics, and each man's preferred assault rifle to replace those lost when they jumped off the oil platform. He also noted a few new toys.

With the team down three men, he would help out with Green Team and have an opportunity to test out the new weapons. Grant would be doing additional medical training with Dr. Irving, while Zach spent his time at the kennels working with Rocky and a new crop of service dogs. Though before any of them did that, Grant and Zach would be joining him today to breakdown, inspect, clean, and reassemble everyone's weapons.

A beep sounded, indicating the door unlocked and opened. Dave expected Zach or Grant, so without glancing back, he said, "I'll focus on Max's gear, you can pick Jake's or Finn's."

"I'll handle my own."

Dave turned and peered at his best friend. "What are you doing here? Can't believe Val let you out."

Jake chuckled. "Good behavior. Besides, Lockwood wants to speak with us."

"About what?"

"Not sure. Let's go find out."

Lockwood's Office

Bryan peered up from his paperwork when Jake and Dave knocked on his open door. "Come in, gentlemen. Shut the door, please, and take a seat."

Both men sat and waited for their lieutenant commander to come to the point of summoning them.

Lockwood said, "Received Farris's after-action report and want to review her findings with you two before she goes over it with the teams."

"I assume it's not pretty," Dave said.

"Exactly." Bryan raked a hand through his hair. "Again, lack of intel before we executed put Zulu in a tight situation. After interviewing all the detainees and compiling details that came to light after you reached the platform, Farris believes this was a manufactured situation with two potential objectives.

"The first is a for-profit scheme. Lawrence Biden, the CFO of Biopetrol, was indicted on charges of bribery related to winning the contracts from Brazil. The company's CEO was unaware and has been cooperative, providing access to records which helped identify other nefarious activities Biden is involved in.

"Chiefly, his attempt to recoup the losses the company would've suffered once the bribery became known. The insurance policy on their platform would more than cover things if an act of terrorism or piracy destroyed the rig.

"The financial records uncovered show Biden paid Baxter two million to stage a fake ransom. The ten crewmen were all demolition experts sent to rig the bombs. They expected to be paid for their services, but Baxter received orders to execute them so they couldn't reveal the scheme."

Jake interrupted, "Did Biden reveal his plan?"

"No. But a trace of funds led the authorities to Barbados, where they apprehended Baxter. Apparently, he slipped off the platform a few hours before we arrived. He filled in the gaps, revealing he ordered his men to kill whoever came to rescue Biopetrol's crew.

"Only his top men knew the full plan and that they killed the hostages days earlier. Baxter talked because he wanted Biden charged with ordering the murders."

Jake nodded. "The CFO was willing to murder to cover up his actions." His gut rolled as he recalled Max's claim, Athole was responsible for Zulu's death, not Preston.

As if reading his mind, Jake turned when Dave asked, "So the second objective you mentioned, do you believe we were targeted specifically or did they not care which team was sent? Because, I gotta say, we've had a run of bad luck with a string of shitty intel and half-baked missions that go to hell in a heartbeat."

Bryan leaned back and studied both men. "No evidence points to them wanting to target Zulu."

"I hear a but, in your tone," Jake said.

A mirthless chuckle emitted from Bryan. "True. But something Farris said, which she didn't include in her report. She expressed concern this package was given to her for Zulu though the op rightly should've gone to Echo, who is on deployment in the South Atlantic."

"By whom?" Jake asked.

"Her superior, Captain Athole."

Jake's gut seized. He gave his word to the kid to keep quiet, but if Athole hand-picked Zulu for this mission, it could mean he wanted Max dead. This would've been a way to make it happen, but only if the captain was aware of the full situation.

The idea of Preston Stirling being Athole's scapegoat began to ring truer, though it would be difficult, if not impossible, to prove. Jake needed to do some covert digging, but he must proceed carefully. He had hoped to talk to Farris, but now he was not certain that would be wise.

"Why did you ask?" Dave queried.

Unable to reveal his thoughts at the moment, Jake said, "Wondered if the package came through the proper channels is all. Does this mean Farris is going to do a better job of vetting our missions moving forward?"

Bryan sighed. "She did comment on that. Feels responsible she sent you all in based on shoddy intel. Though, I think it would behoove us all to ask probing questions in the briefings, within reason, of course, to avoid another shitshow."

Clearing his throat, Bryan said, "I wanted to share the full details with you two before team debriefing, but this second piece, about Zulu possibly being targeted, can't leave this office."

"The guys have a right to be informed," Dave declared.

Jake shook his head. "I agree with Lockwood. Unless there is hard evidence, speculating will only rile the others. Finn might do something stupid, like storm into Athole's office and get himself kicked out of the Navy. Better if the three of us handle this in a calm and collected manner."

"You have a point," Dave conceded.

Bryan gave a curt nod. "That's all for now. Debriefing will be later this afternoon if McBride and Stirling are up to coming in."

"They'll be here." Jake rose with Dave, and as they exited, he thought about trying to convince Max to disclose his story to the team. However, he resolved to maintain Max's confidence should he refuse, as Jake sought to rebuild the trust between them.

Zulu Team Room

Max fiddled with the frayed edge of his sling as Farris finished recapping her after-action report. He stopped and peered at her when her voice changed, a tinge of remorse in her tone.

"Guys, I take full responsibility for putting you in this situation. Had I dug into the company before bringing this to you, I would've been aware of the bribery issue, and no one would've died or been injured. I can only promise to do better."

Glancing around at the guys, Max noted some appeared angry, and more than willing to place the blame for the EOD tech's death on Farris's shoulders. He analyzed what she shared, and something appeared to be missing. Max coupled the missing element with his knowledge of Athole and came to a sinking conclusion. Athole had a hand in this.

Though the rookie, with only two official missions under his belt with Zulu, he couldn't allow them to turn on Farris. "Lieutenant, how long did you have to delve into the details of the package before you paged us?"

Startled by the question, Nicole turned her attention to Stirling. "You were paged before I received the portfolio. Captain Athole said this operation was of the utmost urgency, and he had Larro notify the teams while I ran through the file."

"So, you had what, maybe fifteen minutes before we showed up to review the information provided to you?"

"Sounds about right. Why?"

The entire room full of Zulu, Delta, Sierra, and the technical support members focused on Max, surprised the rookie was questioning Farris in debrief.

Conscious of all eyes on him, Max shifted slightly in his seat. "Well, ma'am, it seems to me, the decision of who to send was out of your hands, and you weren't given adequate time to prepare. And with Baxter's reputation and no knowledge of the inner workings of Biopetrol, the op appeared straightforward and above board. Perhaps Captain Athole should be the one in here taking the blame."

Jake's eyes widened. Their kid was cocky and, in this instance, not thinking clearly to make such a bold statement about Athole. It would highlight the target he believed might already be on the kid's back.

"I appreciate your support," Nicole smiled a moment before her expression became serious, "but as Zulu's intelligence officer, the buck stops with me."

Lockwood stepped in before anyone else chimed in on the subject as he said, "Let's turn our focus to what we can control, the tactical elements. What worked, what didn't, and how we might change things for future ops."

The discussion turned to their movements, and Max noted Finn appeared quieter than he ever saw the man. He was not left to wonder why too long.

Finn surged up out of his chair. "I should've pulled the EOD back faster. Mannings would be alive today if I had."

"McBride, Mannings was doing his job, just like you, and he would never blame you. He chose to stay as long as possible, trying to defuse the bomb, but when he couldn't, he alerted Delta so they could bug out." Bailey took a deep breath. "His, like the one I encountered likely had too many anti-tampering measures. The men who installed the complex devices were experts."

Not mollified, but unwilling to say more on the topic, Finn picked at the bandage around his forearm that covered the new, pink skin where he had been burned. He half-listened to the rest of the analysis wanting a beer to push down the emotions that rose to the surface.

When debrief concluded, Finn stalked out of the room, heading for the team's equipment room to grab his motorcycle keys because he was done letting Jake drive him around like some invalid. He might have a couple of broken ribs, a bit of a concussion, and a burn, but none of that would stop him from riding his Harley.

Zulu Equipment Cage

Max followed Finn to the cages as Jake held back to talk with Grant about something. Dave headed off to help with a Green Team exercise, and Zach went to the kennels. He could tell McBride was still upset, but he decided not to approach him.

He didn't know them well enough to offer support, and he realized the other guys would've likely done something or followed him if they believed Finn required help. So instead, he went directly to his cage and dug for his keys to unlock his door.

Though he wanted to be rid of the damned sling, he wore it because it lessened the dull ache in his shoulder. As he slipped the key into the lock, Max heard Finn slamming things around. *Yep, he's still pissed off about the EOD's death.*

Giving Finn space to blow off steam, he entered and strode to his shelf, deciding to put the shark tooth in his trinket box.

Finn tossed his backpack on the table, annoyed he couldn't find his motorcycle keys. He proceeded to dump the entire contents and began pushing bits and pieces around, trying to locate them as he muttered under his breath.

He didn't realize anyone else came in until a clattering sound came from his right. Finn whipped around and spied the rookie. His first impression of the kid's expression was anguish. He glanced down and spotted a small wooden box on the ground, and the top appeared to be broken.

As Max knelt to pick it up, Finn moved closer. "Need a hand, Fumble Fingers?"

Max pinned a glare on Finn. "No!" He sat back on his haunches, muttering, "Stupid sling," as he ripped the restrictive item off. He lifted his treasure box and examined the busted hinge before setting it down to search for the contents.

His heart wrenched when he found his grandmother's tiny blue and white ceramic owl broken. He reached for the fragments as angry tears flooded his eyes.

Finn crouched down, noting the sagging shoulders and sadness. "What was that?"

Max blinked away the tears and swiped the back of his hand across his face, not pleased with his childish emotional reaction in front of McBride. "Nothing."

"Come on. I can tell it was important."

Staring at the pieces brought back all the feelings Max had as he watched his grandma dying on the living room floor. That day, his life fragmented just like the owl did today.

Finn picked up the well-worn box as the kid remained silent. He spied a photo taped inside and noted the Mustang. The child in the man's arms could be no one else but Max—same blond curls, only longer, and ocean blue eyes like the woman. He deduced the adults were Max's parents.

Glancing at the bits of ceramic in Max's hands, Finn said, "I can fix these. I'm good with my hands. The two classes I got A's in during high school were woodshop and ceramics."

Max shifted his gaze. "It is the only thing I have left from my grandma. It's irreparable."

"Not for me. Won't be like new, you'll likely see a few cracks, but I can restore it to almost new." Finn held out the box. "Put the pieces in here, so we don't lose any."

After dumping them in, Max began scanning the floor again.

"Something else missing?"

"My mom's necklace and my dad's ring." Max spotted the silver locket under the shelf and inadvertently reached for it with his left arm. "Dammit!" he hissed, bringing his arm to his chest.

"Here, let me." Finn ignored the twinge in his ribs as he snagged the chain. He noted the locket. Snooping, he popped it open and glimpsed the baby picture. "Ah, Baby Maxers."

Max stiffened. No one except his dad ever called him Maxers. Grabbing for it with his right arm this time, Max groused, "Thanks."

Finn grinned. "You were a cute baby ... wait, you still are," he teased, endeavoring to lighten the situation. When Max didn't bite back with a retort, he asked, "What's his ring look like?"

Aware of what McBride thought of his father, Max remained tight-lipped as he searched. He spotted it near the center table. Standing, he said, "I found it."

As the kid moved past him, Finn glanced at the photo in the wooden box again. The kid had the features of his father except for hair and eye coloring. If not for that, he might be looking at body doubles. He rose, bringing the little box with him and turned as Max grabbed his father's ring from under the table.

His curiosity grew when the kid clutched the ring to his heart and closed his eyes. The reaction told him these three items were precious to Max. "Can I see your ring?"

Max opened up and stared at Finn. "Why?"

"Why not?"

Realizing if he made a big deal of it Finn would razz him mercilessly, Max showed him.

Finn swallowed hard. "His trident ring."

"Yeah." Max reached for his box, but Finn held on. He wanted to yell 'give it to me!' but remained quiet.

"Hey, I wasn't lying. I can fix the hinge as good as new and put the little statue thingy back together too. Got the tools at my place. Come over for a beer, and I'll take care of these."

Max hesitated. "Why would you do that?"

"Why wouldn't I? You're my *baby* brother." Finn grinned as he emphasized baby.

"Not anybody's baby." Max paused, recalling Jake's words about family. "Okay. Thanks." He placed his dad's ring in the box and shoved a hand in his pocket to withdraw the tooth.

"Hey, what's that?"

"The shark tooth the doctor took out of my leg."

"You should drill a hole in it and wear it around your neck," Finn suggested.

"Only if I want to cut myself. There are serrations on two edges." Max handed the shark's tooth to Finn to view close up.

"I'm getting you a magnetic bracelet like mine. It will keep you from tangling with any more sharks."

Max laughed. Zach clued him into Finn's fear of sharks, and their tacit agreement not to enlighten McBride his magnet was worthless. "Don't need a silly, girly bracelet. Orcas will be there to protect me."

Finn's eyes widened. "Orcas!" He set Max's box down and lifted the right sleeve then the left of the kid's t-shirt.

"What the hell are you doing?" Max asked as he pulled back.

"You're missing something."

"What?"

Finn pulled up the sleeve of his shirt. "This."

Max peered at the Zulu insignia tattooed on Finn's bicep.

"We're going to my tattooist tonight. Gotta make you official."

Jake stood in the doorway, having observed since Max showed the ring. He stepped forward and cleared his throat. "Team trip to the Barnacle and then tattoo."

Max grinned. He knew precisely where to place his tattoo.

Chapter Twenty-Four

The Barnacle

LAUGHTER filled the air around Zulu's table as Finn regaled them with a tale about a dog, a donkey, and a chicken, which might or might not be wholly exaggerated, if not completely fabricated. No one cared, though. They were all in a lighthearted mood and more than willing to enjoy the moment.

On his third beer, none of which he bought for himself, Max glanced around the bar. A sense of belonging enveloped him, something he had never truly experienced. Sure, Red Team and Sierra, except for Babcox, accepted him and made him feel welcome, but with Zulu, it was somehow different … better … almost like coming home.

He gave Jake's words considerable thought, and determined, yes, the choice was his to make. He could lower his protective walls, open his heart, and invite his new brothers in, or continue to let the fear Dick Asshole instilled in him reign and remain alone. Doing the latter allowed Athole to win.

So, Max chose family over fear. Though, he did recognize learned habits would still rear their ugly heads from time to time, something he must be conscious of and mitigate if possible.

Max also mulled over a piece of advice Jake gave him on the way home after he spilled his guts. *Your father's legacy, good or bad, does not define you. Be yourself, and your parents will be proud.*

When another beer appeared before him, Max glanced to his left. He didn't recognize the older man and opened this mouth to ask why he set it there but didn't get the chance.

"This one is on me. Thanks for pulling my rookie's ass out of the fire before he got himself blown up." He stuck out his right hand, marred with scars, and index finger missing. "Name's Derek West. Welcome to the family, Kid."

Max shook Derek's hand as Jake grinned and said, "Not often we find you haunting the Barnacle, DW. What brings you down from your cabin?"

Derek focused on Jake. "Just checkin' on my rookie. Word is you boys encountered a bit'o trouble." He smiled, glanced back at the younger Stirling, and added, "And started a new myth."

"All true, swear on a Bible I saw it with my own eyes," Dave said as he peered at his former team leader.

Max listened as Dave and Jake talked with West, who he learned had been selected as Zulu One after his dad, and the rest of the team died. He also discovered that is when Jake joined Zulu, as number six. Max laughed along with the others as Derek shared tales of rookie Jake, but was taken off guard when Derek stood to take his leave and turned to him.

"Maxwell, I knew your father well. Preston was one hell of an operator and a damned-fine leader. Don't know what the hell happened, but I never believed for one moment he led the team to their deaths ... not his style. If you turn out to be half the operator he was, you'll do Zulu proud."

Swallowing hard, Max nodded.

Jake's mind swirled on this info. Now was not the time, but he decided to contact Derek later and pick his brain. He might be able to provide a clue or two, which might give them a thread to follow and lead to some proof of Preston's innocence and Athole's cover-up.

After Derek left, the team ordered one more round of beer and a shot of tequila before heading out the door. Thankfully, Finn's favorite tattoo parlor was within walking distance of the bar.

Squid Ink

Grateful for the numbing effects of alcohol and numerous distractions over the last hour and a half, Max remained still as Justin filled in the black of Zulu's orca and trident. He enjoyed the antics of his brethren as they kept him, the tattoo artists, and other customers entertained during the late-night session.

Justin and Zulu were the only ones left in the shop when Finn pulled up a rolling stool and stared at the positioning of the orca. "Why'd you want it sideways and on the inside of your bicep?"

Max glanced at Jake before answering. "It's where my dad's tattoo was. Always dreamed of making Zulu and honoring him by getting one in the same location."

Finn had not missed DW's comments about Preston to Max at the Barnacle. Though he might be bull-headed, and still believed the elder Stirling responsible for the deaths of noble men, he conceded, at six years old, Max might've worshiped his father. Therefore, it was not his place to make any nasty remarks.

Dave was the one to broach the subject. "Been thinking about what Derek said. He's always been an excellent judge of character. As Sierra One, he would've worked real close with Stirling on many ops. Do you think there is any truth to his assertion?"

Max's eyes met Jake's, willing him not to say anything.

Jake shrugged. "Not sure. All I do know is that a SEAL should be judged on his own merit. And in that case, the kid is a fine addition to Zulu."

Relieved Jake didn't reveal his secret Max breathed easier as the others agreed.

Fifteen minutes later, Justin set his tool down, cleaned the orca tattoo, held a mirror for his client to view the result, and applied ointment before covering the new tat. "Leave this covered until morning, and then keep it moist until the skin heals. If you notice any fading or spots that need a touch-up, pop back in, and I'll take care of it."

"Thanks." Max grinned as he stood among his brothers after pulling out his wallet to pay, only to be told his team already paid.

Max's Apartment

Golden rays of morning shone in through the window, causing Max to groan, rollover, and bury his head under his pillow. He drank way too damned much last night and had a hangover as penance. He lay still as he relived the night, a smile coming to his face despite the pounding in his head.

When his phone alarm sounded, fingers fumbled on the nightstand seeking to switch it off. With another groan, Max sat up and swung his feet to the floor, simultaneously wishing he didn't have physical therapy today and eager to begin his rehabilitation phase so he could return to operating.

His scrunched eyes spotted two tablets and a glass of water on the bedside table along with a note.

Take the aspirin and eat some dry toast. I'll be by at ten to pick you up. Jake

Glancing at the clock, Max had enough time for a shower and breakfast of toast before Jake arrived. After shuffling into his bathroom, he removed the bandage covering the tattoo.

Max grinned as he raised his right arm to the side, revealing his orca with the menacing teeth. As he flexed his bicep, the teeth moved as he remembered his dad's tattoo doing. On lazy Sunday mornings, he used to beg his father to make the motion and laughed every time.

He chuckled as the sense of belonging, of attaining the family he desired, settled firmly in his heart. *Six brothers, one heart,* Max recalled his dad saying as he moved to turn on the tap.

After taking a long shower, allowing the hot water and aspirin to soothe his headache, Max stepped out, dried off, and applied lotion to his new tattoo. He hurried through the rest of the morning routine, and his toast popped up as a knock sounded on his door.

Grabbing a water bottle from his fridge, and the toast, Max went to the door. "I'm ready. Let's go."

Jake squinted at the kid through his sunglasses. The little shit was too damned perky after a night of drinking.

Base PT Room

Max slipped off his t-shirt to allow the physical therapist to do his initial assessment and added his two-cents. "I'm fine. Aches a little, but that is normal. I'll be good as new in a week."

Mark studied his patient. "You've had a dislocation before?"

"A couple of times." Max's gut clenched as he recalled the first time. Uncle Asshole yanked him by his arm so hard his bone popped out of joint. He had been twelve at the time and failed to do his uncle's bidding fast enough.

Forced to lie when the doctor asked him how it happened, Max confirmed Athole's fabrication. His uncle told them he crashed his bike while jumping off a ramp, and Max didn't dare contradict the story out of fear of another beating. *Hell, I didn't even own a bicycle.* Max shook the memory away and refocused on Mark.

"Okay, then you know the routine. Passive movements first to test your range of movement, and then we'll progress to normal functioning as your body tolerates. My PTA, Cynthia, will take care of warming your muscles first. I'll leave you in her capable hands."

Max grinned at the cute assistant as she placed a heating pad on his shoulder, but his attention moved to Jake on the next table as Mark spoke with him.

"Haven't seen you in here for a while, which I prefer. How're the knees?"

"In great shape."

Picking up the chart, Mark nodded as he read the details. "Bruised ribs, and pulmonary contusion. Not much for me to do. How's your pain level while breathing?"

"Zero. I'm good. Told Dr. Irving I didn't need to come. Just need you to sign off."

Mark snorted, well aware of how Jake ignored his health, preferring to believe he was invincible. "How about a bit of cardio, and I'll assess whether you're ready to return?"

"Fine."

Mark glanced at his third patient—the Mighty McBride. He drew a steadying breath and prepared to grab the bull by its horns.

"Mark, I don't need no PT. McBrides get thrown, and we get back up without no fancy therapies," Finn groused.

"Well, that may be true, but in the case of rib fractures, patience is the name of the game. It's only been three weeks, and bones take time to heal. However, I believe we can shorten your downtime using a few modalities.

"I'd like to start with soft tissue mobilization and functional massage to keep your muscles loose. Kinesiotape will provide stabilization, and I think you would benefit from using TENS therapy to regulate your pain, allowing you to reduce your medication."

Viewing the expected bull-headed glare, Mark almost laughed as he pulled out his red cape, also known as Betty, his latest PT intern. The flame-haired beauty with a light dusting of freckles across her nose came forward when Mark motioned to her. "Betty, this is Petty Officer McBride. Finn, this is Ms. Campbell, my intern, and she will be handling your treatments."

Finn stared, almost gaped, and his face morphed into a smile. He wouldn't mind a massage from her. "Well, hey there, lassie, guess I'm in your hands," Finn laid his brogue on thick. He fell in lust the moment Betty spoke, the light lilt of a Scottish accent coming across loud and clear to his ears.

Across the way, Jake snickered and turned to Max. "Mark's found a secret weapon to get Finn to comply."

Max grinned, watching Finn make an utter fool of himself while flirting with the therapist. The more he interacted with McBride, the more he found the man to be a quixotic mix ... and the more he liked him.

Finn's Apartment

Kicked back on his couch, a beer in his hand, and the TV tuned to the sports channel, Finn breathed easier than he had in weeks. He might become a fan of physical therapy if it meant massages from Betty. Though, in truth, he would continue to go, because he wanted to make sure the kid followed through.

Also, he had no choice. He discovered Dave gave Jake his motorcycle keys, both sets, and Jake told him he would only return them if Finn continued with therapy. Sometimes his senior leaders pissed him off with their hovering.

He chuckled when Jake gave Max a lecture and said if he tried to drive his stick shift before Mark cleared him, he would be running the hills from dusk to dawn with a full rucksack. Jake also laid out the rules to the kid too, expounding on the fact he was now family, and as such, they would always have his back.

Finn almost shit himself when the cub responded with a sarcastic, 'Yes, Dad,' after Jake asked Max if he made himself clear. The scoffing tone reminded him of how Jamie reacted to one of Jake's long-winded lectures, which gave him pause and brought back the Canadian medic's impression of Jake being a papa bear to Max.

Perhaps the relationship went both ways. Orphaned at six and sent to live at a boarding school by eight, meant the kid didn't have a father figure in his life. At least not a flesh and blood one. It was clear to Finn now, Max idolized Preston Stirling. The only problem with idols is they often had flaws, and the kid might never accept his father messed up and got six men killed.

Sighing, Finn took a sip and put those thoughts away. If Jake saw Max as a son, and Max viewed Jake as a dad, who was he to say anything against it, especially when the kid wormed his way into Finn's shielded heart. How the hell Max did that, Finn couldn't figure out, but there he was, and there his little brother would stay … a bond stronger than blood.

Commandough Pizzeria

Jake sat across from Derek after ordering, taking a moment to gather his thoughts.

"Spit it out, Rookie." Derek lifted his lemonade, needing a break from beer, having consumed more alcohol last night than he did in a typical month, which was not much anymore. He used to drink much heavier, but his third wife helped curtail that.

"Tell me about Preston Stirling."

Derek eyed Jake. "Not having second thoughts about drafting his kid, are you?"

"No."

"Good, because that shit won't fly with me. Maxers was a sweet boy, and it is shitty what happened to him after Preston died."

Jake's gaze narrowed. "You knew and did nothing? How the hell could you allow him to suffer?"

Both hands coming up palms outward, Derek said, "Whoa there, back it up. What exactly are you saying?"

Realizing he made an assumption, Jake backtracked. "What did you mean?"

"What do you know that I don't?" Derek lowered his hands and leaned forward.

"You first."

"All I meant is that Max lost the three people he loved in less than a year, and had to go live with an uncle who didn't want anything to do with him. Athole is a cold-hearted bastard, married to his career, and as such, had no time for a wife or kids.

"The way he treated the boy at the funeral … atrocious and cruel. If I had to do it all over, I would've landed a fist to Athole's jaw for telling Max he cried like a pansy. For God's sake, the six-year-old lost his mom, grandma, and dad in quick succession. The kid deserved to cry, bawl, and wail.

"Before I could intervene, Kendrick stepped in and presented Max with his father's flag. Still chokes me up to recall Max saluting Kendrick before he accepted the folded flag and held it to his little chest like a lifeline.

"If I hadn't been going through my second divorce, I would've sought custody of Maxers. Doubt I would've won, but it might've sent a message to Athole. And then Droit approached me about taking over Zulu. A dream come true, at the cost of too many brothers."

Derek took another sip. "Okay, now you. Why did you go on the offensive?"

"Did you keep any contact with Max?"

Derek shook his head. "No." A sickening sensation started in the pit of his stomach. "Don't tell me that bastard ..." he trailed off as the realization came to him. He recalled one of the last conversations he had with Preston when he told him he requested a stand down. "Ah, shit. He did, didn't he? Athole was abusive to him, wasn't he?"

"What makes you draw that conclusion?" Jake didn't want to reveal Max's confidence.

"As I said, Athole has always been cold bastard. But it's something Preston said about a week before his final mission. He loved his son and wanted the best for him. With Lois and his mother both dead, the only biological family left was Athole. Preston worried if anything happened to him, Max would suffer from Athole's hatred of him and his own sister."

Derek clenched his long-ago injured hand, a wound that ended his days on Zulu. His remorse-filled eyes sought Jake's. "I failed Preston and little Maxers. Shit, I should've watched out for him ... he's family ... Zulu protects family."

Jake nodded. "Tell me about Preston. You said you didn't believe he messed up."

The pizza arriving interrupted their conversation, and it gave Derek a moment to realize why Jake wanted to meet so far off the beaten path of any sailor hangout. Finally, someone else who didn't buy the official story.

After swallowing one bite, Derek said, "If I had to give you an example of the type of man and leader Preston Stirling was, only one name pops to mind."

"Who?"

"Jake Marshall." Derek smiled at Jake's surprise. "He was as dedicated and hard-hitting as you. Preston cared about his men and mission with the same passion you carry. He possessed intelligence and a gut that kept his boys alive in some of the hairiest situations. He was an operator's operator, but he was bi-lingual too, spoke cake-eater as well as knuckle-dragger."

Jake chuckled. "Well, that's one thing we don't have in common. I tend to piss off the cake-eaters. Lockwood is my go-between."

"Well, at least you have him." Derek took another bite and chewed, waiting for Jake's next question. Droit had been right all those years ago when he drafted a young buck named Marshall to fill out the last spot in Zulu.

"If you had to guess, what do you think happened on that mission?" Jake lifted his piece, hoping Derek might provide him something tangible to follow.

"The official line is Preston disregarded intel and went in anyway. I call bullshit. If you had been told a building contained massive amounts of explosives, and the HVT was inside, would you rush your team inside? I wouldn't, you wouldn't, and neither would Preston."

His hand clenched again, as Derek said, "But the recording proved he was informed of the details. Preston replied, 'good copy,' right before he said, 'we're going in,' and the building exploded moments later."

"Was there video footage of the op?"

Derek snorted. "I see you forget your roots. We didn't have the toys you boys have now. The answer is no—only the audio. I heard the clip, it was Preston's voice, and that's all brass cared about. They had someone to pin the deaths on."

Jake leaned back. "Audio can be altered."

"True, but it would take a concerted effort to frame Preston. Everyone in TOC would have to be in on the conspiracy. Mind you, perhaps something like that happened, but I'm more inclined to believe the transmission might've been garbled on Preston's end. He didn't repeat back what TOC told him."

For the next hour, the two men discussed the situation as they consumed their pizza. As they stood to leave, Derek captured Jake's gaze, his expression solemn. "Whatever happened, it isn't Maxer's fault. Take care of him, as I should've."

"I will," Jake promised.

Chapter Twenty-Five

Two Weeks Later – Katsaros Gallery of Fine Art

RICHARD strolled through the gallery, eyeing the various pieces of art available for sale as he sipped his wine. The investments he made with Preston's life insurance and the money he received by selling his brother-in-law's house and worldly possessions grew to a sizable sum. He could, if he desired, purchase any of the items, though he was not a connoisseur.

He only attended these events to add to the cultured veneer he refined over the years. Schmoozing here introduced him to many in the political arena. And the connections he established would assist him in his next step upon retiring from the Navy.

Richard had a plan, and the millions he invested in offshore accounts would help him launch his political career. Senator first, but one day he would be President of the United States. He grinned. President Richard Athole had a nice ring to it.

"Good evening, Captain. A pleasure to see you again. Find anything you might like to take home?"

Richard turned a smile on the gallery owner. He had no use for this lowly man but played his part. "Several are tempting. Quite a turnout tonight."

Duff Flanagan nodded. "Yes, indeed. My protégé, Cali Miller, managed a coup by arranging a loan of the Mendelian statues from Italy. So many wish to view them."

Cali's Apartment

"Sorry I'm late," Max apologized when Cali answered the door.

"No worries, I only finished dressing moments ago. Just let me grab my coat." Cali turned and strolled to her closet to select her mid-weight jacket. Now early autumn, the night air would be cool and damp following the recent rain.

Max enjoyed the view as Cali sauntered away. He leaned on the doorjamb, watching the way her hips swayed while wearing high heels. He liked the little black dress. It hugged her curves perfectly. He would prefer her in nothing and wished they could just remain here tonight instead of attending the gala.

But she worked hard on this event, and he wanted to support her. So, Max went head-to-head with Jake and his teammates this afternoon, making a case for why he should be allowed to drive, although the physical therapist had not cleared him to do so yet. He had to make a few concessions; ones that made him feel like a teenager—a small price to pay to be here with Cali.

Returning to the door, Cali slipped on her coat and beamed a bright smile as she teased, "I'm glad your five fathers granted you permission to come tonight."

Max chuckled. "Not fathers, brothers."

"They act more like fanatical fathers, controlling your every move. Do you have a curfew?" She hugged his forearm after pulling her door closed.

"As a matter of fact, Jake expects me to call him when I arrive home." Max escorted Cali down the stairs.

"You gonna call? Wait, don't bother answering. Yes, you'll call." Cali smiled up at Max, so handsome in his suit, but she would take him in whatever he wore, preferably in the bedroom au naturel, scars and all.

"Better than having five fanatics busting down my door if I fail to report."

"True." Cali giggled. "I swear, they're more overbearing than my brothers, and that's saying something."

Max only smiled, happy to have true brothers.

Katsaros Gallery – Main Room

The initial crush of people thinned out after several hours, and Max enjoyed observing Cali in her element as she worked the room. He stayed by her side, although the food table called to him because he had not had time to eat today.

His day started with a long walk, and though he wanted to jog, he refrained because he only had one more week of therapy. If all went according to plan, he would be cleared to engage in full workouts and rejoin his team.

After the walk, he took a shower and barely stepped out, when his phone buzzed. Jake was on his way over to transport him to base because Farris required his language skills to translate some critical chatter. Max spent the rest of the day in TOC.

Unfortunately, except for the brief discussion to obtain permission to drive himself tonight, Max had no time to breathe, let alone eat anything, so he was famished. When Jake dropped him off at home, Max swiftly changed before jumping in his car to race over to Cali's place to pick her up for the event.

Accepting a second beer from the server making the rounds with beverages, Max froze when he spotted his uncle. *What the hell is he doing here?* A moment later, Cali's boss, a man Max liked, approached them and spoke to Cali.

"There's someone I would like you to meet. Captain Athole is admiring the marble statues and has a few questions," Duff said.

"Certainly." Cali made her excuses to the group, snagged Max's arm, and followed Flanagan.

Max's mind spun a mile a minute. He wanted to avoid a confrontation with Uncle Asshole in front of Cali. Hell, he didn't want Asshole to be aware he knew her. Many scenarios about what Athole might do with the knowledge ran through his mind. When his gaze locked with Athole's, Max squared his shoulders, preparing for battle.

Duff made the introductions, wholly unaware of the familial connection between Athole and Stirling. He took his leave, moving on to speak with other potential customers.

"What can I tell you about the statues?" Cali asked.

Richard held in his surprise to find his nephew in attendance. He chose to act as if they were strangers. It would not serve his purposes to acknowledge the pissant in this arena. He counted on Maxwell following suit, and for once was not disappointed.

As Cali engaged in answering Athole's questions, Max stood and listened. Though it felt a bit like lying, he didn't want Cali to know he was related to Athole. She might assume they liked one another, and he didn't want to air dirty laundry in public. Better this little white lie and he would explain later if things moved in a more serious direction with Cali.

Thankfully, the encounter only lasted a short time, and they moved on to other guests. Fifteen minutes later, Cali ended up surrounded by a group of her professor friends, many of whom discounted him as Cali's fad and believed she would wise up one day and kick him to the curb.

When the discussion moved into esoteric babble, Max leaned over and whispered, "I'll be back in a moment."

Cali peered up at him. "Where are you going?"

"Men's room."

"On the way back, would you snag me a glass of white wine?"

"Sure. You want any hors-d'oeuvres?" He hoped yes because his stomach ached to be fed.

"I'm famished, some of the fried mushrooms, please."

"Alrighty." Max moved off to find the nearest restroom. On his way, he eyed the Mendelian statues, appreciating the effort the artist put into carving them.

Katsaros Gallery – Men's Restroom

After taking care of business, Max was washing his hands at the sink when two men entered. They were guys he met at one of Cali's posh parties. He didn't care much for either of them, but he put up with them because they were Cali's associates.

"Hey, Max, right?" Morgan stopped next to Cali's boyfriend.

"Yeah." Max reached for a paper towel.

"Can't believe Cali brought you to this high-class affair. You stick out like a sore thumb," Frank sneered. He never liked the guy Cali chose to date and was not above letting him know how much he didn't fit.

"Guess it isn't so classy if you're here," Max retorted.

"Shouldn't you be off killing innocents in some foreign country to fulfill the dictates of this fascist regime?" Frank flung back.

Any response was cut off by the sound of gunfire. Max rushed to the door to find out what was happening, while Frank and Morgan ran to cower in the stalls.

Crouching at the doorway, Max scanned the main gallery, searching for Cali. His pulse beat a rapid staccato until he found her in a group being herded into a corner. He counted five gunmen armed with assault rifles. Although calling 911 would be most people's first inclination, Max hit Jake's contact after he retrieved his cell from his front pocket.

"Hey, Kid. You're home early."

"No. I'm still at Katsaros Gallery. Five men carrying AK-47s entered and fired off several rounds. From my vantage point, I can't tell if anyone is dead or if there are more hostiles."

Jake stood and signaled to Dave as he put the phone on speaker. "Where exactly are you?"

"In the men's room on the first floor. Cali is in the other room with the gunmen. I want to go to her."

"Stay where you are. I assume you are unarmed?"

"Not quite. Got my pocket knife." Max fingered his small knife.

"Don't join a gunfight with a knife. You call the police?"

"No, you came to mind first."

"Sit tight, Kid. We're coming. And Max …"

"Yeah?"

"Don't do anything foolish. You're almost qualified to return to active duty, and I don't want you on the injured reserve again."

"Copy." Max inched back into the restroom, allowing the door to close, fighting his desire to rush out there and protect Cali.

Katsaros Gallery – Main Room

Herded with everyone else to the corner, Cali scanned for Max. Her heart raced, but she refused to cower or cry like many of the others. She hoped Max remained hidden wherever he was because there were too many armed men for him to take them on by himself.

When one of the men pulled Duff from the group, she took a step forward, wanting to help, but found herself yanked backward and a voice urgently whispered in her ear, "Don't draw attention to yourself."

She turned and spied Captain Athole. The man gave her the creeps. Cali found his questions earlier insipid, and she didn't miss the glare he shot toward Max. Though she wondered if the two men knew each other, neither acknowledged the other. Of course, the Navy had thousands of men, so the likelihood this officer and her enlisted boyfriend having met seemed slim.

"They have Duff. I can't stand here and do nothing."

"What do you think you can do against automatic weapons?" Richard whispered. He'd been playing with ideas of how he might use the pissant's girlfriend to his advantage. Befriending her, and laying a seed of doubt about Max to ruin their relationship might work in his favor until he found another way to rid the world of Preston's spawn.

Though Cali didn't want to admit the captain was right, she did, gaping with horror as they pushed Duff to his knees and placed a gun to the back of his head. A shiver ran down her spine as one of the men spoke.

"Stay where you are. No talking. No moving. If anyone tries to be a hero, he is dead." Jean-Luc Fouquet eyed the hostages and then ordered, "Grab four more and check the bathrooms. I don't want any stragglers."

A surge of power ran through Fouquet as the sheep complied. Getting kicked off the Toronto Police Force, thanks to charges of firing without cause, coupled with his previous disciplinary actions due to his run-in with Daniel Broderick, pissed him off.

After being fired, he hooked up with several felons and other former officers who had been discharged years before for their part in teaching Broderick you don't rat on your fellow officers to Internal Affairs. The life of crime was much more lucrative than being a constable, and their skills gave them an advantage, an understanding of the tactics the police would use.

Fouquet decided to flee Canada, branching out to the U.S. when things became too hot after he received a visit from three men, a black-haired man, an amber-eyed man, and one as fierce as an enraged highland warrior with a scar across his face. They informed him if he ever so much as frowned in Blondie's direction again, he would forfeit his life.

He asked who Blondie was, and the raven-haired man's hazel eyes erupted in flames as he said, 'Constable Daniel Broderick.' Fouquet believed them, and leaving Canada appeared to be in his best interest. Besides, here he and his team were unknown and not in any system yet—not that they planned on getting caught.

Outside Gallery

Breaking the speed limit, Jake and Dave made it the gallery in Chesapeake in record time. The trip should've taken at least twenty-five minutes, but only took Jake fifteen. While en route, Dave called 911 to report the incident and followed up with a text to the guys. Jake parked, and they hurried to the crime tape the police erected to set their perimeter.

They found Zach already there, and he explained he was at the Greenbrier Mall on a date gone bad, so he ditched the woman and hightailed it to the scene as soon as he got Dave's text.

With no authority to operate on home soil, all three SEALs became frustrated since they could only stand here and observe the local authorities.

Finn, pulled from Glitter Girls where he had been enjoying the dancers before the message, strode up to join them about five minutes later. His hands shoved in his jacket pockets to ward off the unseasonably cold night he asked, "What's the sitrep?"

"SWAT arrived a few moments ago and so did a negotiator. They are trying to contact those inside, to no avail."

Grant jogged up, almost slipping on a patch of wet leaves downed by the recent storm. "The kid. He okay?"

"So far, so good. He's still in the bathroom. Indicated no other shots fired since the initial rounds. He's antsy, though. He can't stand Cali being out there without him." Jake raked a hand through his hair as he stomped his feet, needing the physical activity to keep warm, having raced out without a jacket.

"Don't blame him. If it were Cathy, yeah, I'd be chomping at the bit to go to her. And Jake, so would you if it was Val." Dave met Jake's gaze and received a nod.

"SWAT is gearing up." Zach pointed to the group of seven men checking their weapons behind their armored vehicle.

Jake shouted, "Sergeant! I have information for you."

Sergeant James Fox turned and viewed the man who yelled, noting he waved to him. Leaving his men for a moment, he strode over through the wet leaf debris littering the road. "Who are you?"

"Master Chief Jake Marshall and one of my men is inside. He called and gave me details you will find useful."

"Make it quick."

"He was in the latrine when the shots rang out. Two other friendlies are with him. Stirling spotted five hostiles with AK-47s but is unsure if there are more. They rounded up the attendees and put them in the far corner. I told him to stay put."

"Why didn't he call the police?"

"Training."

"What?" Fox's brows knitted together.

"Pounded into his head, I'm the first person he calls if the shit hits the fan. His name is Max Stirling. You can call him if you need updated intel."

"What's his number?" Fox pulled out his cell phone and punched in the digits. He halted before pressing call, concern lighting his features as he asked, "Will his phone be in silent mode? I don't want to put him in danger."

Jake grinned. "Yeah, the kid is smart. Would've been the second thing he did."

"Second?"

"First is to call me."

"Got it. Thanks." Fox hit send, and when it answered, he said, "This is Sergeant Fox, am I speaking with Max Stirling?"

"Yes."

"Your master chief said you might be in a position to provide us with additional info." Fox moved back to his team.

Max sighed. *So they're out there, probably pissed off they can't do anything, just like me.* "Yeah, give me a moment to take another scan."

"I don't want you leaving your cover." Fox put it on speaker so the rest of his men could listen in.

"I now see eight men, three more than the five I spotted earlier. Appears they moved everyone, about forty people, to the south corner near the marble statues."

"Can you hear anything?"

"No one is talking. Their faces are all covered in white, plastic masks, but they're all wearing suits like the guests."

"Anything else you can tell me?"

Max focused on two men who set a backpack on a table and unzipped it. "Crap, they have a shitload of C-4." He watched for another moment. "They're handing it out to the others, and they appear to be taking it to various locations." Max's gut seized when one man put a block of the moldable explosives near Cali. "They're placing some around the hostages."

"Thank you, Stirling. Let's keep this line open, and you can feed me any new developments."

"Shit, someone is coming towards the bathrooms. I'll leave my phone on in my pocket, try to feed you what I can without giving it away."

Chapter Twenty-Six

Katsaros Gallery – Men's Restroom

MAX barely slipped the phone into his breast pocket before the bathroom door slammed open. He managed to position himself out of sight behind a half wall, hoping to get the drop on the man. Though Jake and the cop said stay, he couldn't. The armed man would find him anyway, so he formed a plan.

Waiting for the door to swing closed and the man to come close enough before launching his attack, Max's kick sent the submachine gun skittering across the tiles. The hostile staggered backward, stunned for a brief moment before he reached for his handgun.

Not allowing him to draw the pistol, Max engaged the masked man in hand-to-hand. When his moves were countered Max, gathered he was up against a well-trained male. They exchanged several fast blows before ending up on the floor. Ground fighting would favor Max, he enjoyed taking Judo lessons beginning as a teen, and his SEAL training took him to the next level.

Peeking out of their stalls, Morgan and Frank only stared as the two men fought it out.

Max managed to flip the man, got him a chokehold, and applied pressure until the male went limp. He held tight a little longer, ensuring he was out. Pushing the unconscious man to the side, Max got to his knees and peered at the two cowards.

"Thanks for the help," Max replied with sarcasm before he yanked off the mask, removed the guy's belt and blue tie, then began undoing his own red tie.

"You killed him," Morgan stated with disbelief at having watched someone kill for real. His stomach turned.

"Not dead. Down for the count." Max unholstered the pistol and tucked it into the waist of his pants at the back.

After Max stood, he grabbed the shoulders of the insentient man, dragged him to the handicap-accessible stall, and positioned the goon with his back against the toilet's base. Max pulled the arms up and round to the other side and secured the man's wrists with his red necktie.

"What are you doing?" Frank asked.

"Isn't it obvious?" Max turned to the dense and cowardly men. "Give me your ties."

"Use his. Mine is French silk," Frank groused as he pointed to the guy on the tiles.

"I need his. Give it over, or I'll take it." Max glared.

Morgan began undoing his. "Why do you need that guy's tie?"

"Cause I'm going out there." Max took Morgan's tie, knelt, and bound the hostile's ankles before shifting the legs towards the hands. A quite uncomfortable position for the man now in a backward C. He knotted the fabric from both ties to the inert man's buckled belt, effectively hog-tying him around the toilet. The assailant wouldn't be going anywhere.

"You don't need mine. He's secured." Frank refused to remove his expensive tie.

Standing, Max moved into Frank's personal space. "Tie. Now!"

Frank gulped at the menacing, ice-cold glare, took a step back, ran into the wall, and began taking off his necktie, unsure why Max needed it.

Once he obtained the length of material, Max unrolled a mass of toilet paper and shoved it into the restrained man's mouth before fastening the makeshift gag with Frank's tie. Rising, he said, "Now he can't yell for his buddies."

Going to the sink, Max raked his fingers through his unruly curls to put them in some semblance of order, re-tucked his shirt, and put on the blue tie before retrieving his cell from the floor where it fell during the scuffle. "Fox?"

"What the hell is going on?" Sergeant Fox demanded, having overheard the commotion and snippets of conversation.

Max sighed with relief. *Still working.* "One assailant secured. I'm going to wear his mask and go out there to gather intel."

"No. Too risky." Fox stared at the Katsaros building. Whoever planned this knocked out all cameras, so they were completely blind. He didn't like going in without understanding what his men would face. The negotiator failed to elicit any response from anyone inside, though he continued to try.

"With all due respect, sir, I'm trained for situations like this. You need to know what you're up against, and frankly, I'm not leaving my girlfriend, and the others out there unprotected right next to explosives. You don't want forty innocent people to die any more than I do."

"Will you blend in?"

"Yeah. This guy's suit and mine are both navy, we're both wearing white shirts, I took his tie, and we're about the same build.

"I don't like this, but don't have much choice," Fox bemoaned.

"No, you don't. Tell my boss … ah, never mind. I'll tell him myself when this is all over. I'm not gonna be able to hear you, but I'll feed you details."

"Understood. When we breach the building, at the first flashbang, you hit the deck, remove your mask, and stay down. Do I make myself clear?"

"Crystal." Max pocketed his cell, retrieved the rifle, and peered at Frank and Morgan. "You two stay here and lock the door."

"You're not actually going out there?" Frank asked.

Max pulled the mask over his face. "Yes."

When the door shut, Morgan turned to Frank. "I think we've hastily judged him. We never gave him a fair shake. I can't believe he is willing to risk his life to give the cops details."

Frank shrugged. "Still don't like him and all he stands for. If it weren't for violent men going off to play war in countries that don't want us there in the first place, the world wouldn't always be attacking us."

Morgan shook his head. "You will never recognize your faulty logic. A strong military protects us and maintains our freedom. Men like Max put their lives on the line every day so we can sit here and speak our minds."

When Frank only smirked, Morgan stopped wasting his breath. *Some people will never understand the vital role the military plays in keeping America the Land of the Free.*

Katsaros Gallery – Main Room

Max stopped at the end of the hall and surveyed the room. He noted many of the females appeared frazzled, a few crying. The men were not in much better shape. He smiled; glad the mask hid his face when he spied Cali. She was no fragile flower. She stood erect, fearlessly scowling at their captors.

However, the fact Athole stood behind her soured his stomach. He hoped like hell, if his uncle recognized him, he would keep his damned mouth shut. *One positive going for me, Uncle Asshole didn't appear intoxicated earlier. An inebriated Athole is unpredictable, whereas a sober one is cold and calculating.* Max preferred the sober version.

Taking stock of the situation, Max whispered, "Fifteen armed men in the main area. Five are guarding most of the guests in the far corner. They separated five older male hostages. They're on their knees in the middle of the area. One guy is behind them, holding a pistol to the back of a hostage's head, threatening to execute him."

Max recognized the man in immediate jeopardy and wished he could do something to prevent Flanagan's death. Cali's boss was a decent man who enjoyed knocking back a stout ale in a pub and didn't come across pretentious like several of the snobbish people in Cali's crowd.

Moving forward, he headed straight for the C-4 stuck to the wall near Cali. Luckily, the other masked men appeared to be engaged and didn't pay any attention to his movements. Approaching the explosive, he allowed his eyes flick to Cali.

Cali released a soft gasp but quickly stifled herself. She would recognize Max's blue eyes and blond curls anywhere. For a fraction of an instant, she wondered if he might be involved since he disappeared shortly before the gunmen entered. Almost as fast as the thought came, she dismissed it as a load of rubbish. *If not involved, what is he doing dressed like them?*

Max realized she recognized him and gave a slight shake of his head as he silently pleaded. *Please don't say anything. Don't give me away.* His gaze flicked to the plastic explosive and back to her, trying to communicate his intention. He deliberately didn't peer at his uncle, hoping he wouldn't recognize him.

Athole tracked the movement of the man who returned from the bathroom. An observant man, Athole noted a difference in body carriage and hair coloring. He had not located Maxwell among the crowd, and recognition flooded in as he caught sight of the ocean blue eyes.

A prime opportunity to kill his nephew presented itself. All Richard needed to do is out him. But he couldn't. Not in front of so many politicos. It would crater his future ambitions. He must remain silent and hope the little shit screwed up and got his brains blown out, attempting to be a hero.

Relief surged through Max as Cali only gave him a scarcely noticeable nod. Whether she understood or not he was grateful she didn't give him away. Heading to the first bomb, he reached for his pocket knife and flipped it open. After glancing around to make sure he wouldn't be observed, he severed the detonator lead and made it appear as if the device was still armed.

Cali's eyes widened at Max's actions. *Oh my God, he is risking himself to save us. If they catch him, they'll kill him like they did the security guard at the front desk.* As he turned, she caught his whisper and realized Max must be communicating with someone outside.

"One explosive defused. Moving to the next." Max's gaze once again landed on Cali, their eyes meeting and communicating more than words. He took the chance to speak a little louder so she might overhear him, "At the first bang, drop to the floor, curl up, and don't move. Pass that along to the others."

He pivoted and started for another block of C-4. His brain endeavored to determine who these men were and what they were after. They appeared well organized, and the explosives military grade. As he skirted the guy holding a pistol to Flanagan's head, Max overheard two of the armed attackers speaking French.

Halting at the second device, Max listened as he disarmed it. He only picked up fragments of what they said, but enough he filled in the rest, figuring out their plan.

Moving again, Max whispered, "This is a heist. They're planning to blow the place to cover their thefts. They are dressed like everyone so they can ditch their masks and blend in when things go to hell. You got about fifteen minutes to get in here before they set off the fireworks."

Outside Gallery

Fox paced in the inclement weather as the rain began to fall again, and he addressed his six-man team. "Facing fifteen armed subjects is a suicide scenario. No way we can take them into custody without fatalities. We don't have enough time to call up another team. Anyone got suggestions?"

The team rookie waited for a moment, hoping someone would have a better idea than him. Sarge likely wouldn't go for it, but when all the others shook their heads, Felix spoke up, "Sarge, this is somewhat unorthodox, but I think I have a solution."

"What?" Fox peered at his rookie, a former sailor who joined the force after his enlistment ended.

"Well, I recognize Master Chief Marshall and the other men. Marshall runs one of the top SEAL teams. I worked in logistics and loaded their supplies on many occasions. With one of their brothers inside, they'll jump at the chance to assist us."

Turning to view the men, Fox considered the possibility. It wouldn't be out of bounds. Although not law enforcement, they would be well versed in tactics necessary to end this situation. They only lacked protective gear and weapons.

"Sarge, the backup tactical gear is still in the truck from our last training exercise," Felix added.

"Grab five sets and locate some weapons. I'll go ask." Fox strode over to Marshall.

Jake spotted the sergeant moving towards him as did the others. They all became quiet as Fox stopped.

With no time to spare, the sergeant got straight to the point. "Marshall, my rookie tells me you and your men are SEALs. We have a critical situation that doesn't permit me time to bring in another SWAT team. We need your help.

"According to Stirling, fifteen armed men plan to use explosives to cover a heist in about ten minutes. It would be foolhardy to go in with only seven men and most likely end with fatalities, both civilians and my officers. We can provide weapons and Kevlar vests if you are willing to lend a hand."

"Hell, yeah!" Finn exclaimed before Jake answered. He wanted to do more than stand here, worrying about their kid.

Jake nodded. "What do you need us to do?"

"Come with me. We can plan tactics while you suit up."

Dave lifted the police tape, and all the guys ducked under, glad to be able to do something other than wait.

Katsaros Gallery – Main Room

So far, luck had been on Max's side. The person who designed the bombs used an identical and simplistic mechanism on each one, with no countermeasures. Also, none of the hostiles picked up on his activities.

As Max casually worked his way to the last one, he glanced again at the five men on their knees. He realized they were being used to control the rest of the attendees. No one would attempt to run if one of their friends or colleagues would be executed.

Approaching the food table, Max's stomach rumbled when he spied the fried mushrooms Cali wanted. Tempted to pop a few in his mouth to sate his increasing hunger, Max resisted so as not to draw attention to himself.

Reaching the final device, Max pulled out his knife again, flicked it open, and set to work. Although at first, he kicked himself for not being right beside Cali when things went down. Now, he was glad he was in the restroom—a fortunate fluke that worked to everyone's advantage.

"Fabien, que fais-tu?" Fouquet yelled at the last-minute addition to his group after Pierre came down with the flu. The new man appeared to be somewhat of a feckless explosives expert who tended to keep quiet. When Fabien didn't respond, Fouquet grabbed a fish from the table and flung it, whacking Fabien in the back of the head.

When something hit him, Max whipped around and spotted the fish on the floor. *What the hell ... flying fish?*

"Fabien, pourquoi tu joues avec les bombes?" Fouquet shouted, pissed off the guy ignored him.

Oh shit. Guess I'm Fabien. Wants to know why I'm fiddling with the bombs. Will he recognize I'm not him if I speak? Taking a chance, Max mumbled he was only making sure they were armed properly, "S'assurer juste qu'ils sont bien armés."

Fouquet nodded, turned, and headed to the back where several others gathered the artwork, which would fetch them millions from the right buyers.

Athole clenched his jaw to stop himself from alerting the criminals to what Maxwell had done. His desire to watch Preston's brat die almost outweighed his common sense, but he reined himself in before he acted rashly. *There will be another chance that doesn't blow my career to smithereens.*

Max blew out a relieved breath when the man walked away, believing he must've responded appropriately. "Final explosive disarmed," he whispered to Fox. SWAT would take things from here, so Max slowly began to make his way toward Cali.

Outside Gallery

Geared up and ready for action, Zulu planned to enter from the rear while SWAT breached the front. Their two-pronged approach would split the focus of the hostiles, giving both teams an advantage.

As Finn adjusted his grip on the MP5, he said, "Our fair-haired boy better hit the floor, or I'm gonna beat his ass."

Grant glanced at Finn; surprised Jake allowed him to participate with his still-healing ribs. But on the other hand, trying to keep the red-headed door-kicker down when a brother was in peril would be as successful as shoving a full-grown bull into a thimble ... not ever gonna happen.

"You'll have to stand in line, Jake will have first shot," Zach quipped.

"Quit flapping your jaws and focus. Tangos will look like the guests, and we don't want any friendly fire fatalities," Dave scolded for Jake, who transitioned into full Zulu One mode.

The men all shut up and prepared for the go signal from Sergeant Fox.

Chapter Twenty-Seven

Katsaros Gallery — Main Room

HALFWAY to Cali, flashbangs erupted, and Max spied the man who threw the fish at him, grabbing Cali to use her as a shield. Instead of going down as ordered, he ran flat-out in her direction since he couldn't take the chance of gunfire hitting Cali. He had the foresight to drop the AK-47 and rip off the mask so that he wouldn't be mistaken for one of the criminals.

Zulu entered, taking out the active shooters firing at them. All understood cops worked under different protocols, and they had been given a brief rundown. As some fled, they pursued them to take them alive.

Fox's team stayed in formation as they moved inside, breaking off into two groups. As Felix followed his sergeant, he spotted one subject running for the hostages, taking off his mask and dropping his weapon, hoping to fit in. Another one grabbed a female and yanked her towards him as he fired at him.

Felix aimed and fired off a round in the same split-second the running felon went flying at the one holding the woman. A cry rent the air as someone yelled, "Cali down!" Both men hit the floor. The rookie couldn't believe his eyes as the one on top struggled with the still masked man on the bottom. He didn't have time to consider more as bullets sprayed near him. Felix, sarge, and his teammate dove for cover behind a marble statue.

On the ground, Fouquet stared into a face he didn't recognize. *This isn't Fabien.* He registered the explosions didn't go off as planned when the police breached the front door. He attempted to point his handgun at the man.

Max grasped the barrel of the pistol, struggling to move it off him. He and the criminal rolled over and over as he fought to gain control. On the fifth roll, the gun went off.

Athole grinned as Cali screamed when Max's body draped over the man who tried to seize her. "Max! Noooooooo!" Staying low, Cali crawled to him as more flashes erupted around her. In a fog, her world fracturing into a million pieces, Cali believed she witnessed Max's final moments of life. She fumbled to pull him to her and roll him over.

Her first glimpse of the man beneath took her breath away. Lifeless brown eyes stared back at her. Flicking her gaze to Max, her heart fluttered, finding his blue orbs open. "You're alive."

"Yeah," Max breathed out as gunfire ceased. After a glance around, noting SWAT had a handle on things, he sat up then stood. Pivoting, he clasped Cali's hand and drew her up to him. He framed her face with his hands, staring into her frightened eyes. "Thought I wouldn't reach you in time."

Her knees going weak at the thought of Max almost dying, Cali clung to his jacket and moved her head to his shoulder as she became faint with emotions washing through her. His strong arms encircled her, holding her up.

A surge of fury came forth, and Cali pulled back. Her voice came out fierce, "Why did you do something so foolhardy? You could've been shot!" She slapped his upper arm. And when her hand came away bloody, her legs gave out. She would've sunk to the floor if not for Max supporting her. "You were shot."

"Nah, it's that guy's blood. Come on." Max put his arm around Cali's waist and guided her towards the officers helping the hostages pick themselves off the ground. He noted Athole acting like he was in charge as he spoke to an officer wearing sergeant stripes. Without qualms, Max interrupted, "Sergeant Fox?"

Fox turned at the familiar voice. "Stirling?"

"Yes, sir."

"Thank you for your help. This would've been a fiasco without you defusing the bombs. Got some help from your team too." Fox nodded towards Zulu, who led several cuffed men to the front to hand off to officers flooding into the building.

Athole seethed as Max inserted himself, and the sergeant dismissed him in favor of thanking the pissant.

"Sir, the man over there," Max pointed to the dead man, "we fought for his gun, and it went off. He's dead. I expect you'll need an after-action report from me."

"Yes." Noting the blood on the woman's hand, he said, "Ma'am, are you injured?"

"No only transfer from …" her head turned to the man lying in a pool of blood.

"If it is alright, I would like to take Cali out of here." Max understood the aftereffects of adrenaline would start to make her shaky, and he wanted her closer to EMS in case she became shocky.

"Fine. Stay close, and when we're ready, I'll find you."

Outside Katsaros Gallery

Riding the downward crest of his own adrenaline rush, Max maneuvered Cali outside and to the first EMS gurney under a canopy. "Sit and let them check you over." Cali opened her mouth to protest, and Max said, "Humor me, please."

Cali nodded and sat. She began shivering and appreciated the blanket Max requested and draped over her shoulders before he stepped back to allow the paramedics to take her vitals.

"Sir, do you need to be checked out?" a medic asked.

"No, I'm fine."

Several minutes later, as it began raining heavily, an officer hurried over and asked, "Are you, Stirling?"

"Yes."

"Please, come with me. The sergeant is ready to talk with you."

As Cali started to get off the gurney, Max shook his head. "Stay here. I won't be long. I promise. No need for you to get wet."

"Okay." Cali reached out a hand to him. When he grasped it, she pulled him close and whispered, "Thank you for saving me."

Max grinned and kissed her forehead. "Be back in a moment." He hurried through the rain, following the cop to where Fox stood outside under an overhang.

"Stirling, this is Detective Hanson, he'll take your statement, then you'll be free to go."

Max reached behind to his waist, gingerly withdrawing a firearm with two fingers. "You'll be wanting this. I took it off the man I tied up in the bathroom." Hanson pulled out an evidence bag, and Max dropped the pistol in as he asked, "My team?"

Fox replied, "They'll write out their statements and debrief with us at the station. Good work, in there. No civilian or police fatalities when we breached because of you. Thanks again."

"Glad to help."

Hanson said, "Let's start with your full name."

"Maxwell Stirling, but I prefer Max."

"Please start at the beginning and tell me what occurred."

Before Max began, a colleague interrupted the detective. Waiting for their conversation to end, Max started to feel the shakes that came with the end of his adrenaline surge. He tried to hide the tremors, clenching his fists, but the chill of the wind blowing through his soaked clothes didn't help.

As Hanson's dialog dragged on, Max leaned against the brick building, unexpectedly fatigued, more so than a typical drop in his epinephrine level. He lifted an arm to wave at Jake and the others as they walked past, and the aches in his body from two fights let themselves be known.

Becoming dizzy, he wanted to sit down. This was not a normal come-down from stress. His eyes sought out Grant, but his vision tunneled, and his legs began to give out as he tilted to the left.

Grant stopped so abruptly Finn ran into the back of him.

"Forget how to walk?" Finn grumbled.

"The kid. Something isn't right." Grant changed directions. His pace quickened as Max's gaze fixated on him.

"What the hell?" Finn joined Grant when Max's legs appeared to buckle, and he slid down the wall. Finn called over his shoulder, "Jake! Max's down."

As Max descended, his world folded in on itself.

Jake turned from speaking with Fox, and his eyes landed on Max as the kid's body slumped to the sidewalk. He was running in the next instant, along with Dave and Zach, all following Grant and Finn.

Hanson shouted, "I NEED HELP OVER HERE!"

Grant pushed the officer out of the way. Dropping to his knees, he carefully shifted Max's body to the concrete on his back. He tapped his cheeks several times until Max's eyes fluttered open. "Hey, Kid, what happened?"

Disoriented, surprised to find Grant above him, Max mumbled, "Um, … unsure. Lightheaded."

Finn blew out a breath. "Pretty boy fainted."

Max frowned. "Prefer passed out."

"Is he injured?" Jake asked as worry ratcheted up a notch.

"What's going on over here?" Fox inquired as he joined the group, and gazed at Stirling.

"Give me some light," Grant said as he wiped the wetness off his hand from turning Max over.

Hanson flicked on his flashlight.

"Shit he's bleeding," Dave stated.

"Not mine. Belongs to the guy I took down to save Cali," Max muttered as he fought to stay with them.

"Grant?" Jake wanted a reason for his rookie to be lying flat on his back and semi-conscious. His gut seized, hoping he had not been injured again.

"Not sure. There were a lot of bullets flying in there. Let's remove his jacket and make sure adrenaline isn't covering a wound." When Jake and Finn sat Max up, Grant pulled his navy jacket from him.

Although crimson discolored the white shirt, Grant couldn't find any wounds. He took Max's pulse, noting a slight elevation. "Could be a post-rush drop in blood sugar. Anyone got a candy bar?" When they all shook their heads, Grant peered at Zach. "Go ask one of the medics for a glucose packet."

Zach sprinted off into the rain.

"When did you last eat?" Grant asked as he tucked Max's blazer under the kid's head.

"Um." Max blinked open. "Yesterday. Had two beers tonight."

Finn crouched, his worry ebbing. "Idiot. Alcohol on an empty stomach ... even I'm not that dumb. Why didn't you eat?"

Still fuzzy, Max mumbled, "Busy, late, no time."

Dave huffed as he eyed Jake. "He was in TOC all day. We should've brought him some lunch."

Realizing the situation was in hand, Fox said, "Once you get your man squared away, I need your team to come to the station to fill out paperwork."

Jake nodded as he spied Zach skidding to a halt at one of the many paramedic rigs.

"Need glucose gel and a couple of blankets."

The paramedic eyed the man in street clothes and tactical gear.

"My teammate is down, over there." Zach pointed behind him. "Do you have any?"

"Yeah, sure. Hang on a second." He grabbed two tubes and two emergency blankets. "Need my services?"

"Nah, Grant's got Max covered."

Cali hopped off the gurney. "Is Max hurt?"

Zach shook his head and chuckled. "Fainted due to low blood sugar. He's not gonna live this one down for a long time."

Athole overheard their conversation, and it confirmed his belief. *The pissant is still a little wuss. Never could handle the stress. Zulu won't tolerate the pansy much longer.* Tired of waiting to give his statement, he turned his attention on a young officer. "I'm Captain Athole. I have important matters to attend to, so I need to provide my account next."

Using the blanket as a shield from the rain, Cali followed Zach. She didn't much like the razzing she overheard as she approached. Sure, she understood 'guy talk' and 'brother behavior' with five of her own brothers, but she was in no mood for hearing Max belittled, even if in fun.

As Zach covered Max in one of the blankets, Cali used the tone she reserved for rebuking her recalcitrant brothers. "Cut him some slack. Max risked his life, defusing multiple explosives, and saving over forty people and countless irreplaceable works of art."

She hid her smile as the guys halted, giving her contrite expressions. Cali knelt beside Max and grasped one of his hands, noting the slight tremor, as her other hand moved to brush the wet curls from his forehead. She remained quiet as Grant opened one of the glucose tubes and squeezed a bit into Max's mouth.

Mortified beyond belief, Max kept his eyes closed. Cali might've stopped the teasing for tonight, but he would be razzed about this for a long while, at least until someone else did something more embarrassing than fainting.

Grant gave Max the last of the first packet and rechecked his pulse, finding it back to normal.

"Feeling better?" Cali asked, as his hand steadied.

"Yes, ma'am," Max answered as he dared to lift his lashes, hoping not to view mirth in his brother's expressions. He released a sigh when instead he found Jake's reproachful mien.

"You are not to ignore your health. I thought we went over this clearly the other day."

"I was busy," Max tried to interject.

"Not so busy that you couldn't ask someone to grab you lunch." Jake raked a hand through his hair, his own pulse increasing as he glared at the kid. He was angry … at himself. He expected immediate change, but in reality, Max would need time to learn what it meant to be part of a family.

"You didn't have lunch. Why didn't you tell me? I assumed you weren't hungry, or we would've swung by the food table." Cali stared at Max.

"You were having such a wonderful time. I enjoyed being with you. I can handle going without eating."

"Apparently not, Princess Fainty," Finn quipped, but quickly clammed up when Cali gave him the evil eye.

"Ready to try sitting up?" Grant asked.

"Yeah." Multiple hands reached out to help him as Max shifted up, and they leaned him against the wall. Grant handed him the other tube and instructed him to consume it before attempting to stand. His head clearing and vision returning to normal, Max peered at the detective. "Sorry for making you wait."

"No worries. You faint—"

"Blacked out," Finn overrode the man. He was all for teasing his little brother, but he'd be damned if he would allow anyone else to disparage the kid.

Eyeing the red-headed man, Hanson changed his words. "I can wait until you're ready."

Max sucked in a bit more of the sugary gel before he launched into his account from the moment the gunfire erupted while he was in the bathroom. His tale left his teammates, Cali, and Hanson spellbound for several moments after he concluded with, "Cali crawled over to me, and pulled me off the man."

Grant was the first to break the silence. "Did you screw up your shoulder?"

Max chuckled. "No. Works fine. Told the PT I'm ready to be cleared."

Cali's Apartment

Tucked under warm covers, his stomach sated with a delicious omelet Cali whipped up for him, Max enjoyed cuddling with his girlfriend as she slumbered peacefully. Both were wiped out from their ordeal, and neither was up to having a romp tonight.

He grinned as he recalled the guys giving him guff over driving home alone until Cali stopped them in their tracks when she said, *'What makes you think he is going home?'* God, he could fall hard for this woman if he dared to open his heart again.

Having his fill of being considered the girly-man due to fainting, Max insisted he drive to her place. He chuckled when Jake told him to take tomorrow off to rest. Max had no intention of resting, leastwise, not when he and Cali woke up.

If the weather remained rainy, he wouldn't mind spending the entire day at Cali's, just the two of them. However, if the sun came out, a hike would be a fun way to spend the afternoon. Though, he expected she would need to go into work for an hour or two to help Flanagan with inventorying the artwork and noting any damages for the insurance claim.

A smug expression briefly came to Max's face as he thought about Athole. Whether his uncle acknowledged it or not, Asshole bore witness to the fact Max was not worthless and saved the captain's life along with all the other guests. Max also wondered how Frank and Morgan would react the next time he encountered them at one of Cali's events.

Max drifted to sleep with more pleasant thoughts … being part of a brotherhood where they dropped everything to come to his aid. He didn't need blood bonds to be part of a family who cared about him.

Chapter Twenty-Eight

Two Weeks Later – Training Field

S MOKING the rest of the team, Max sprinted to the top of the hill first. His face-splitting grin greeted each one as they joined him. "Five cases of beer coming my way," he gloated.

"I'm getting you the hoppiest, most skanky, foreign beer I can find," Finn retorted.

Max chuckled, happy to be on active duty as of today. Last Friday, seven days ago, had been an act in futility to get Jake to let him return although the doc cleared him. All Jake replied to his repeated requests was, 'We're leaving for deployment soon, so go have fun with your girlfriend for the next week.'

So he did. They took a trip to Cali's boss's cabin. Flanagan happily gave Cali paid time off after an exhaustive assessment determined the Mendelian statues survived in pristine condition, and only a few minor works had been damaged. The respite would be his way of thanking both Cali and Max.

They enjoyed lazy days of curling up in front of a roaring fire in the log cabin. Quite romantic Cali claimed, and he relished spending their nights engaged in passionate lovemaking. Both returned yesterday, fresh and ready to tackle the future.

Jake grinned, glad to have the team whole again. He took to heart Valarie's suggestion to allow Max and Cali time to solidify their new relationship before Zulu left for three months.

Val said the young lovers would need a durable link if they were to survive the rigors of SEAL family life. A brief time of being free and easy would allow each to draw upon pleasant memories when the crap hit the fan, as it inevitably would. If his marriage was to be used as a bellwether, his wife was dead right.

"So how many more laps does the kid have for leaving the men's room when you told him not to join a gunfight with a knife?" Grant asked.

"Hey, my knife came in handy," Max retorted but waited for the ax to fall for disobeying Jake's order to stay in the bathroom. He squinted as the sun peeked over the horizon.

Jake nodded as he peered at his men. "True. And the kid did what was necessary. Forty-three people, Max included, are alive because he courageously acted when others cowered." Jake captured Max's gaze to drive home his point. "I'll never firebrand your ass for taking calculated risks, and that is an example of one. You used your brains and your training."

Max couldn't help the smile that flourished at the compliment.

Finn shoved Max and teased, "Don't be letting that make your head swell, Princess. You might faint again."

"I didn't faint. I passed out," Max countered.

"Same thing."

With Finn's ribs fully healed, Max launched himself at the man he who was fast becoming a best friend, taking him to the ground as he declared, "Is not! Fainting is girly, and I'm not."

"You got goldie locks hair ... so, yeah, you're girly," Finn laugh, enjoying razzing his little brother.

Max got Finn in a chokehold. "So, you're gonna tell people you lost to a girl?"

The two brothers wrestled as the sun climbed higher in the sky, and the others grinned. All understood this was nothing more than friendly fighting—brothers hassling one another—family fun.

After several minutes Finn tapped out, and a victorious Max rose ready to gloat until McBride stood and declared the rookie had to clean all their gear before going to the ball game.

Zulu Equipment Cage

Max thought Finn had been joking about him cleaning all the team gear, but once they returned to the cage, everyone piled their crap on the center table, and Jake gave him *the glare*, which he now understood as *'get to it,'* before everybody else left.

He brushed boots until he got dried mud out of the ten soles. Max broke down, cleaned, and reassembled all their rifles, though he knew each one of the guys would redo it themselves later—they were all picky about their weapons. He wiped down their helmets and night vision then inserted fresh batteries in both the NODs and their radios. His last chore … reload all their mags.

With no doubt in his mind, Max decided this was a first deployment rite. Being the new guy could suck at times, but today, doing this didn't faze him one damned bit. He belonged on Zulu, and they accepted him. He reached his dream, made his parents proud, and gained the family he always wanted … so cleaning their stuff was not an issue for him.

He also proved Athole wrong. He was worthy, and one day, with the help of his new ally, Jake Marshall, he might actually be able to restore his father's honor and take Athole down. After Jake shared what Derek West told him, Max considered Jake's suggestion he reveal his secret to the rest of the team. But Max believed, for their protection, at least for now, details of Athole's treachery needed to remain between them.

Max stood back and viewed his accomplishment. Though the task took him several hours, and he had not seen any of Zulu for the same amount of time, a job well-done left him satisfied. Something his mom instilled in him at an early age. Some might've called him weird, but as a little kid, he liked all his playthings put away neatly, that is before Athole threw out all his toys.

Refusing to sour today, Max put thoughts of Asshole away and focused on the positives. He eagerly anticipated going on deployment with Zulu. Yes, he would miss Cali, but they could do video calls. And they still had a few weeks before they left. So, he would make the most of their time together.

The door opening and his brothers strolling in brought Max out of his thoughts. He turned to them with a grin. "All done."

"Merry Maid did a decent job," Finn said as he picked up one of his clean boots.

Max rolled his eyes as the others chuckled.

Jake perused the items; glad Finn came up with an idea that allowed them to finish with their plans with the kid none the wiser. "Time to go win the annual baseball tournament." Jake grinned as he clapped a hand on Max's shoulder. "No black-eyes this time, Kid."

"Copy." Max strode out, happy as a lark today.

Ballfield on Base

After Zulu won the game against Alpha by one point, making them this year's champs, Max would be content to lay on the blanket with his head in Cali's lap for the rest of the afternoon. His eyes tracked a couple of birds flitting around trees with green, red, gold, orange, and brown foliage. He liked the colorfulness of Fall and the visible signs of the changing of the seasons.

Shifting his gaze to the beautiful woman in his life, Max counted his blessings. During their trip to the cabin, he decided to open his heart and take another chance at love. No, he was not anywhere ready to talk marriage yet, but in time, Max hoped he and Cali would move in that direction. Only time would tell, and until then, he would enjoy the journey.

Taking pleasure in the slow afternoon surrounded by Max's team and their families, Cali picked up another blackberry and hung it over Max's mouth. "Want more?"

"Sure." He opened, and she dropped the berry in. The burst of sweet and sour tickled his taste buds.

"What are you thinking about?" Cali carded her fingers through his blond curls as she gazed into his ocean-blue eyes.

"Never had such a good birthday," Max let slip out.

"WHAT? TODAY IS YOUR BIRTHDAY!" Cali shouted as she dumped Max's head on the ground and jumped up.

Sitting up and rubbing the back of his head, he peered up at her. "Yeah."

"Why didn't you tell me?" Her hands went to her hips as she glared at him.

"'Cause it isn't a big deal."

"Yes, it is. You planned a dinner for me and gave me wine glasses. I didn't know, so ..." Cali became frustrated. "I don't even have a present for you."

"Spending time with you is gift enough." Max tried to placate her. He never truly gave the day he was born a thought. It was like any other day, and no one gave a damn about it after his parents and grandma died. Uncle Asshole never acknowledged his birth unless it was to denigrate him.

The team overheard their loud conversation, and after a quick, whispered plotting, they removed the beer from the cooler full of icy water, and snuck around behind Max.

"ARRGH!" Max yelled and bolted to his feet after they doused him in ice and frigid water.

Everyone laughed at the shocked and offended expression on Stirling's face.

Finn quipped, "Kid owes a case of beer."

Shaking ice out of the back of his shirt, Max asked. "Why?"

"Peter Pan didn't tell his girlfriend today is his birthday," Finn stated matter-of-factly.

"Another case for the kid's first birthday with us," Grant said.

"One more 'cause he's a quarter of a century-old now," Zach chimed in as he petted Rocky.

Max only shook his head. *Brothers! Pain in the asses, every last one of them, but I wouldn't have it any other way.*

Jake handed Stirling a beer and a towel. "This one is on me. Happy birthday, Kid."

The blanket now soaked; Max moved to one of the picnic benches. He set his bottle down, and covered his head with the towel, rubbing briskly to dry his hair. When he removed it, Max found almost everyone standing on the opposite side of the table.

However, in front of him, Draper held an orca-shaped cake with twenty-five flaming candles. His mouth gaped as Kira started the group singing the birthday song. When they finished, he said, "You knew?"

"Of course, I did. I'm all-knowing, remember?" Kira chuckled. "Now, blow out your candles and make a wish."

Max inhaled deep. *I wish not to owe another damned case of beer, and my tenure with my brothers is a long one.* He blew out all the candles with one breath. "Let's eat cake."

Taking a seat, Max realized the guys likely read his birth date in his personnel jacket, but them going to the trouble of getting him a cake surprised him. Not since his sixth birthday had anyone celebrated … until today. This one would always be special because it was the first with his new family.

When Cali sat next to him, Max asked, "Did you know about all this?"

"Nope. Honestly." She leaned close and whispered seductively in his ear, "You'll receive my present tonight … in bed."

To cover the rising heat of a blush, Max turned and kissed her. "Perfect. Can't wait," he murmured as he pulled back.

"Aidan, no," Cathy called out, too late to stop her son from scooping out a piece from the cake with his bare hands.

Everyone laughed as the three-year-old smeared icing all over his face as he shoved the chocolate cake into his mouth. Not to be outdone by her twin, Nadia followed suit, much to Cathy's and Dave's chagrin.

When ten-year-old Tommy tried to do the same, Jake caught his wrist. "I don't think so, sonny boy."

Tommy chuckled. "Worth a shot."

Jake tousled his youngest's hair and shooed him away as Val and Kira began cutting pieces and handing them out. Once everyone was seated, Jake nodded to Dave.

Rising, Dave moved to the plain, brown bag near his family's stuff and pulled out a small box. He returned to the table and set it in front of Max. "Happy birthday, Kid."

Max stared at the wrapped package before peering back at Dave. "Gifts aren't necessary."

"No, but they are desired. Open it." Dave grinned.

Watching as their rookie carefully slit the tape, and almost reverently unwrapped the present, brought home Dave's thought again. Max's childhood had been stark. Jake's recent innocuous remarks, especially when he told them he wished to throw a surprise party for the kid, jibbed with his own thoughts.

Max opened the box and discovered a ballcap with Zulu's insignia on the front. He laughed when he spotted KID embroidered on the back. After putting the cap on backwards, so KID showed prominently, Max asked, "How's it look?"

"Good, except Dave should've embroidered Princess Fainty instead," Finn chimed in.

Ignoring their breacher, Zach retrieved a card from his pack and slid it to Max. "Hope you like."

"You didn't have—"

"We already established that fact. I wanted to."

Max tore open the envelope and found a photo of Rocketeer and another dog. Confused, Max turned to Zach. "Huh?"

"That's Rocky and the mother-to-be of his pups. When the litter is born and old enough, my gift to you is that I'll teach you dog training techniques if you want to help me work with the puppies. Will be handy when you adopt a dog of your own."

"Cool. Absolutely. Would be fun."

Grant cleared his throat and then pushed a bag over to Max. "These might come in handy too."

After Max unrolled the top and peered in, his brows drew together. He pulled out an infrared thermometer and several glucose packets. "Um, don't quite—"

"I'm a practical kinda guy. Figured the best gift I could give you is something useful. And with the last few missions, and passing out after the gallery, I thought I should be better prepared with you on the team." Grant reached for the bag. "I'm adding them to my standard medkit.

Though somewhat embarrassing, and definitely practical, Max appreciated the thought. Before he could thank Grant, Finn shoved his trinket box in front of him.

"I finished this last night. Sorry it took so long, but its good as new as promised. Look inside." Finn popped a toothpick in his mouth and rocked back on his heels, eager for the kid's reaction.

Max lifted the lid, and the first thing he spied was a picture taken at the welcome barbeque of him and the guys.

"Figured since that's where you keep important stuff, you'd want that in there too."

Speechless, Max nodded as he picked up the photo and showed it to everyone.

Kira smiled and gently nudged Finn's arm as she teased, "Aww. You're such a softie."

"Am not," Finn grumbled, but grinned, waiting to the for the most significant reaction.

Max's eyes lit on his grandma's owl. His fingers cautiously touched the blue and white figurine. "It looks brand new." He turned it around, searching for cracks, but not finding any. His eyes sought out Finn's. "How?"

"Told ya, I got an A in ceramics, and these hands are golden." Finn grinned.

Max blew out a breath as he clutched the owl, and noted the curious gazes, so he explained. "After my dad died, I was only able to salvage three items that belonged to my parents and grandma before my uncle got rid of everything. I broke my grandmother's owl recently, and Finn fixed it for me."

Cali leaned in closed. "What are the other items?

"My mom's locket. My father gave it to her the day I was born. And my dad's ring." Max laid his owl back inside and closed the lid as Jake approached him.

"This one is from the entire team." Jake handed over a thin, floppy rectangular package.

Max tore off the paper, and his grin grew as he discovered a Zulu flag. He couldn't wait to hang it up in his apartment.

Holding out a tiny box, Jake met Max's gaze, his expression attempting to communicate pride. "This one is from me, Kid."

The hushed silence around him, made Max a bit unnerved. He broke his gaze with Jake and reached for the gift. He swiftly opened the black box. Utterly floored, Max stared at a trident ring.

"There's an inscription," Jake softly said.

Max rotated the ring as he read the engraved words on the inside. **Like father, Like son. Two generations of honor.**

Jake settled a hand on Max's shoulder and gave a slight squeeze. It would be up to the kid, when and if, he shared his secret with the guys, but he wished to make one thing crystal clear.

His voice steady and firm, Jake said, "Blood bonds aren't required for family. True brothers are those who you are willing to bleed for and who will bleed for you. Now and forever, you are a member of Zulu's brotherhood. Happy birthday, Max."

Unable to express the true depth of his emotion, Max only nodded. *Six men, one heartbeat. Team is all the family I need.* Peering at everyone's smiling faces before landing back on Jake's, Max grinned and finally managed to utter, "Thank you."

Keep reading for a sneak peek
at Laura Acton's third novel
in the **Strike Force Zulu** series.

Sneak Peek:

WOUNDED
HONOR

STRIKE FORCE ZULU
Book 3

Newport News, VA – Seaside Star Restaurant

LIEUTENANT Nicole Farris squeezed lemon into her water as the man joined her at the table. "Thanks for meeting me for dinner on such short notice."

"I'm surprised you called after the way we left things five years ago. Why did you?"

Nicole gripped her glass to steady her hand. Usually, she would be rock solid, but the reason for this encounter rattled her to the core. "Let's order first."

George's eye caught the slight tremor most wouldn't detect. He only nodded and waved over the waitress. He ordered the sea bass for himself, and Nicole ordered a shrimp salad. When she fidgeted again, he realized whatever she had to say hit her deep, but he waited for her to engage.

Steeling herself, Nicole said, "I need your help. I understand if you're reluctant, but you're the only person I trust." She lowered her voice, "The matter is highly sensitive, and I believe people's lives are at stake."

"Who's lives?" George leaned in closer. Nicole was spooked; he was sure of it now.

"I can't tell you yet. You need to promise me you won't divulge what I tell you to anyone, and I mean anyone. Not even those you are certain you can trust."

"Nicole, what have you gotten yourself into?" Concern lit George's weathered features.

"Promise?"

"I give you my word. I hope it means as much to you now as it did years ago."

Nicole inhaled sharply, regretting the words she said to him the last time they met. She hoped he heard the sincerity in her tone, "It does, or else I wouldn't be here now."

George smiled and reached a hand across the table, letting her reach out if she desired. His grin grew when she grasped his hand. "Tell me, sweetheart, what's got you worried?"

Drawing strength from his touch, Nicole said, "Dad, I think my boss is trying to kill my team and blame me."

George Farris believed his daughter without reservation. "Never trusted Athole. What do you need from me?"

Virginia Beach - Near Chuck's Creamery

A light breeze blew as Max and Cali strolled down the sidewalk arm in arm. With Max leaving on deployment in three days, Cali enjoyed their simple date tonight; a stop at her favorite ice cream shop and a double scoop of mint chocolate chip. She teased Max about him getting plain chocolate topped with orange sherbet. The combination seemed odd to her.

Max halted at the corner, scrunched his face and hissed.

"What's wrong?" Cali's eyes surveyed him, searching for a non-existent injury ... still jumpy from the few he suffered.

"Brain freeze," Max groused.

Cali laughed.

"Hey, not funny." Max cracked open one eye.

"Told you not to eat so fast," Cali replied with no sympathy, still grinning.

The pain ebbing, Max's face relaxed, and he chuckled. "Been a long time since I had ice cream. Didn't want it to melt."

"No fear of it doing that today. Perhaps in the middle of summer, but not now."

Something about Maxwell Stirling made Cali willing to risk being in a relationship with an elite warrior who could be called away at any moment. The more time she spent with Max, the more drawn to him, she became. Instead of focusing on what the future might or might not bring, she endeavored to take pleasure in the simple things life offered, like a lazy stroll downtown.

Cali leaned in to kiss his cheek, but a tiny ball of energy plowed into Max as it rushed around the corner.

Max peered down at the child who ran into his legs and now sat on the ground, gaping at him with surprise.

"Sorry, Kami's excited about visiting Chuck's Creamery." Kami's mother said.

Crouching, Max grinned at the little girl, who appeared to be no more than four years old. "I like ice cream too. Make sure you don't eat too fast. Brain freezes are no fun." He helped her up as he stood.

"I like chocolate. Mommy said I can have fudge on top too," Kami said in a cheerful voice, her brown eyes alight with delight.

"You should try orange sherbet with the chocolate. Yummy," Max suggested.

"I love orange!" Turning to her mother, her bright eyes begged. "Can I, please?"

Smiling, Kami's mom reached out her hand to her daughter. "Sounds interesting. Let's do it."

For several moments, Max stood in place with a grin on his face as he watched Kami skip, hurrying her mom along to get her frozen treat. Cali wrapped her arms around Max's waist as she stood behind him. "You're a softy."

"Yeah, well, don't tell my brothers."

"Your secret is safe with me." Cali promised.

Their pleasant night erupted in chaos in the next moment. A ball of fire exploded from Chuck's Creamery, sending glass, debris, and people flying. They stared in horror as the tiny girl and mother, who just reached the shop, were flung in the air and came crashing down on the sidewalk.

Heedless of the fragments of glass, brick, metal, and plastic raining down, Max raced forward into the hectic scene as others ran from it. He knelt next to Kami, and his breath caught in his throat as he shielded her tiny body.

His action would not change the result. Lifeless eyes, which had only moments ago held such promise and joy, stared up at him. His face screwed up in agony, and his eyes teared up. He would claim they were from the acrid smoke billowing out of the now-destroyed creamery, not the senseless loss of life.

Max had no idea how long he covered Kami, but when multiple pairs of hands pulled him up and away, he sat back on his heels, and the scene came into focus. Firefighters, cops, and paramedics swarmed the area. Blankets covered several bodies. A sheet draped over Kami as sound returned to him.

"Sir, are you hurt?" a paramedic yelled in his face.

"Cali?" Max frantically searched to his left, his pulse beating a rapid staccato, fear he might've lost another love.

"I'm here," Cali's quavering voice said to his right.

Max turned to her and pulled Cali to him, his embrace bruising as he clung to her. "She is gone. She never …" He couldn't finish. There were so many 'nevers' for Kami. Never got to try orange sherbet with chocolate. Would never grow up. She never stood a chance being so close to the blast.

Pulling back, difficult because Max didn't want to release her, through tears, Cali peered into his eyes. "I know. You need to let them look at you. You're bleeding."

"I'm okay." Max scanned Cali's body. "Are you hurt?"

"No, I was standing behind you. I'm fine. But you have a myriad of cuts on your face. Allow them to clean you up, at least."

Max stood and shook his head. His gaze methodically moved as he surveyed the area, and his stomach clenched at what he observed. "This isn't supposed to happen here. This isn't a war zone. Children don't die in explosions here."

Cali waved off the medic as she said, "I'll take him home and clean him up."

An officer stopped them and asked if they witnessed the explosion. Neither one provided much detail, only that the blast occurred. They didn't see anything or anyone out of the ordinary before the tragedy. Dazed, they wandered back to Max's place.

Though Max's external wounds were minor, the one to his soul, only visible through a pair of troubled ocean-blue portals, would require a different curative.

About the Author

Laura Acton, author of the *Beauty of Life* and *Strike Force Zulu* series, was born in Phoenix, Arizona, and raised with two older brothers by amazing parents. Her American father's poetry inspired her love of the written word, and her Canadian mother provided her with a role model of a loving and courageous woman who always strove to find the beauty in adversity. After Laura's high school sweetheart returned from the Navy, they married and raised three sons.

Laura graduated summa cum laude from Western International University with a Bachelor's of Science in Business with a minor in e-Commerce. For thirty-five years, she worked for high-tech companies as a Business Analyst, developing quality processes, documenting system requirements, and writing training materials.

From the time Laura was a teen, delivering newspapers in the early mornings, she occupied herself by crafting stories in her mind but never had time to write them down. After her beloved husband passed and her sons no longer needed a Mom taxi, she had after work hours to fill. One quiet night with soft music playing, Laura discovered her passion for writing fiction.

Writing became an obsession, prompting Laura to retire early from the corporate world to become a full-time author. Now her dogs keep her company while she writes novels about valiant men and women who forge bonds through emotional and physical adversity. Laura enjoys creating brotherhood and family sagas filled with Special Forces and SWAT action, hurt, comfort, intrigue, romance, drama, angst, twists, turns, and connections.

Visit Laura's website for info on her latest novels
and to sign up for Laura's email list:
https://www.lauraactonauthor.com/

Made in the USA
Las Vegas, NV
09 December 2020